CARMAN

KATHLEEN DESALVO

ISBN: 0615443826
ISBN-13: 9780615443829

Prolog

In 1898 thousands of Italians came to America to make their fortune, but not Juana and Paul Duva. They came to find their son John, who barely seventeen, had come to America and mysteriously disappeared. Although they could not speak or understand one word of English, they set out for America knowing only that somewhere in that vast country was their son. Nothing was going to stop them. Unhappily something did.

Shortly after their arrival in America, their youngest son Anthony, who had withstood all the rigors of an Atlantic crossing, came down with a mysterious fever. It took months of care, and almost all the money they had brought with them from Italy, to make the boy well.

Paul sent a request for money to his trusted cousin who had been left in charge of Paul's home and vineyard in Italy. Despite countless letters, an answer never came. Paul could not understand why there wasn't an answer. He wrote to a friend in his town of Benevento, to try and find an answer for him. When finally he received news from home, he was devastated to find that his cousin had been using all his assets for his own gain.

It was time for Paul to look for work and make money, not only for his family in America, but to go home and reclaim his property. The only jobs available to foreigners were as common laborers. Paul's experience was running a winery. Sadly he was on the wrong coastline for that endeavor. New York was where he landed and where he would stay until he made enough money to continue his search for his son and then, to go home to Italy.

Learning English was another matter. Although he was quick to understand the language, he had a difficult time speaking. He was embarrassed by his Italian accent and was reluctant to hold a conversation in any language but Italian. Through one of his new Italian friends, he was hired temporarily as an apprentice mason. He spent long hard days working in the hot city sun learning the trade.

From the time he was ten years old he worked in the vineyard with his father. Hard work was not alien to him. It felt good to feel the strength in his body return. In a short time he became an expert at masonry, and was proud of his new profession. In winter when the weather was too cold to use cement he was content with the spare jobs he would find. If you were a good worker, diligent and reliable, odd jobs were not hard to find.

Juana was happy that her little son was well again and growing like a weed. She was also delighted to find herself pregnant again. Paul would have gladly gone home to Italy so that the baby would be born there, but that was impossible.

Anxious about his home and vineyard, he waited patiently for any word from his cousin. At long last a letter arrived telling of failed crops and the need to mend fences, and a leaking roof. Paul's plea for help was completely ignored. He knew the letter was a sham but was powerless to act.

The more he tried to save, the more they needed to get by. With Juana's help they managed to put aside enough money to move to a small house, where they could rent out a room or two. She could not bear to have a new baby born in an apartment crawling with roaches, mice and the occasional rat. Living in a house they could save the money they would get from their boarders.

Two days after their move, Juana went into labor. The birth was so quick that the midwife was never called and Paul delivered his own baby. He was exhausted by the experience but overjoyed that he had another son. Juana was hoping for a girl, but grateful the baby was strong and healthy. Besides she thought to be the mother of three sons was a gift from God.

He was a good baby and in no time he was smiling and laughing. He resembled both of his brothers, although darker that either one. Little Anthony just loved him and would spend hours playing with him. He was a beautiful baby who grew into a handsome little boy. Everyone seemed to love him, especially the women. He learned to speak Italian from his parents and English from his brother. His parents sent him to catholic school where the nuns were known for their preferential treatment of Irish children. However, for this little Italian boy they made an exception. He charmed his way right into their Irish hearts.

Chapter One

1929

Except for the glow of his cigar, the room was completely dark. He gazed out of the window and realized it was snowing heavily.

"Just what I need, a snow storm," he thought. He was hoping for a clear, beautiful day tomorrow, an omen, any sign that what he was about to do was right.

At least he was home in his mother's house. Mama understood she was never judgmental. A remarkable woman small in stature and frail in appearance, but she radiated a strength that was both reassuring and intimidating. He could count on Mama to be there for him, to shore him up, if need be, or attack anyone or any thing that stood in his path.

There were few courageous enough to stand up to her. Perhaps Papa could. He stood well over six feet and was strong as an ox. Most men were intimidated by him but certainly not Mama. This tiny woman could leave her husband speechless with her antics. He was usually unwilling to spar with her verbally or otherwise. He knew that she was absolutely loyal to him and that was enough for him.

Mama was a full time Catholic and part-time sorceress. She was the oldest daughter of an oldest daughter and had been taught all the sacred prayers handed down from generation to generation needed to ric the worthy of any physical or mental distress. She had the ability to dispel the dreaded "Malocchia", evil eye, with a strange ritual using common olive oil. She could cure a high fever with a prayer learned at her grandmother's knee. Moreover she was capable of relieving pain with just her hand on your forehead as she murmured her secret prayers. Her most famous remedy was mending a broken heart, which she cured by tender caring words and superior advice.

Without fail, rain or shine, she attended daily mass. Her bedroom resembled a miniature church with dozens of religious statues complete with burning candles. Her family, including the boarders she took in whenever cash was short, was convinced that any day the house would go up in flames. Regardless of her peculiar ways, Carman adored this little dynamo, his mother "Juanna".

Tonight he could hear her shuffling to the kitchen, as she called out, "hey Carman, you sure you couldn't eat a little something? How about some coffee, huh?"

"Coffee sounds good," he answered "what are you doing up at this hour?"

"Making coffee," she said, "You want a little whiskey in it?"

"Si Mama" he said. He was cold and a cup of Mama's coffee with a shot of booze was just what he needed to warm up.

She came in his room and turned on the light.

"No light Mama, I prefer the dark tonight," he said as she flicked the light off.

"Here bambino, drink your coffee," she said handing him the steaming cup. She turned and quietly and left him to his reverie.

As he sat drinking his coffee, Carman closed his eyes and remembered a time when life was simple and he was young and free without a care in the word. Remembering wasn't difficult at all. In fact, in a strange way it was comforting. Maybe he could find an answer.

1911

Carman was thirteen and about to graduate from St.Mary's School. He remembered it, as if it were yesterday. It was the day Father Paul came into his classroom to talk to the boys about a possible two-week stay at St. Simon's Seminary in the Catskills. The young priest talked on and on about the virtues of entering the Priesthood. He managed to capture the imagination of several boys in the graduating class, including Carman. Two weeks in the Catskills was enough reason for Carman to consider going to St.Simon's Seminary. He'd never seen mountains or been out of New York City for that matter. He knew his mother would be delighted to see him visit a Seminary. Every Italian mother visualized her son as a priest. Paradoxically, Papa would be outraged and shout in Italian that no son of his would spend time with "Those Hypocrite Priests."

Mama would take care of Papa's histrionics and manage to get some extra pocket change for Carman's trip while she was about it. Because of her, Carman's name was added to Father Paul's list.

Father Paul considered himself successful if more than one name appeared on the list from Sister Amelia's graduating class. When five names appeared on the list he was ecstatic until he saw the last name Carman Duva.

"This is going to be a very interesting two weeks at St. Simon's. God help them. Of all the boys in St. Amelia's class, Carman was the least likely candidate for the priesthood. Unless of course, they allow priests to marry some day," the priest wondered thoughtfully. As Carman's confessor Father Paul knew that Carman had lost his virginity under bizarre circumstances, to an older girl, more than a year ago. The priest was also aware of Carman's continued success with several of the young women of the parish who were willing to share their wares with the young stallion.

Every Saturday afternoon, Carman would "bare his soul" to the astounded cleric. As the weeks passed and the priest listened to the boy, he became less critical of his behavior, realizing the boy was completely without malevolence and definitely exaggerating. He was convinced he could not have committed all those transgressions. It wasn't until pretty, twenty-year-old Annette Gasperino came to confession with a tale very similar to Carman's encounters that Father Paul stopped doubting the boy's prowess.

The idea of Carman becoming a priest was ludicrous, but since his name was on the list and his parents had signed all the necessary paper work, Father Paul reluctantly included Carman in his arrangements for the trip to St.Simon's. He was relieved that this year he would not be accompanying the boys to St. Simon's, but knew instinctively that something would go wrong.

Chapter Two

St. Simon's Seminary

On a beautiful May morning the boys from St. Mary's graduating class arrived at St. Simon's by horse and wagon. Although it was almost summer in New York City, the air in the mountains was crisp and felt cold to the boys as they jumped off the wagon. It was barely eighty miles away from home but the temperature has dropped at least twenty degrees. The stillness and beauty of the horizon captivated Carman. The mountains in the distance were breathtaking beautiful.

"What a place," he whispered to his friend Marty who nodded his head in agreement for he too was in awe of the beauty surrounding them in the Catskill Mountains. Waving to the farmer who had picked them up with his horse and wagon from the train station in a town called Hurleyville, they marched silently with the young prelate who had greeted them upon their arrival. The boys were both tired and hungry after two hours on a train and a bumpy hour drive on a farmer's old wagon. They barely noticed the beautiful statue of the Blessed Virgin as they passed under an ornate iron archway onto the grounds of St. Simon's Seminary.

The prelate directed them up three long flights of stairs and motioned to them to follow him. They stopped at a large double door that opened into the rooms of a very old visiting priest who was there for a long deserved rest and had asked to meet the young boys upon their arrival. They were ushered into an elaborately adorned apartment and told to stand in line to meet Monsignor Ricco, the visiting priest. Carman was pushed and shoved until he was the first one in line. The Monsignor, a small man only five feet tall but almost as wide, dressed in flowing robes of his office entered the room. The old priest looked at them without comprehension completely baffled by their appearance. Hoping to jar his memory the young prelate said, "Monsignor here are the boys you asked to see."

"Oh yes, yes" replied the Monsignor. "Very nice, very nice" He started at the back of the line and embraced each boy lightly kissing them on both cheeks. When the old priest finally got to Carman he looked completely confused and grabbed the boy kissing him fiercely on the mouth. Unknown to anyone watching the old priest stuck his tongue in Carman's mouth. With the quick reflexes of a thirteen-year-old Carman kneed the Monsignor causing him to fall to the floor howling.

"My God boy, what have you done? Have you lost your mind?" shouted the prelate.

"What have I done?" screamed Carman. "Do you know what he did?"

"Out get out all of you and wait in the hall," cried the prelate as he tried to lift the rotund Monsignor. Needless to say, Carman was taken to the Rector's office and chastised for his outlandish, barbaric behavior toward the Monsignor.

"Didn't he realize how old the Monsignor is? What harm could a mere kiss on the lips be? Thank God the Monsignor wasn't hurt," shouted the Rector.

Carman was never asked why he kicked the Monsignor and he never told anyone. He was content that they allowed him to stay, on the proviso that he would curb his blatant temper and do penance for his behavior. The old priest was questioned by the Rector but was unable or unwilling to remember anything about the incident. For some strange reason the old priest had a great deal of difficulty urinating, but decided not to mention that to the rector either.

On the second day at the seminary, the boys of St. Mary's committed another small indiscretion. After an exceedingly boring lecture by one of the priests at the seminary and a light lunch, the boys were encouraged to walk around the giant complex and enjoy the beautiful grounds. By mid-afternoon the boys were starving and unfortunately came upon a pen of unusually large chickens. Lucky for them, Vito, the butcher's son, was one of them. Carman coaxed one exceptionally beautiful chicken over to the edge of the fence and grabbed it. Running as if their lives depended on it, the boys headed deep into the woods surrounding the seminary. Once there, Vito skillfully twisted the chicken's neck as he had done countless times in his father's butcher shop. He then carefully slit the chicken's neck with his knife, a weapon most of the boys from the Bronx carried. In a matter of minutes Vito had the bird defeathered, cleaned and ready for the fire and spit the boys had fashioned.

After they finished eating the chicken they settled back to rest before returning to the complex.

"That had to be the best chicken I ever ate," said Marty.

"Nothing like a picnic in the woods," added Carman licking his fingers. Suddenly, out of the bushes jumped a young prelate, whose name the boys later learned was Father Hugh. The prelate was aghast at the sight of the beautiful feathers blowing in the breeze.

"God help me," he whispered. "You've eaten the Bishop's Rifle Bird."

"What do ya mean, Rifle Bird? It was just a chicken," exclaimed Vito.

"The Bishop brought that bird all the way from New Guinea and had its wings clipped to keep it penned," replied the prelate shaking his head in disbelief. Realizing the severity of what the boys had done he yelled, "Quick boys cover up that fire. If anyone else sees the smoke they'll be out here investigating and there will be hell to pay. Bury those bones and keep your moths shut. Play dumb if anyone asks you about the bird. Don't say anything at all, and you guys better eat a big dinner tonight." The boys did the best they could to cover up the evidence and meekly returned to the seminary.

The next day the boys were taken to the chapel for confession. On the way, one of the Seminarians asked Carman if he knew anything about the missing bird. In reply, Carman gave him an emphatic "no" and continued on his way to confession. It was the shortest confession Carman had had in a very long time.

"Bless me Father for I have sinned. I have lied once" was all he said. Pleased with himself that that was all he had to confess, he was surprised by the hefty penance the priest gave him which was a rosary said while kneeling at the altar rail. Father Paul only gave him a penance like that when he confessed that he had slept with a girl.

"Was it possible this priest knew exactly what he lied about?" he wondered.

The remainder of the two weeks passed uneventfully with lots of prayer, lectures and an increase in portions of really great food. All the boys returned home looking healthy and rested. Carman came back with a life long friend, Father Hugh, affectionately called "Father Hugh Who." Carman asked Father Hugh why he had covered up for the boys. The young prelate could not explain why. He said it was just the comical sight of boys licking their fingers, surrounded by those beautiful feathers.

"What was more important anyway, a boy or a chicken," was his final reply. It was because Father Hugh circulated the possibility of a "wild Fox" kidnapping the chicken that got the boys off the hook.

When the butcher's son Vito entered the seminary, Carman sincerely considered becoming a priest himself. Unfortunately, the memory of that strange kiss from the Monsignor stayed with him. Then there was this beautiful young widow who subsequently took a fancy to him. He was never really sure which reason had kept him from the priesthood.

Chapter Three

Home Again

Carman remembered how his brother Anthony had taken him under his wing after his memorable stay at St. Simon's Seminary. Of course Mama was disappointed she wanted a priest in the family. Not especially Carman, any Duva would do.

"It never hurt to have a little leverage in heaven" she'd say. Papa, on the other hand, was relieved to have Carman home again. The thought of his son celibate was unimaginable for him.

"No man was meant to live in that state. It isn't natural", he growled.

One day close to Carman's graduation from grammar school, Anthony asked him to take a walk with him to Morris Park Avenue. Carman of course went and while the brothers strolled Anthony said, "Carman, everybody has to work, even you little brother". They were standing outside of Similetti Piano Emporium.

"Are you talking about working at Similetti's by any chance?" asked Carman.

"What's wrong with Similetti's, I work here?" replied Anthony.

"You're thirteen now," he continued," Its time you earned your own way."

"Come on Anthony. I've got to finish high school. How will I get into college if I don't finish high school first, huh?" Carman replied with his voice cracking.

"Sister Amelia said that I got the highest mark of anyone who took the entrance exam for St. Michael's High School. She said I might be eligible for a scholarship to St. Michael's. If my grades are good enough I can even get a scholarship to Fordham. Imagine Anthony, Fordham University!" he said reverently.

"Well, if Sister Amelia pays all your other expenses and gives Papa two dollars a week, maybe we can work a deal," answered Anthony smiling.

"Think Carman," he continued seriously, "even if you do get a scholarship, who's gonna pay your way? We have to help Papa. He hasn't worked in six months and he's counting on us."

"Does Mama know you're taking me for a job?" asked Carman.

"You know Mama wants you to go to school. She's already lining up new boarders to take in to help pay your way. We both know Mama can't do any more work than she's doing now. I've never seen her sleep, have you?" Anthony questioned.

"No, I've never seen her sleep either," answered Carman, lowering his head. "It's just that"...he couldn't finish, he knew the inevitable.

"Come on," said Anthony softly, "you get a job now, make some money and we'll see, maybe I can help you."

"Sure" thought Carman, "then he'll never sleep either. Well, how do I look?" said Carman brushing his hair out of his eyes.

"You look fine. Just remember to stand up straight, and don't smile, look serious. Nod your head to everything he tells you. Mr. Similetti likes that," said Anthony looking at his brother and realizing what a good looking kid he was with those coal black eyes and jet-black hair. No wonder some of his friends' call him "Blackie." You'd never guess we were brothers.

Anthony was as fair as Carman was dark. He had hair the color of flax, and hazel eyes, but he had the same good looks as all the Duva boys. Their brother John, a mixture of the two younger Duva's was unquestionably the most handsome.

Carman entered Similetti's Piano Emporium and was surprised by the number of pianos that lined the walls. He had never seen so many in one place. They literally glowed in the afternoon sunlight. Fortunately, Carman didn't realize that the shine on all those pianos would be his responsibility.

Anthony introduced Carman to Mr. Similetti and Mr. Similetti took to Carman almost immediately. As he questioned Carman he was impressed by the boy's contemplative responses. Surprisingly, Carman was hired on the spot and started the day after graduation from grammar school.

Sometimes late in the evening, long after Mr. Similetti had gone home for the day, Carman would sit at the jet black Wurlitzer. To his surprise, Carman discovered he had a gift for music, something he never would Anthony introduced Carman to Mr. Similetti and he took to Carman have known if he had not gotten his first job waxing pianos. At first the music he played, if you could call it music, was discordant almost ethereal.

Eventually, he could play on the piano the melodies he heard in his head as he entertained the cleaning woman as well as himself. It was always difficult for him play to the Wurlitzer. When he would finally arrive home Mama would always ask why he was so late. She suspected it was one of those "fast women" that she had heard about at the market. To ease Mama's vivid imagination, Carman would sing to her the song he had made up that night. The words were usually hilarious and Mama loved to hear them. Carman's singing voice left much to be desired, which made the songs he sang even funnier.

One evening Carman arrived home early.

"Did you eat, Carman?" Mama asked.

"No Mama, where would I eat if not here? Who is the best cook in the entire Bronx?

"You know just how to get around your Mama. Now sit and I make you a nice frittata, but be quiet, your Papa just got in and he is very tired" she whispered.

"Mama" he said, "you sit and tell me about your day. I can make an omelet. I never get a chance to talk to you anymore." He suddenly realized looking at his mother that her hair was sprinkled with gray. Even her walk was slowed. She used to literally fly around the kitchen. Her beautiful face was getting old.

"Carman," she said as she dropped into a chair, "if you came home earlier we could talk. We could even start making plans for you to go to high school. I have a lot to tell you about," she added.

"I've decided to wait awhile before I go to high school. I have a good opportunity at Similetti's."

"Sure you have. Polishing pianos is a profession," she said in her halting English. "There's a big demand for piano polishers. In fact I bet if I could read a newspaper, I'd see big ads for "Polishers." What are you talking about? You're gonna go to high school and then to college and make something of yourself. God gave you a good mind. You can't waste it. That would be a sin."

"Please Mama, I promise you I will go to high school and then college, but not now - soon. Mr. Similetti wants me to help in the office with the accounts. Anthony told him that I'm good at math, and he said he'd give me a chance. The regular clerk is sick with pneumonia."

"Mrs. Misetti's boy?" she queried.

"Yes Mama."

"Is it bad Carman?"

"No."

"You've been in the office with him there sick."

"No."

"Good Carman, it is not that I am not sorry that the Misetti boy is sick, I just don't want you to get pneumonia. You'll get a raise Carman?"

"Yes Mama."

"Good boy Carman." She said as she got up and kissed his cheek. "You still have to go to school right."

"Right Mama, now go to bed. I'll clean up here."

"You know Carman; I'm a very lucky woman to have such good sons."

"Good night Mama."

"Good night Carmino."

He ate his omelet and wondered if ever he would get back to school. He could hear his little sister Dominica coughing, and then his mother going into her room. He was certain Mama was giving his sister one of her famous but foul tasting remedies. Bad as they were, Mama's concoctions usually worked. Thinking of little Dominica always made him smile. She was such a happy little girl and he just loved her. He could make her feel special by just calling her Dominica. Everyone else called her Mamie. A name she hated but seemed to be stuck with. Dominica, with the face of an angel was as dark as her brother was. Carman was certain that little Dominica would break a lot of hearts on her way to becoming a woman. Time had a way of flying by unnoticed, but he resolved to closely watch the phenomenon. He was determined to see her grow into a beautiful woman.

Just as he started to wash the dishes, the kitchen door opened and Anthony came in carrying giant bag of groceries.

"You're not going to believe me Carman but I've got a girlfriend and her Papa owns a grocery store."

"Get out of here," Carman answered convinced that his brother was kidding.

"I swear it's true. Her name is Pauline and her father is a grocer and he actually owns several stores. He likes me and he insisted that I bring home as many groceries as I could carry."

Listening to his brother ramble on, he was certain that there was a catch here somewhere. Apprehensively he asked, "What does Pauline look like?"

"Carman she's a beauty. I can't understand why he gave me the groceries either."

"Anthony, this is your first girl friend and you're acting as if you're in love. I thought you were gonna be the priest in this family?"

"Carman, me a priest? Well, to be honest I have thought about it, but not anymore. You won't believe your eyes when you see her, I know I can't."

"Enough," shouted Carman," I'll be fourteen next week and I've had - I don't really know how many girlfriends. You can't be in love so quickly. Please Anthony," he begged, "don't be in love. I thought that in a few years I'd be old enough to hang out with you and we could get to know all the girls in the neighborhood together."

"Don't worry little brother, I'm not married yet. We're gonna have plenty of time to hang out together. In fact, I expect to learn a lot from you. Now help me put these groceries away."

Chapter Four

1929

The snow continued to fall but Carman ignored it and walked quietly into the kitchen. "What a wonderful room," he thought. It was almost completely white. There were white tiles on the floor and the cabinets were painted white. Even the counter was white. The crockery was white. There were always fresh flowers in season displayed in a white porcelain jug on the kitchen table. It was the brightly colored curtains that gave the room warmth. He walked to the sink and washed the coffeepot and made another pot of coffee. As he watched the water percolate, the wonderful aroma of the coffee permeated the kitchen. When the water turned a dark brown color that could be seen in the small glass dome of the pot, he knew that the coffee was ready. He poured himself a cup and reached for a bottle of rye whiskey from the cabinet above the sink. He poured a hefty shot into the coffee. He called it "Coffee Royal." It was the perfect drink for a long night. He carried his coffee back to the parlor. As he sat drinking it, his mind wandered back to the night so many years ago when he first saw Anna.

"My God," he said aloud, "was I that young when this nightmare began?"

1911

He remembered sitting in the dimly lit back office of Similetti's, his fingers numb from the cold as he added countless rows of figures checking them over and over looking for his error. He stood up to stretch and remained with his arms over his head immobilized by the sight of her. She had blond hair flowing in ringlets down her back that fell softly to the tiniest waist he had ever seen. She turned and in that moment Carman's life changed forever. Never had he seen anyone to match her beauty. Her eyes were the color of turquoise coral, and her skin was lightly colored by the touch of the sun. He couldn't begin to describe her mouth. He was fascinated.

"Hello," she said breathless from running up the narrow stairs to the office with the speed of a gazelle.

"So you're the boy my father keeps raving about, the boy with, what does he say, oh yes the boy with a head for figures." She stepped closer with hands on her hips and remarked with a sigh, "I thought you'd be much older."

"Sorry to disappoint you," replied Carman lowering his aching arms. "You've got to be Anna.

"Well who else would you expect to see in his store this late at night, a thief?"

"Which one are you, a thief or Anna?"

"Don't be a fool boy."

This is a cold one, thought Carman as he eyed her carefully looking for imperfections and finding none.

"How old are you exactly?" he asked finally.

"On my next birthday, I'll be eighteen," she announced proudly although a little unnerved by his unwavering gaze.

"That's pretty old", he said.

"Well how old are you, 16?"

"Right on the head, 16." In two years he said under his breath sitting down at his desk.

It was in the light of the small desk lamp that Anna finally got a good look at Carman; she froze with her mouth open.

"My" was all she said.

"My what?" asked Carman? Anna was not the first female to be startled by Carman's dark good looks. Fortunately he never took his appearance too seriously. Well, almost never.

"My," she repeated as she spun on her heel and ran down the stairs as if her life depended on it.

Carman sat back in his chair and thought, "beautiful, she's just beautiful. Not for you Carman, this one is for you. He returned to his work and finally found his error and was able to go home.

ANNA

Anna lay in bed twisting and turning unable to sleep. Just who was this strange boy Papa had hired? It was her curiosity that had gotten the better of her. After listening to Papa rave about the boy he had hired to polish his pianos, and who now was doing his books, she just had to see him. Now she could not sleep thinking about him. Those eyes, my God those eyes. He looked at me as if, as if, she sat up in bed with a start, "as if he could see into my soul," she said aloud. Anna was not prepared for the impact this curious boy had on her. She was unaccustomed to think about anyone, except herself. Thinking about Carman was very disturbing, especially remembering the feeling of being trapped in that little upstairs office. Her desire to flee was more compelling than her attraction to this young boy. Was he really two years younger? Perhaps he was almost seventeen. After all she was barely eighteen.

"What's the difference he's only a boy, she thought as she tried in vain to fall asleep. Completely exasperated she threw back the bed covers off, put on her robe and slippers, and headed for the kitchen for a glass of warm milk. A glass of wine would probably work much better but Papa would find out and the backlash wasn't worth the effort.

Mama called out from the top of the stairs to see if she was all right. Anna answered wearily that she was completely fine and told her mother to go back to bed. Anna could never understand how her mother could detect her roaming through the house since every room was so richly carpeted. The ornately carved staircase was so thickly carpeted that she imagined a horse could gallop soundlessly up and down the stairs. "Maybe my door squeaks." Quietly Anna warmed a pot of milk on the wood stove. When it was ready she poured the milk in a glass and carrying it carefully, she slowly crept back to her bed where she eventually fell into a troubled sleep.

Anna awoke the next morning cross from her lack of sleep. Since she was always irritated about something, her lack of sleep went unnoticed by everyone. The servants heard her shouting and knew she was up.

"Rosa, come help me dress," she shrieked.

"Where were you," she continued as Rosa entered the room with bowed head knowing that no matter what she answered, Anna would continue to harass her. She waited until the barrage was over and set about laying our Anna's clothes all the while thinking, "God help the poor bastard this one marries, and please let it be soon."

She knew Anna very well and was wise enough to escape her wrath with a few techniques she has learned taking care of the spoiled, pampered, mollycoddled "witch". The name she was called by most of the household staff. In fact some of the kitchen help were convinced that Anna had some mystical power and avoided any contact with her whatsoever.

Dressed in the finest clothes money could buy, Anna set out to find her father. She was determined to learn as much about Carman as possible. Anna considered herself very clever and she had decided on a scheme to get close to the boy. She found her father reading his paper in the study.

Sweetly she whispered in her fathers' ear, "Papa, do you have one little minute for me?"

"For you, Papa always has a minute," he answered putting his paper down.

"Well Papa, I've been wondering if I could learn about the piano business. Maybe you could use me in the office to help with some of the paper work?"

"What do you know about paper work?"

"Well Papa, that's it exactly. I don't know anything about your business and since you're always talking about the new boy, I thought, well, I'd like to learn something, and maybe he could teach me."

"Ah, so you've met Carman and now you want to know about the piano business."

"Meeting Carman has nothing to do with it. He seems to work very late and I thought that I could help."

"Anna, Anna, Carman likes to work late to make more money. You my darling daughter belong here with you Mama, not in a cold damp office."

"Oh Papa," she replied with tears in her voice.

"You seem very interested in this boy Anna. He may look older than he is but believe me, he is just a boy."

"Oh Papa please. I try to show a little interest in your business and you think I'm only interested in a mere boy. You know perfectly well that I am engaged to Guardo."

"Anna my bambino, don't get upset. I am very pleased that you want to help out. Papa will find something for you to do. Now go and help your Mama," he said as he led her out of his study.

"Too bad Carman isn't older," thought Mr. Similetti. "He was by far a more preferable suitor than Guardo was for his Anna. Carman's family came from money in the old country. I wonder what happened to it." He was very fond of Carman. There wasn't anything that the boy was not eager to learn. He was just born a little too late and a little too poor for his Anna.

"What a shame," he thought as he went back to reading his paper.

Chapter Five

1912

Carman walked home whistling a melody that had been racing through his head most of the day. "If I could write music," he thought, "I wouldn't have to rely on my memory for the melodies that come and just as quickly leave." He was determined that someday he would learn. It wasn't enough to be able to play what you heard. You had to be able to write it down. Deep in thought, he didn't notice his brother running to catch up to him, until he tapped him on the shoulder. Carman jumped at his touch.

"Hey Carman, it's me Anthony, take it easy. What's the matter, did I scare you?"

"You scared the shit out of me."

"You got the knife Papa gave you?"

"I've got it Anthony, don't worry. If I lost it Papa would give me one kick with his boot and I wouldn't walk for a week."

"The old man is tough all right, but he gave you the knife for protection," answered his brother as they walked matching strides down the dark street. They decided to go to Guardo's for coffee and crumb cake. Anthony wanted to talk, and Carman was hungry, freezing and willing to listen. Anthony put his arm around Carman as they walked the rest of the way huddled together against the cold. Sitting down at one of the back tables sipping hot coffee, Carman asked, are you ok, you look really pale?"

"I'm fine," Anthony answered looking around the dingy little restaurant.

Guardos' was completely devoid of atmosphere, and by most standards was definitely grimy. But the prices were right and the crumb cake divine.

"Ok Anthony, what's the story?" asked Carman as he dunked the crumb cake carefully into his mug of coffee and took an enormous bite.

"Well," Anthony answered in almost a whisper; "I'm in love." Carman started to choke on his cake causing Anthony to pound him on his back. Tears rolled down his face he was laughing so hard.

"Anthony you've got to be more careful when you tell me things. Do you want me to choke to death?"

"Maybe if you didn't put a whole cake in your mouth at one time you might have a little room to breathe," he answered laughing.

"Come on Anthony, are you really in love?"

"I think so. Well, I know so. Well I better be. I just asked her to marry me."

"Her who?" said Carman.

"I told you about Pauline. Remember the groceries?"

"Ah, you're gonna marry the girl so we can get free groceries?"

"Carman don't make fun, I'm serious."

Carman could see that he was serious and leaned over the table and gave his brother a big hug. "What the hell," he said, "Why shouldn't you be in love?"

"What do you really think, Carman?"

"I think you should marry her. Knowing you the way I do I'm sure you've just been shaking her hand goodnight, right?"

"Hey, some guys respect women. Not everybody can be like you, although you better be careful for one of these days..."

"I know, I know. I'm just a boy. I'm not a man yet."

"God help us Carman, when you're a man."

"So you're going to marry Pauline?" said Carman eager to get the conversation away from his exploits.

"Yes," he answered loud and clear.

"You sound rally sure."

"I am Carman."

"How are you going to support a wife on the salary Similetti pays you?"

"I'm getting a job at the Telephone Company."

"Sure Anthony and your Mama's name is Mary Leary."

"Carman, I've got it all set up. Marty Fagan, a friend of mine, is taking me downtown for an interview. I'm going to start as a lineman."

"Be sensible, the Telephone Company never hires Italians."

"Who's Italian? You're talking to Steve Duval. My parents were born in France."

"Well you sure as hell don't look Italian but where are you going to get proof?"

"Marty's getting a baptismal certificate with my new name on it."

"You think that's all the proof you're going to need?"

"Carman, they only ask for proof if you look like a real "WOP.""

"Christ, if you weren't my brother I'd bop you one. I can't stand that expression."

"I'm sorry. Hey, when I get you into the Telephone Company you'll be French too."

"Yeah right, have you ever noticed how dark I am?"

"We'll think of something," Anthony replied.

"Ok, so you get a new fancy job, what then?" asked Carman wondering why anyone would marry so young. He planned to live the life of a happy bachelor, loving and leaving them.

"Pauline and I are going to have the bans announced next week and be married June first. What do you think?"

"I think you're nuts to marry so young. Have you gotten permission from her father yet?"

"Incredibly her father said yes right away. He did say that Pauline was delicate and that I'd have to take very good care of her."

"There's more here than meets the eye. Your Pauline is really a beautiful girl. There's got to be plenty of guys lining up for her hand. How come her father gave you the nod?"

"You gotta start calling me Steve now, kid. Anyway, Pauline loves me and that's enough for her father. Besides our grandparents came from the same town and that means a lot to him."

"Yeah, I bet he thinks you're going to own Papa's vineyards again,"

"No, it's nothing like that but someday I'd like to go back to Italy and claim our land. We could be rich if I can get that ungrateful cousin of Papa's to relinquish his claim on our vineyards."

"I never realized that you were such a dreamer "Steve.""

"My brother is going to take a lot of looking after if he really believes all the nonsense Papa feeds him," thought Carman as the brothers ambled home. "It must be because Anthony was born in Italy that he has such a tie to the old country. Sometimes late at night, when everyone was asleep, Carman would hear his father and Anthony planning their return to Italy. Too bad the only thing I ever get from Papa is a boot in the backside and a promise of more. Papa doesn't consider Dominica and me Italian because we were born in America. Only Anthony and John have that distinction because they were born in Italy.

When they finally got home, Mama was waiting for them with a bowl of spaghetti for Carman. Papa insisted that real Italians eat macaroni and so there was a bowl of "Ziti" too, for the real Italians in the family. His mother, as usual, stood waiting with a towel over her arm ready to serve them.

"Mama, why do you stand there every night waiting for us to ask for something? You're not a waitress, you know," said Carman

"It's the custom," she replied in her beautiful Italian. "My Mama and her Mama before her stood waiting as their men sat down to supper. Maybe someday the custom will change. I'd like to think that my Dominica would sit down and eat with her family. But for now, I stand. After all, you work all day long."

"But Mama you work all day too. You even work after everybody goes to bed."

Refusing to sit, Mama said, "you are the man and I am the woman. Now eat and be quiet."

After everyone finished dinner and left, Mama started to clear the table. Carman stayed behind and insisted that she sit down and let him clean up. Reluctantly she did saying, "Carman tell me about your day."

"Not much to tell Mama except. . .

"What is it Carman, you want to ask me something, go ahead. You look so serious. You're not in trouble are you?"

"No Mama, he answered, "I was just wondering what you know about Anthony's girlfriend Pauline?"

"Is that all? You had me worried for a minute. Well "she continued, "Pauline is a nice girl. I think it will be a good marriage. The only thing that worries me is she's a very delicate girl. She was a sick child and it left her weak. Her Papa is afraid for her. He knows Anthony is a good man and will take care of Pauline no matter what happens. Your brother loves this girl and she loves him. In the end that's all that really matter. You too are a good man. But you are different than Anthony in many ways. Life to you is very exciting and challenging. I pray every night that life will be kind to you. Afraid to break your spirit, I let you grow up a little wild. In some ways my Camino, you are untamed like your Papa. Someday you too, will be hit by the thunderbolt and fall in love like your brother."

"I hope not Mama, at least not until I'm an old man." He replied.

"Now I go to bed," she said as she got up wearily and kissed her young son goodnight.

Carman finished the dishes and turned out the light and headed for bed.

Juana lay in bed listening to the rhythmic sound of her husband's snoring, which usually lulled her to sleep. Tonight, tired as she was, sleep would not come. After talking to Carman about Anthony it was impossible not to think of her oldest son John. "My sweet boy, how I miss you," she thought. The only thing she knew how to do when she thought about John was to pray. So Juana prayed until the dawn came up when she finally fell asleep.

Chapter Six

JOHN

The first child born to Juana and Paul Duva was a son named John after both of his grandfathers. This beautiful child more than compensated for the many disappointments the young couple had endured during their first few years of marriage. By the time John was a year old he was babbling contentedly. Although only Juana could decipher exactly what he was saying, everyone agreed he was an extraordinary baby. He grew into an enchanting child eager to please and delight. He was obviously loved by his father Paul who spoiled the boy. This was unusual of Paul as he was detached and outwardly dispassionate, but John was his father's pride and joy. He flourished in the beautiful countryside surrounded by love and attention. Juana was afraid that without restrictions the boy would grow up irreverent and superficial but was helpless to deny him anything for she herself, was enchanted by the child. In spite of the deferential treatment, John grew to be an earnest, serious and very sensible young man

Paul inherited his father's vineyard despite the objection of his father's brother Louis. His Uncle Louis felt that he should have inherited at least half of his brother's wealth since he had worked side by side with his brother to make the vineyard a success. Paul realized the inadequacies of the will and gave his uncle one quarter of the vineyards to plant and harvest for himself. Although outwardly grateful, Louis Duva conspired and planned for the day that the entire vineyard would be his.

Almost eight years later, after several miscarriages, Anthony was born. Paul was content having two sons would continue the legacy of the Duva vineyards. Life went on uneventfully but happily, for the Duva family with Mama waiting on her men as was the custom in an Italian household, and Papa happy as the "Padrone." Although considered wealthy, the family lived simply for the most part, except when it came to educating their sons when only the best would do. As John grew he became more involved with his studies. Secretly he longed to be a physician but was content to learn as much as he could. John believed that extraordinary possibilities awaited him and learning was the road to all goals.

At fourteen, John became quite the ladies man. He was good-looking and appeared much older than his actual years, a fact not lost on the young girls of the village. His Uncle Louis encouraged his philandering hoping that in some way he could discredit the boy to his father.

By the time John was barely sixteen he had impregnated not one, but two of the girls in the village. Both girls were beautiful and from very good families. The dilemma was too involved even for the village priest who had been called in as a mediator for the three families. In very rare cases like this it was usually the errant man's brother who came forward to rectify the situation by marrying one of the pregnant girls. Unfortunately, John's brother Anthony was only eight years old and not a candidate. What to do? Even Mama, who could usually resolve almost any situation, was baffled.

John was so young he could not think of any way to change the situation. His only thought was to flee, but his guilty conscience prevented that. If there were a way out of this predicament he would take it.

"Papa, what am I going to do?" John asked in frustration.

"My God son, you've got yourself cornered, I don't know what to tell you. Do you love one of these girls perhaps?"

"Of course Papa, do you think I go to bed with any girl?"

"Well who is it?" his father asked wearily. .

"It's Rosa I love Papa, and she loves me. Maria was just there."

"What do you mean, Maria was just there."

"It's true Papa, I had too much wine and Maria was there and before I realized what I was doing it was over. It was just one time Papa, I swear."

"Did you realize Maria was a virgin?" asked Papa.

"Rosa was a virgin too, Papa," added John.

"Mama Mia" exclaimed his father.

Loud screaming was heard coming from the road. Both Papa and John ran outside to see what was happening. Standing in the middle of the road was Carlo Fementi, Rosa's father. In his arms was the lifeless body of his daughter. Children from the village school had gone to the lake for a picnic when they discovered Rosa's body floating at the waters' edge.

"Look what you have done John Duva, you have killed my Rosa," cried Mr. Fementi.

With tears running down his cheeks, John ran to Mr.Fementi.

"Please let me carry her, he begged, it is too much for you."

As Mr. Fementi reluctantly handed over his daughter to John, he fell to the ground in exhaustion. John's father bent to help him up as he whispered words of comfort. Holding him up, Paul Duva guided the distraught father to his home.

John, clutching Rosa to his chest, was unaware of Maria following quietly behind. As they reached the Fementi house Rosa's mother stood in the doorway with her hands covering her face unable to witness the terrible scene.

John entered the house and went to Rosa's room. There, he laid her down as gently as possible. Carefully he removed her matted hair from her face and gasped at her beauty, even in death.

"Rosa, Rosa, I am so sorry, so sorry, forgive me," he murmured over and over again. Maria, who had followed John into the room, tenderly turned John to herself and held him tightly as he sobbed in her arms. Gently she led him out of the house and back to his home, where Mama took over.

The entire village went to Rosa's funeral. Old Father Bruno, who had seen too many innocent deaths in his lifetime, was determined to bring peace to Benevento. There was no one else in the village who could calm the people like he could. He knew that Rosa's family was grief stricken and capable of doing great harm to young John Duva. His first proclamation was to declare Rosa's death an accident thereby giving the family the right to have a Mass in church and to bury Rosa in consecrated ground. This act alone was enough, for the time being, to defuse the family's wrath. Father Bruno also asked John not to attend Rosa's funeral, as he feared for John's life. Vendetta in this part of the country was undertaken for far less grievances.

John acquiesced to the priest's request and remained home with his grief. Through all of his misery Maria was by his side, although at times he was unaware of her. Maria's gentle hands would massage his aching head, as she would softly whisper encouragement into his unresponsive ear. He finally pushed her aside and begged her to leave him alone in his sorrow.

The weeks passed and he came to terms with Rosa and his unborn child's death. He made a decision that would have far reaching consequences to the entire Duva family. He would quietly marry Maria and go to America.

John approached his father with his plan but his father was distraught with his decision and tried to dissuade him

"I must go Papa, Maria carries my child and I will not have this baby brought up in the shadow of my stupidity. I lost both the girl I loved and our unborn baby. I cannot take the chance of losing Marie and her child too. Can you understand Papa?"

Paul grabbed his son and held him close. John was his oldest and dearest son and his heart was breaking at the prospect of never seeing him again. With tears in his eyes he told John he did understand and would give him whatever he would need to start a new life in America. Mama was not told about John's leaving until the day of his departure. There were no histrionics, just tears that never seemed to stop.

Maria and John spent their honeymoon in Rome. As they made love, all their cares seemed to disappear. One touch of John's hand on her body caused Maria to respond. His tender kisses drove her wild, and as he caressed her breasts, kissing them delicately, she was in ecstasy. As they made love again and again, John could not believe his passion. Even watching her sleep, he was aroused by her beauty. Although he prayed that he would grow to love her, the memory of Rosa still haunted him.

Maria had loved John from the time that they were children in school. She would have gladly had his child without marriage. Rosa's death had made it possible for her to have it all, John and the baby. Maria refused to feel guilty about Rosa, but continued to give of herself to John with all the love in her young heart. She was convinced that, John eventually would love her, as she loved him.

Chapter Seven

1929

Carman didn't know why or how, but Madelyn came into his mind. Thinking about her was always pleasant. He couldn't help but smile remembering her lovely face.

1914

It was an ordinary day, but one he would not forget easily. On his way to Similetti's he saw her and called, "Madelyn, wait up." She turned at the sound of her name and Carman running toward her. Her heart skipped a beat at the sight of him.

"I can't believe this, is it really Carman?" she thought.

Standing still, afraid to move, she thought, "what should I say to him, how should I act, God help me? I think I'm going to faint."

Catching up to her Carman exclaimed breathlessly, "Is it really you, I can't believe it? I've never seen you around here before, how are you?"

"I'm just fine," she answered shyly.

"Well you look terrific," said Carman.

He was clearly shocked by her appearance. She never looked this good in school. She was absolutely gorgeous.

"Thank you "was all she could reply, afraid to trust her voice talking to him.

She was remembering all those years in school hoping he would notice her, but he just seemed completely unaware of her existence.

"I can't get over you, you're beautiful."

"Please, you're making me blush," she said trying to hide her flushed face.

"Being beautiful is nothing to be ashamed of. It's just that I never noticed it before and now I'm making a complete fool of myself?

"You could never be a fool."

"I appreciate that," he answered, wondering why his hands were trembling.

"Where are you going? You do realize you're in an Italian neighborhood?"

"Of course, I work here," she answered smiling broadly.

"Where?"

"Caesar's Tailor, around the corner from Similetti's," she answered.

"I work in Similetti's,"

"You're joking, Carman.

"No, I swear."

"I can't believe it," she said.

They stood gazing at one another and suddenly laughter erupted from both of them. They started to talk, interrupting one another as their laughter engulfed them all over again.

Finally Carman said, "go out with me tonight. I'll take you to a very, and I mean very, reasonable restaurant for supper. What do you say?"

"I say, yes." What time do you get off?"

"Not until eight."

"Me too, " she lied eagerly. I'll meet you at Similetti's at eight."

"It's a date," he answered as he ran to work.

Madelyn fairly danced into Caesar's Tailor. She could not believe that Carman had asked her out. "Thank you Lord, I'll never ask for another thing," she whispered

Sitting at his desk, Carman could still not get over Madelyn's transformation from a skinny little girl to beautiful young lady! "Could someone change this much in such a short time? Perhaps it's been a year and a half, well maybe two years," he thought as he dragged out his accounting books. "Who knows, I've lost all track of time since I started work. Christ I'll be sixteen in August. Where did all that time go?

Forget it. I've got to come up with some money for tonight. I'm sure Mama will give me some if I ask. I just hate to ask. But it's for a good cause. Maybe this is the thunderbolt Mama keeps talking about." In his heart he knew it wasn't. He wouldn't have to ask himself if it were.

He was caught up in figures adding and subtracting all morning.

At lunchtime, he hurried home to get some money for his date. Luckily Mama was busy and didn't ask why he needed the money. She just handed him her purse and said "take what you need."

This he did gladly. He changed his shirt, splashed some of Anthony's cologne on his face and carefully combed his hair. He ran all the way back to work.

Dashing up the stairs he saw Mr. Similetti's daughter Anna sitting at his desk.

"Gad, what does she want?" he wondered. "Boy, she's real pretty, a little crazy too. But she's too old, and too damn rich." he thought.

"What can I do for you, Anna?" he said as he came into the office.

"Not a thing Carman. I just stopped by to look at you," she replied calmly.

"Boy, she really is nuts," thought Carman. Ignoring her reply he calmly asked,

"Can you go to the post office for me?"

"How can I look at you if I go to the post office?"

"Come on Anna, be serious, will you go?"

"I am serious. I can't seem to stop thinking about you. I've decided to look very hard at you to see what it is about you that I am attracted to. "Is that ok with you?" she asked.

"Anna, you're my boss's daughter and I really think you're terrific. But maybe you haven't noticed I'm just a little young for you. You don't want to be accused of robbing the cradle do you?"

"I know Carman. That is a problem, isn't it? I'm almost twenty-one. It's just an infatuation, nothing more then that. I will just have to ignore it, won't I?"

"That's a great idea. Now please go to the post office for me and on your way think of your fiancée, Guardo."

"Please Carman, I always think of Guardo. I'm going to marry him some day. It's just that you fascinate me. For no apparent reason, you seem to invade my thoughts."

"Anna, do you think you should talk to me like this? It's a little strange isn't it?"

"Why not Carman, you work for my father and you are only a boy. What's the harm?"

"The harm is that you embarrass me."

"Carman, I doubt that in your entire almost sixteen years, you've ever been embarrassed. Now, where are the things you want mailed?"

"Right here," he said handing her a large bundle. "And please get me some stamps too,

"Ok Carman, but I have to get money from Papa. Bye Carman," she said as she sailed down the stairs.

"God help poor Guardo, she's really nuts."

Carman sat down to his figures and forgot everything; even his date with Madelyn, until he looked at the clock and saw that it was already seven forty-five. Rubbing his eyes from the strain of working with numbers all day, he closed the lights and ran down the stairs to keep his date.

He opened the door and saw Madelyn standing under the street light.

"God," he thought, "There is nothing as beautiful as an Irish girl. He had, of course come across a few who could stop a clock, but when they were beautiful, no other nationality could compare. This opinion comes from an unbiased full-blooded Italian.

"Hi, waiting long?"

"Not long at all. It's so beautiful out tonight with the scent of summer in the air; I could stand here all night."

"My favorite time of the year," replied Carman.

"Mine too. Well, where are you taking me for dinner."

"To a little Italian restaurant, where the food is great."

"What's it called?"

"Lamana's, and its just a few blocks from here," he said as he took her hand.

Madelyn caught her breath as she felt the pressure of Carman's hand. Chills ran up and down her spine as if she were coming down with a bad cold. He turned to her and smiled, completely unaware of his effect on her. It was a beautiful evening and as they walked hand in hand, passersby looked at them and smiled. They were young and radiant. It was impossible to ignore them.

As long as they stayed in the Italian section Carman felt safe, but he knew that if he would wander out of little Italy into the Irish section he would probably find trouble.

"I can't worry about that now," he thought "there's something about this girl that makes me feel great."

As they got closer to the small neighborhood restaurant, they could smell the tantalizing aroma of Mama Lamana's cooking.

"Can you smell that Madelyn, isn't it glorious?"

"What is it Carman, remember I'm Irish?"

"It smells like fried Calamari."

"What's Calamari, Carman?"

"It's squid," he answered.

"Oh God Carman, people really eat squid?"

"Don't worry, I'll order for both of us and I won't tell you what you're eating. I guaranty you'll love it."

"Ok, Carman anything you say, but please no squid."

As they entered the dimly lit restaurant, Mama Lamana called from the kitchen; "Carman how's your Mama?"

"She's fine," he answered.

"Good, sit down with your friend, I've made something marvelous tonight."

Looking around the tiny, immaculately clean restaurant with the little red candles flickering on each white table cloth and all the colored bottles of wine and oil lining the walls, he was glad he had brought Madelyn there.

"Oh Carman," she exclaimed, "what a lovely place. I can see myself in the shining floors, and look at the beautiful flowers on all the windowsills. I love it."

"You're gonna love it even more after you taste Mama Lamana's cooking,"

When their food arrived, Madelyn could not identify any dish. With Carman's prompting she managed to try everything. The only thing she could not abide was the little black fish lying on their appetizers. Carman assured her that a lot of Italians didn't like them either. On the other hand he seemed to relish them and she was more than happy to give him hers.

After eating they sat looking at one another over the remains of the little red candle. They could barely move after the feast Mama Lamana had cooked for them.

True to his word, everything was delicious and aside from the little black fishes, Madelyn never asked what she was eating.

"Carman, I really can't move," she said.

"Neither can I, don't worry we'll take a stroll around the park and we'll feel fine."

Carman had his arm around Madelyn's waist as they left the restaurant. He was holding her up and unconsciously drawing her closer to him. They entered the park, which was crowded with couples walking hand in hand. After they walked a little while Carman asked, "are you feeling better?"

"I feel fine Carman," she answered snuggling closer to him.

"I feel fine too, let's head for the lake and sit down for awhile.

It was relatively quiet as they approached the lake. Most of the strollers had gone to the bandstand to listen to the music. You could hear it as it drifted softly down to the lake. With the reflection of the moon on the water, you couldn't ask for a better setting.

Looking at this beautiful girl, Carman found himself overwhelmed with desire. He was suddenly shy, unwilling to take advantage of this lovely girl. Taking a deep breath he turned to Madelyn and said,

"Well Madelyn, tell me about yourself, what have you been doing since graduation?"

She tilted her head, and with a knowing smile kissed Carman softly.

It was the sweetest kiss he had ever felt. He grabbed her fiercely and kissed her deeply. He had to get control of himself. He wanted to make love to this girl but was afraid. What he felt for Madelyn was very different than anything he had experienced before. He jumped up from the grass they were sitting on, grabbed Madelyn by the hand and ran from the park. They stood breathless on the street. Madelyn stood on tiptoe and kissed Carman on the cheek.

"Thank you," she murmured. She too had experienced overwhelming desire and was afraid she could not break the spell herself.

"You're very welcome, he replied, feeling pretty good about himself.

"I don't think it's a good idea for you to walk me home. You'll be out of your neighborhood and perhaps in a little danger."

"I'll just have to chance it. I want to make sure you get home ok. We'll go the back way and if we're lucky, we won't meet anyone on the way."

They snaked their way safely into the Irish neighborhood. When they arrived at Madelyn's house Carman kissed her lightly and made a date to meet her on Sunday afternoon. He retreated the same way he had entered without an incident.

Walking home, Carman was struck by the notion that something wonderful was happening to him. He didn't know what the feeling was, but wondered if it could be love. Then again, maybe what he was feeling was good old-fashioned lust. No, it couldn't be lust. It was something entirely different. Could I be in love? No, no way, I'm just a kid. No one falls in love this young. Besides I can't let it happen. I've got too many things to do. I'm not ready for any responsibility. Not yet anyway. When he entered the courtyard he saw his mother sitting at the window waiting for him.

"Carman" said his mother as he opened the door, "come talk to Dominica. She has been crying all evening and she will not tell us what is wrong. Your Papa is very upset. You know how he worries about her. Please bambino, see what's the matter with her."

"Sure Mama, I'll find out what's wrong," he answered as he walked down the hall to his sister's room. He could hear her crying as he approached her room.

"Mama Mia, is there no peace for me, "he said as he knocked softly on her door. When there was no reply he opened the door and asked, "Its Carman, can I come in a minute?"

When she still didn't reply he went slowly into the room and saw her huddled, clutching one of her dolls.

"And I thought you gave up playing with dolls years ago, although you look very sweet with a little dolly in your arms."

With that remark, Dominica flung the doll at Carman and cried, "what do you know about me looking sweet. Everybody teases me because I am the tallest girl in the class. Even the boy I like called me a string bean today, and Papa won't let me get a new dress for graduation and Mama say's I'm too young to wear a long dress any way and Paul says---"

"Stop, please," pleaded Carman. "just one problem at a time. There is nothing that you have said so far, that cannot be fixed. Now start at the beginning." Getting into a prize fighters pose he asked, "who called you a string bean anyway? I'll knock him out."

"Oh Carman, Dominica said laughing through her tears. "You are funny."

Sitting down on her bed he said, "brothers are supposed to be funny to their little sisters. Now tell me, one at a time, all your problems.

Listening to Dominica, he knew he could take care of her dilemma. It seemed that the boy Dominica wanted to take to her graduation dance thought she was too thin and definitely too tall. Not a problem, he would talk to whatever his name was, and make the boy understand just how perfect Dominica was. By the time Carman had finished talking, the boy would be delighted to take Dominica to the dance as well. Carman could be very persuasive. Getting the long dress was going to be a little more difficult. When you deal with Mama and Papa together, you had to use some fancy footwork. His ace in the hole would be buying the dress for Dominica himself.

Carman asked Dominica if he could talk to this boy. Dominica was a little apprehensive about Carman talking to her date Victor, but she trusted her brother. If Carman said he could fix everything, he would.

"Yes," she thought, Carman will make everything all right.

And he did, even though the dress that Dominica wanted was almost a weeks' pay, the picture of his beautiful sister on the night of her graduation dance never faded from his memory. For the rest of his life, whenever he thought of his Dominica, he saw her the way she looked that night, absolutely beautiful.

1929

"Is it possible that fifteen years have passed since Dominica went to her first dance?" thought Carman glancing out of his window at the falling snow?

What a vision she was that night. I will never forget the look on Papa's face when Dominica came into the parlor to show everyone her new dress. Mama could not stop the tears that ran down her face and Papa, unlike himself, put his arm around Mama and kissed her wet cheek. Even the day that Dominica married Victor, she didn't look as beautiful as she looked that night. It was definitely worth all the extra hours I had to work to pay for the dress that she wore that night.

Life was good. Everyday was another surprise or marvel. Youth, how wonderful it is, full of enchantment. If I had it to live over again, I wonder if I'd really change anything. Who knows he thought, as he sat staring out at the snow billowing around the corner covering everything in sight with a magical coat of white?

Thinking back to that time in his life, he could still visualize Madelyn Keeley with those glorious blue eyes and radiant red hair.

1914

The following Sunday Carman met Madelyn as planned and they spent another wonderful day together. Carman was careful to keep his distance from her for fear of losing control, advice given to him by his friend Marty who said, "Carman you can't get in trouble if you just hold a girl's hand. Anything else is too risky, so listen to me and touch nothing else, just her hand."

Carman followed his advice to the letter and the day went on without any awkward developments. Carman was proud of his behavior, but essentially he was relieved. He felt out of control in Madelyn presence and had almost decided not to see her again. The only contact he made was lightly holding Madelyn's hand. He was actually humming to himself as they reached her door.

"I hope you had a good time today Madelyn" he asked.

"How could I not, being with you." She touched his face lightly with her cool hand.

He visibly moved back from her. She looked at him wondering what she had done to startle him.

"Goodnight" whispered Carman.

"Will I see you again?" she replied doubtfully

"Sure, next Sunday same place," he answered rapidly. He ran down the street with his heart beating wildly. "I'm losing my mind. This can't be happening to me," he thought as he raced back into his neighborhood. It wasn't until he turned the corner to his house that he finally stopped running. He leaned against the light post to catch his breath and tried to understand what exactly was happening to him. To his surprise and relief he saw his brother coming down the street.

"Anthony," he called, "you're just the person I need."

"Steve, remember its Steve now, not Anthony"

"Oh yeah, I forgot Steve. Do you have time to go to Guardo's for coffee?

"Sure no problem," he replied as he put his arm around his brother's shoulders as they walked to Guardo's.

"So what's your problem, women?" asked Steve as they sat at a table in the back of the little restaurant.

"No," said Carman, "just one girl."

"Oh, oh Carman this sounds serious, women I can handle, one girl is another bag of tricks. Ok, start at the beginning and don't leave anything out."

As Carman explained to his brother in detail his utter fascination with Madelyn the reality of the situation caught him. Before he finished, he looked at Steve and said in a voice so low that his brother had to bend closer to hear him. "My God, I think I'm in love."

"Not a chance Carman, you're too young to be in love. It's just passion."

"Oh, I'm so relieved, it's just passion. Come on, I've had passion before, it wasn't like this."

"Correct me if I'm wrong," answered his brother, but until now when you were in the throes of passion did you satisfy that urge with the lady of the moment?"

"Well yes but it was over as soon as, well you know Steve."

The following Sunday Carman met Madelyn as planned and they spent another wonderful day together. Carman was careful to keep his distance from her for fear of losing control, advice given to him by his friend Marty who said, "Carman you can't get in trouble if you just hold a girl's hand. Anything else is too risky, so listen to me and touch nothing else, just her hand."

Carman followed his advice to the letter and the day went on without any awkward developments. Carman was proud of his behavior, but essentially he was relieved. He felt out of control in Madelyn presence and had almost decided not to see her again. The only contact he made was lightly holding Madelyn's hand. He was actually humming to himself as they reached her door.

"I hope you had a good time today Madelyn" he asked.

"How could I not being with you," she said touching his face lightly with her cool hand?

He visibly moved back from her. She looked at him uncertainly wondering what she had done to startle him.

"Goodnight" whispered Carman.

"Will I see you again?" she replied doubtfully

"Sure, next Sunday same place," he answered rapidly. He ran down the street with his heart beating wildly. "I'm losing my mind. This can't be happening to me," he thought as he raced back into his neighborhood. It wasn't until he turned the corner to his house that he finally stopped running. He leaned against the light post to catch his breath and tried to understand what exactly was happening to him. To his surprise and relief he saw his brother coming down the street.

"Anthony," he called, "you're just the person I need."

"Steve, remember its Steve now, not Anthony"

"Oh yeah, I forgot Steve. Do you have time to go to Guardos' for coffee?

"Sure no problem," he replied as he put his arm around his brother's shoulders as they walked to Guardo's.

"So what's your problem, women?" asked Steve as they sat at a table in the back of the little restaurant.

"No," said Carman, "just one girl."

"Oh, oh, Carman this sounds serious, women I can handle, one girl is another bag of tricks. Ok, start at the beginning and don't leave anything out."

As Carman explained to his brother in detail his utter fascination with Madelyn the reality of the situation caught him. Before he finished, he looked at Steve and said in a voice so low that his brother had to bend closer to hear him. "My God, I think I'm in love."

"Not a chance Carman, you're too young to be in love. It's just passion."

"Oh, I'm so relieved, it's just passion. Come on, I've had passion before, it wasn't like this."

"Correct me if I'm wrong," answered his brother, but until now when you were in the throes of passion did you satisfy that urge with the lady of the moment?"

"Well yes, but it was over as soon as, well you know."

No," answered Steve, "it was just passion or lust or being sixteen. This feeling you have for Madelyn is the same thing. Take my advice don't see this girl anymore or you could get into trouble. It's not worth it Carman. You're too young to get seriously involved with anyone, not with a libido like yours. Before you know it you'll have her in the family way and you will be taking your vows from Father Paul. Your whole life would be over. Listen to me and don't get involved. Not now anyway, perhaps in a few years when you know where you are heading. What happened to your dream of going to high school and then college? This is not the time to be serious about a girl. Wait until you're a grown man. Then it will be time enough to fall in love. Now is the time for great passions that come and go. Now is the time to break away from everything and find your dream. You can't get tied down to one little redhead, and an Irish girl at that."

Carman listened to his brother and knew that he was right, not about being in love, but about everything else. It's not the time to get involved with any girl. Steve is right, I'd never want to tarnish Madelyn's reputation and I would if I kept seeing her. She hasn't got a clue about what's been happening here and I'm not going to be the one to break her heart. I know I'd never be able to give up Angie or Lilly or even Lola. Steve is right as usual. This isn't love. Thank God!

"What's the matter Carman, you're smiling. Is everything ok?"

"Steve I don't know what I'd do without you. You have a way of putting everything in perspective."

"Come on Carman, let's go home. Mama will be sending out a search party for you and I'm really tired.

"The two brothers walked the familiar route home, each deep in their own thoughts.

Not seeing Madelyn again was much harder on Carman than anticipated. One thing he had learned in his short life was that every obstacle teaches you a lesson. He needed to feel a little pain losing his first love. It made him softer and more vulnerable and less conceited. In the end, he grew up a great deal in a very short time. Carman didn't know how to break up with Madelyn without hurting her. It was the first time in his relationships with the female gender that he was moved to compassion. In the end he sent her a letter explaining that he had enrolled into Erasmus High School and was determined to graduate and that he would absolutely have no time available to see her, etc etc.

He read the letter over several times, each time almost tearing it up, but in the end he sent it. He was so depressed that Mama asked Steve to find out what was bothering him. Steve told Mama not to worry it was just an affair of the heart. Mama was especially kind to Carman and miraculously he lived through it.

The most important development that occurred was his enrollment into Erasmus High School. With the help of Sr. Amelia, Carman entered night school and started his long journey toward a degree.

One sunny Sunday afternoon a few weeks later, Carman saw Madelyn as she strolled down Morris Park Avenue on the arm of Billy Kenna, a big brute of an Irishman. She hardly glanced at him as he passed by but out of the corner of his eye he saw her wink. He certainly looked the young scholar carrying an armload of books.

"Here I am, up to my eye balls in study, broken hearted over Madelyn and she's found a new boy friend. Is there no end to my misery?" he thought as he laughed all the way home.

Chapter Eight

One day slid into the next as Carman tackled going to work all day and to school every night. After work he'd stop home for dinner and then he'd go straight to Erasmus High School. By eleven o'clock every evening, completely exhausted, he was in bed fast asleep. Although tired most of the time, he found school exciting. A whole New World opened up to him making him eager to graduate and go on to college. He had no idea where the money for college would come from, but was determined that nothing would stand in his way. Being without funds was a constant. He always found a way to make it. Now was no exception. He was convinced that any sacrifice was worth the reward.

With hard work and determination Carman got his high school diploma in barely two years and was anxious to start on his degree. Unfortunately, life has a way of altering your plans. Sometimes the most innocent behavior can cause disaster.

He continued to work at Similetti's Piano Emporium and was considered by Mr. Similetti to be invaluable. Advancement was guaranteed with or without a degree. Mr. Similetti was delighted with Carman's attitude and encouraged him monetarily as well as verbally. He treated him at times more like a son than an employee. Mr. Similetti's only regret was that Carman was too young for his prized possession, his daughter

Anna regarded Carman as a peer and was reluctant to relinquish her affection for him no matter how many times she was told that he was much too young for her.

Carman being completely immersed in schoolwork and the endless figures that needed to be correlated identified and corrected at work was oblivious to what was happening around him.

He failed to recognize the significance of Anna's constant presence. He saw Anna as a pretty but lonely young woman and was reluctant to dismiss her for fear of hurting her feelings. He never encouraged or dissuaded her from being in his little office. The more

Anna came to know Carman the more fascinated she became. Without understanding the depth of her feelings for Carman she fell head over heels in love with him. Carman unaware of Anna's affection for him, treated her with kindness which she regarded as fondness.

The realization of Anna's emotional involvement manifested amazement in Carman. He was totally unprepared for the devotion she displayed. He could not escape her. She showered him with little gifts, which he refused. Then the gifts became bigger and better and more difficult to turn down. But he remained steadfast but Anna was relentless and eventually wore him down with tickets to see the Great Caruso. She, of course, was part of the gift. Reluctantly, with a great foreboding, Carman escorted Anna to the Opera to witness Caruso in "The Barber of Seville". It was a night he'd never forget.

1929

Carman sat staring into space remembering that fateful evening when he took Anna to the opera. Even now he understood why he had given way to Anna's. She was a remarkably beautiful young woman, and he was flattered by the attention. Unquestionably lonely with only his books and figures to keep him company, he was ripe for picking.

He remembered how difficult it was for him to give up Madelyn. It would have been impossible if he hadn't thrown himself into work and school.

"Carman" called his mother bringing him back to reality, " are you never going to bed tonight?"

"Not tonight Mama, I have too much reminiscing to do, and only one night to do it in."

"Carman, you would think you were going to the gallows tomorrow have a little faith, everything will turn out fine, eventually."

"Mama, nothing can turn out fine, if I get caught only God can save me."

"But Carman" his mother answered, God will always save you, have no fear my son, he will take care of you."

"Sure Mama, sure, go to bed and let me continue my memories while I still have them, good night."

"Goodnight my son, I will pray very hard for you and something will turn up, you'll see,"

"Now where was I?" he chuckled.

"This is really too painful but how many men get the chance to reach back into their memories no matter how fanciful they become, and try to find where exactly they lost their footing?"

"Where was I? Oh yes my beautiful deranged Anna.

How thrilled I was to be going to see Caruso.

1914

Carman could not believe it. He was actually going to see Caruso in person. Mama was excited at the prospect and Papa smiled when he heard the news, which was a lot for

Papa, even his brother Steve got caught up in the preparations. Steve was the only one in the family who owned a new suit and true to his nature, he surrendered it to his little brother, who was bigger than he was. Miraculously Carman managed to squeeze into the suit.

Confusion reigned in the Duva household. Papa had decided that Carman needed a haircut and was clipping away merrily while Carman groaned in despair as his black locks cascaded to the floor. The outcome was surprisingly good. Carman looked very handsome and much older, impressing even Mama.

What a night it was it would have been wonderful if the entire family could have gone to see Caruso. But if only one could go, it was agreed, it should be Carman. Besides, Anna Similetti didn't invite the family, "just Carman'" Mama was quick to remind them.

Mama watched Carman walk down the street to pick up Anna when suddenly; she clutched her chest and shuttered visibly.

"What is it Juanna, you look white as a ghost?"

She lifted her head as if in a daze, unable to reply.

Paul looked at his wife with such concern that Juanna forced herself to speak.

"I'm sorry, it's just that an undeniable feeling of doom came over me."

"Juanna please what could happen? Your youngest son is going off to see Caruso."

"That's not the problem, it's that Anna, I just don't trust her. She is a very strange one.

There is something not quite right about her. If it weren't for Caruso, I would have found a way to stop Carman from going out with her."

"Come on Juanna, you worry for nothing."

"I must be getting old," she answered trying to smile. "Carman is almost a man and here I am frightened. Ah, I am crazy. Come I'll make some fresh coffee. I baked a nice cake for you. Anthony, come have some coffee with Papa and me and tell us about your Pauline."

"Mama, please why can't you call me Steve like everyone else?" he said coming into the house from the back porch.

"Hey, I christened you Anthony and Anthony you will stay. Come have coffee, and I'll think about calling you Steve every other time."

"Mama, you are crazy," Steve replied hugging her as they walked into the kitchen,

"Every other time you say? Oh Mama, only you would think to do that."

Carman whistled as he walked down the avenue to the Similetti house. He felt wonderful. For the time being his studies were over, and at last, he had a diploma from high school. As soon as possible he'd apply to all the colleges in the area. He had to get an engineering degree. Undeniably he would have been ecstatic if he could go to school for a degree in music but he knew you could not have everything. He wasn't prepared to spend his life struggling as a musician. Engineers, on the other hand, could always make a good living and he was determined that he would live well no matter how difficult it was to achieve that goal.

Nearing the Similetti house, he wondered what he would say to Anna. She was a strange one, buying him presents and always around under his feet in his tiny office. She was a beauty though, and only four years older than he was. But she was unusual.

Oh well, we're going to see Caruso, not get married, he thought, and continued whistling as Anna opened the door to his knock.

He was stunned at the sight of Anna who was dressed in a long silk blue gown the exact color of her eyes. With her almost white hair piled on top of her head, she resembled a Botticelli Madonna. Carman was speechless and could hardly whisper, "hello".

Anna realizing her effect on Carman smiled broadly as she ushered him in to meet her mother.

Mrs. Similetti was an older but darker replica of Anna. She had hair and eyes as black as Carman, and a happy countenance that put him at ease immediately.

"So you are Carman, I am very happy to meet you young man. Between my husband and my daughter, I do not know who holds you in higher esteem. You must be a remarkable young man. Come and tell me about yourself," she said as she ushered him into the Similetti's palatial living room. It took Mrs. Similetti less than a minute to have Carman completely at ease, confessing his most secret ambitions for the future. She was impressed by the young man and sorry that they had so little time to get acquainted.

"It was a pleasure meeting you and I hope to see more of you," said Mrs. Similetti as she gave Carman her hand and bid him good night. Mr. Similetti stood at her side beaming at Carman, so happy that Carman had made such a good impression on his wife.

"Our carriage will wait for you and Anna, so enjoy yourselves," said Mr. Similetti shaking Carman's hand.

Carman led Anna down the steps to the waiting carriage for their trip to the Metropolitan Opera House to see Puccini's Tosca, starring Enrico Caruso.

Anna and Carman sat in wonder listening to Caruso sing. Although fluent in Italian they had to pay close attention because their dialects got in the way. Anna sat clutching Carman's hand at the death scene, tears rolling down her cheeks. Anna held Carman's arm and as the music intensified, so did Anna's grasp on Carman's arm. So much so that he had to remove her fingers one by one to return the circulation in his forearm. Anna did not seem to notice, and he smiled at the look of intensity on her face. He settled back to listen in ecstasy as Caruso sang. It was a remarkable evening, filled with delight from the moment Carman had fetched Anna at her home. His mind kept drawing back to Anna's mother and her exceptional Italian beauty and charm.

As the Opera continued with its glorious strains and magnitude Carman thought, "If I could write music like this I wouldn't need to get an engineering degree. You're some dreamer Carman."

The Opera came to an end, the audience stood up and cheered even in the orchestra where they were sitting the applause was deafening, and they both chimed in shouting their praises. As they left the Metropolitan, hand in hand both in their own reverie, several people stopped to admire the handsome couple, but Carman and Anna were completely unaware of the attention. Reluctantly they entered the Similetti carriage that was waiting for them at the curb. Neither of them wanted the evening to end. When they drove past Central Park Anna asked the driver to take them through the park. Halfway around the park in a very remote area Anna whispered, "why don't we walk for a while it's such a beautiful night".

Carman was anxious to leave the carriage after sitting so long at the Opera, and he wanted to be alone with Anna, just for while. He was surprised at his own desire to have Anna to himself for awhile. With his arm protectively over her shoulder they walked down a lonely lane in the park and stopped in the moonlight and as if on cue they kissed passionately and deeply, completely overcome by desire. They paused breathlessly and Anna murmured over and over "more Carman, more." Together they lay on the grass as Carman kissed her neck and softly bit her earlobes as she moaned in his arms.

Carefully he eased her dress off her shoulder baring her ample breast that he touched gently. He bent his head to capture her breast in his mouth and was lost in the wonder of the taste of her. Tenderly from breast to breast he fed like a small animal. Anna grabbed his head and pushed him to her breast until he sucked so harshly that she cried delighted, in the pain he caused.

Unable to stem the flow of passion and without realizing how, he was straddling her body tearing at his clothes. Anna lifted her skirts and removed her scant undergarments as she skillfully maneuvered her warm moist body to engulf him. She gasped in pleasure as he began his slow rhythmic climb. They moved in unison as if they had loved many times. Both of them were completely unaware of their surroundings and luckily were uninterrupted by sight or sound. The outcry of pure joy escaped from their lips as they climaxed together. Lying limp in each others arms until the stirrings of desire overcame them once more and again they came together to relive the unbelievable joy of their pure, unadulterated passion. They lay for a long while still as one. Being young he was able to take her one last time, finally satisfying the hunger that had taunted Anna from the first day she had first seen Carman.

They were completely exhausted as they lay on the grass catching their breath. Sitting up surrounded by moonlight they looked at each other and smiled broadly and then started to laugh. At first softly and then so loud they had to cover their mouths to avoid being caught completely nude in the middle of Central Park.

Trying desperately to get control of himself, Carman began to help Anna back into her dress. She in turn found his pants and shoes and sat on a rock holding her sides as she watched Carman try to put himself back together. It was only then, as he carefully tied his shoes that Carman realized it was not the first time for Anna. He was surprised and relieved at this discovery. He didn't want to be her first, even though given the circumstances he doubted if it would have mattered. He knew that passion hadblinded him and reasoned that the older he got the more control he would have.

After inspecting one another's clothes, they went in search of the carriage, grateful that they had been undetected. In a few minutes they found the carriage with the driver sound asleep and the horse enjoying a meal of dew covered sweet grass. The driver awoke with a start as they climbed into the carriage. Grateful for his nap he slowly drove them home. Surprisingly, neither Anna nor Carman uttered a word. They seemed to be lost in their own worlds. Carman trying to understand the consequences of what happened and Anna completely delighted that it did.

Chapter Nine

1929

Carman could not help but laugh at the irony of what had ultimately been the turning point in his life. The realization of the repercussions of that one night on his life eluded him until this moment. Then, he had no idea of how his life would change and how all his dreams would disappear. He could remember as if it were yesterday, how mature and adult he felt then. With certainty he addressed the world and himself. Confidence inundated his demeanor as he strolled down the avenue assured of his absolute confidence in himself. Carman laughed at the sight of himself at sixteen a mere boy playing at being a man. Carman's laughter echoed through the house, alarming Mama who called out, "are you alright?"

"Of course Mama, I'm sorry for waking you I will try to have a little restraint.

He was the epitome of a self-possessed youth. It would be sensational to experience that wonderful feeling now. Carman recalled the exact moment he finally understood the reality of his union with Anna. It was when he told his brother what had happened on his supposedly innocent night at the Opera.

1914

Carman did his best to avoid Anna as much as possible after their encounter, more for his sake than hers. He still refused to believe the impact of his actions and tried to carry out each day in her presence as if absolutely nothing had happened. It wasn't until the following Friday, when Carman met Steve at Mama Lapoli's for some fried calimari and spaghetti marinara, that reality set in. After the brothers had ordered Steve sensing something very strange about his brothers' demeanor asked, "what's the matter." The words were barely out of his mouth when Carman poured out the whole ignoble affair with Anna. Words failed Steve as he sat stunned looking at his brother wondering when exactly Carman has lost his mind. Sighing deeply, Steve murmured "Dio mio."

"Is that it Steve, is that all you have to say? No words of warning, no shouts of dismay? Just "Dio mio" I need more than that, I need help, I need counsel, I need to relive that night, Jesus Steve I need a God damn miracle."

"If she's pregnant, then you'll need a miracle. Now you could use a smash right in the head. Are you completely crazy? You know, Anna is not quite right in the head, not exactly a mental but she's really strange, She's also a very forceful young woman, who is used to her own way and will stop at nothing to get it. Never mind the fact that you work for her father and that she is engaged to none other than Guardo Ponsetti, who out weighs you by 150 pounds and is ten years older than you, and I might add just as a reminder is "Black Hand".

"Steve easy, easy, I just made love to the girl, just once. Well maybe more than once but just one night.

"Just once, oh that makes it alright. Gee I guess I should remember that and only do it one time but with different girls. Wait, what do you mean maybe more than once? How many times did you do it?"

"You don't want to know. I really don't remember exactly how many times."

"What are you taking about you don't remember how many times. Jesus Carman you're starting to scare me. How many times did you make love to the girl?"

"To be honest, I think it was three. But I'm not sure."

"Holy shit, he's not sure maybe three times. All in one night?"

"Yes, I told you it was only one night."

"Holy shit," was all Steve could say as he stared in complete wonder and dismay at his little sixteen year old brother talking casually about the sex he had and here he was just dreaming about it. Finally he whispered.

"I've been engaged to Pauline for six months and feel guilty if I kiss her too long, and you tell me you made love to Anna three times in one night. Dio mio."

"It looks bad, hah Anthony?"

"It's Steve remember, I'm working for the telephone company now, I'm not even supposed to be Italian any more, I thought that was supposed to be the big dilemma."

The brothers sat looking at one another and simultaneously began to laugh until tears rolled down their cheeks and Mama Lapoli came over to quiet them.

Steve first to get hold of himself smiled at Carman and calmed him down and promised him that no matter what happened, that he would stay at his side. As long as Anna wasn't pregnant everything would work out. The only thing he had to worry about was if Mama and Papa ever found out. Then there would be hell to pay. They finished their dinner in silence each thinking of alternatives to the situation. As they strolled home after dinner, Steve said, "Carman just pray you didn't get Anna pregnant. The rest of situation can be handled if you use your head and treat her kindly and put as much distance between you two as possible., capito?"

"Si, answered Carman, I think I should join the Army. That's the only place she can't get at me."

"Don't be crazy. You just have to keep your head."

"Hey Steve, you don't know what it's like to make love to Anna. I really think I should join the Army."

The two brothers walked home enjoying the beautiful summer night and wondering how life could become so convoluted in just one night.

About a block from the house Steve stopped walking and turned Carman so that he could speak to him face to face.

"When I said you should stay away from Anna, I meant a little distance not an ocean. Joining the Army in not what I had in mind. There's a good chance I could get you into the Telephone Company. You have your high school diploma and plan on going to college. There's no reason they wouldn't hire you. You just have to change your name and nationality. No one has to know our family came from Italy. Besides you're too young and Papa would never sign the papers for you to join the Army. There are simpler solutions to this dilemma, let's wait and see what happens, there's no need for a hasty decision now."

"It's not just Anna, replied Carman, I've been seriously thinking of joining the Army before any of this happened, I want to join the Calvary."

"What do you know about horses?" asked Steve.

"Absolutely nothing, that's why I want to join the Army so that I can get into the cavalry. It's the closest I'll ever get to become an American cowboy," he added winking.

"You read the papers and you know as well as I do that we will eventually be involved in the war in Europe. If I join now I'll have a choice of joining the Calvary. I don't see myself as a foot soldier and I want a little excitement and adventure in my life, I'll be seventeen in August and all I've ever done is work and go to school. If I'm lucky I get a chance to make love to a woman, and look where that's gotten me.

"Well you're one up on me Carman, all I've done is go to school and work. I lost my virginity to Lola, like most of the guys in the neighborhood, I've never had a woman who didn't charge me for the experience, and I've got six years on you. So tell me exactly what women? Where do you find them? More importantly does Father Paul know? When I told him about Lola in the confessional, I thought he would have a stroke.

"You know you may be six years older than me, but when it comes to sex, I'm definitely the older brother.

Carman could never equate sex with sin. He believed that something as wonderful as sex could never be a real sin. Maybe it could be a venial sin but never a mortal sin. Making love to a woman was a natural progression. There was a line he would never cross, at least not knowingly. He could never make love to a married woman. Not a mortal sin, maybe a venial sin.

Finally answering he said," Father Paul is used to me confessing making love. Somehow I don't think he believes me anyway. I only started about two years ago."

"Two years?"

Steve lost his virginity when he was twenty and thought he was too young. The idea of his little brother at fourteen being with a woman was almost comical. Sure Carman was always tall for his age and I guess he looked older that his years. How could anyone mistake a fourteen-year-old boy?

Smiling at the absurdity of Carman's remarks he replied, "fourteen is a little young isn't it?"

"No, Steve, I wasn't too young, I was thinking about it a long time before I decided to - you know, - do it.

"And when exactly was that? "Wher. you were eleven perhaps, he asked unwilling to believe the preposterous story his brother was weaving?

Suddenly Carman realized that his brother didn't believe him and he laughed to himself knowing that he hardly believed it himself.

"What possible reason could I have to make up a story like this. The first time it happened I was only fourteen and whether you believe me or not the circumstances were a little bizarre, but it happened.

No one, even his brother would be convinced by what really happened on that glorious day at Star Beach.

Star Beach was a very small isolated watering hole used by neighborhood kids. Just like every other boy in the surrounding area, Carman would go to Star Beach every chance he got. It was an overcast day and as he walked along the almost barren sandy drifts he looked for a small hill to sit on so he could gaze at the water and breathe in the fresh smell of sea air. Looking out to sea he could erase all the mundane worries that hung over his head. The sky was gray and the clouds were moving rapidly across the sky, which should have been a warning to him but instead he was thrilled at the glorious array of images that cascaded over his head. Vapor seemed to rise above the water and touch the low hanging clouds. The last rays of the sun floated across the shallow water masking the danger that was rising in the air. The clap of thunder followed by an enormous show of lightning startled him. He started to run for cover and stumbled on a beautiful sunbather who had fallen asleep on the beach. Roughly Carman woke her and literally dragged her to shelter into an old abandoned boat house.

The young woman was dripping wet as she clung to Carman petrified by the thunder and lightning that shook the small enclosure. The only place to sit was on an old mattress that was surprisingly clean, in the middle of the shack. The more that storm raged the more the young woman held onto Carman until they were both entwined lying on the mattress wrapped in each others arms. Totally unaware how Carman began to caress the beautiful girl who in turn kissed him willingly and before you know it the two of them were making mad passionate love, with lightning flashing and thunder rocking the shack back and forth adding to their frenzy. They undressed totally and lay gazing at one another hesitating only long enough to acknowledge each other's willingness to go on. He kissed her hair, her neck her breast lost in the wondrous joy of her body. Without fear or doubt he entered her and together they rode the lightning to total ecstasy. As if on cue the storm ended as they climaxed. Unashamed they dressed and quickly left the shack to find their way home. Carman never saw her again but was forever grateful to her for his lost virginity. Thinking back he knew that his brother would never believe it. As time passed he had a difficult time believing it himself.

Finally Carman said to his brother, "what earthly reason would I have to lie to you. I had my first encounter when I was fourteen, believe it or not."

"I believe you Carman. I'm just jealous. I always thought you had to love a girl to make love to her."

"I have to say Steve, I always like the girl a lot that I make love to. I just don't love them. You know Steve there are a lot of really good girls that like to have sex. They don't think it's wrong either. Everyone is different; I just do what comes naturally, and so far so good. Actually since Anna, I've lost my urge to, you know."

"I know", replied Steve, more astonished than ever.

As they walked up the stairs to their apartment they could hear Mama shouting at Dominica for coming in late. Lucky for them they went to bed undetected. They both stole into their rooms, escaping any questions from Mama. Unfortunately, they forgot about Papa. Although he was a very quiet unobtrusive man, he was an observer and usually knew everything that was happening in the family. Most of the times he just watched and let Mama deal with the problems. But sometimes he would intervene, and this was one of those times. Papa knocked softly on Carman's door and quietly slipped into his room, grateful that Anthony had fallen asleep.

"Carman, it's time for us to talk."

Startled by his father's appearance, he whispered, "sure Papa, we talk tomorrow, ok."

"Ok, don't forget, sleep now my son tomorrow is time enough."

Carman looked at the closed door amazed at the appearance of his father in his room. He had never sought him out before and Carman was astonished at the stealth of a man his size. The next day was Sunday and true to his word Carman went to his father and the two of them went for a walk on the avenue,

"So Carman are you in a little trouble?"

"Not yet Papa, I think everything will be alright."

"It's that crazy Anna, Si."

"Si, Papa, but how did you know?"

"Carman, I work all over the Bronx as a mason, there is very little I don't know. Madelyn is a very pretty girl but Irish."

Carman looked at his father in amazement.

"I'm not too fond of the Irish. They're a little too arrogant for me. I've had a few fights since I've been in this country and they have always been with the Irish. They're overconfident and they drink too much."

"Papa, you had fights - fist fights?" Carman asked astonished at his fathers' revelation.

"Sure, there are other ways to knock a man down".

"Did you win?"

"Of course I win, your Papa's a good fighter. Carman, do you ever fight?"

"A couple of times Papa, how do you think I broke my nose."

"Ah I forgot, besides you look much better with a broken nose, you were too good looking, now you look, well now you look like Papa."

"There's no one I'd rather look like than you. I only wish that when I'm your age I look as good as you, inside and out."

"Carmino, I like that, I wish Anthony was a little more like you. He's too good. He's a strong man. It's just that he's almost like a saint, not like you or your rascal brother John."

"You know Papa every family needs a saint, someone we can all admire and appreciate. That's Steve Papa, he'll be fine. Pauline really loves him and together they'll have a good life."

"Carman, I want you to promise me, that if something happens that you can't handle, you'll talk to Papa."

"I will I promise, so tell me who did you fight?"

"Well there was this one big Mick, named O'Donnell."

Papa went on and on astonishing Carman with his exploits and confessing finally that there were plenty of Italians that he knocked down in his day.

Shocked by his father's revelation that he knew all about Anna and even the brief encounter he had with Madelyn, Carman was convinced that he needed to get away. Life was becoming too complicated for him to handle. He needed a place where no one could influence him. He desperately needed a place to hide for awhile. He was genuinely fascinated with the war in Europe. Being young and naïve, the more he thought about his dilemma the more the thought of joining the Army became appealing.

Leaning new skills and perfecting old ones made working at Similetti's exciting for him. He was content to work with numbers and found great satisfaction when his sheets balanced. Now he was always uncomfortable. Anna seemed to be everywhere watching his every move. The most disquieting development was his physical reaction to her presence. He was torn between resenting her and wanting her. He couldn't really decide what he felt. Whenever she came close to him his mind became clouded with sheer desire to hold her in his arms. He couldn't understand what was happening to him. He just knew he had to get away.

Carman began to read everything he could about the war in Europe. He found himself drawn to anyone with news about the war. His friend Marty was his only ally. Together they became experts on what was happening overseas.

After several sleepless nights, Carman woke up one morning determined to put an end to his torment. He knew the longer he stayed near Anna the more likely he would lose control. The feelings he had for Anna frightened him. He knew that she would eventually wear him down. It wouldn't take much. She stirred emotions in him that he couldn't harness. The longer he thought about his predicament the surer he was that only joining the Army could save him.

He set out for the only induction office that he was aware of. Fortunately, the office was located on Fordham Road and the Concourse. He walked from Morris Park Avenue to Pelham Parkway, where he could catch a trolley that would take him to his destination. He stood in the early morning sunlight and was suddenly relaxed. In a few minutes the trolley arrived and he got on and quickly found a seat by the window and watched the beautiful homes with manicured lawns that lined the parkway.

He was surprised how good he felt playing hooky from Similetti's. He hadn't missed a day of work since he was hired. There he was sitting in a trolley car with the sun shining and cool breezes blowing his carefully combed hair askew. When the trolley stopped at the Botanical Gardens he had to force himself to stay seated and not jump off the car.

"Another day" he whispered to himself. On this beautiful summer day the flowers would be in glorious profusion. It was a pity that he would miss the spectacle.

The next stop on the trolley line was the Bronx Zoo. The only thing that saved him from an unscheduled stop was the appearance of a lovely blond woman who entered car. All thoughts of the animals in the zoo flew out of his mind when she sat down next to him. He literally gasped. Judging by the ring on her finger she was obviously married. She turned and smiled at him. He smiled back wishing he were ten years older. He sat back and spent the rest of the trip inhaling her expensive perfume and dreaming impossible dreams. He almost missed his stop and went scrambling apologetically off the trolley car.

He stood outside of the Army Induction Center watching a young sergeant through the glass seated at a desk. He was groomed to perfection. His haircut extremely short, his uniform pressed and his shirt starched.

Suddenly genuine fear crept over him and he was unable to open the door. He hand grasped the handle but he couldn't budge it. Finally the young sergeant looked up and smiled beckoning Carman to come in. Miraculously he opened the door and stood stock still unable to speak. The young sergeant beckoned for him to come in and sit at the chair in front of his desk. Carman sat down facing the recruiting soldier.

"What can I do for you young man?"

Finding his voice, Carman announced proudly that he wanted to join the Cavalry.

"That's a fine ambition son," the young sergeant replied. "May I ask how old you are," he added.

Reluctant to lie, Carman told him truthfully that he would be sixteen that August. The sergeant explained carefully how difficult it would be for someone so young to withstand the rigors of training for the Cavalry.

Undaunted Carman tried to convince the young man of his ability to learn quickly and that he was very strong and rarely, if ever, did he get sick or even catch a cold.

"Well young man as soon as you're eighteen you come and see me and I will do all that I can to get you into the Cavalry."

"Is there any way I can join now? Carman pleaded.

"Actually you could get your father or guardian to sign you in, but believe me you're really too young. Go home and think about it. We're very close to war. You don't want to make a hasty decision. I doubt if your father would be fool enough to let such a young boy join the Army. Think long and hard. If you sign, up it will be for five years. You'd be twenty-one when you got out. That is if we don't have a war. The best part of your youth would be spent in the Army. Don't do it son. Wait at least until you're eighteen."

Disillusioned and disappointed Carman rode home on the trolley.

He made a decision to avoid Anna at any cost. If the Army wouldn't take him he wasn't going to let Anna have him. He knew deep in his soul it would be the hardest thing he had to do but he was determined to resume his life. Didn't that sergeant tell him this was the best time of his life? Well it was time for a new girl in his life and Carman started a campaign to go out with every available female in the Bronx. In record time Carman was back in full swing, redirecting his entire being to fun and frolic. Ultimately he realized how unhappy he was with the new life he had created for himself and toned down his exploits with the ladies, focusing on trying to get into a college. He felt he had procrastinated long enough.

No matter how he tried he couldn't get Anna completely off his mind. He needed to fill his head with study and so with hat in hand he went back to Sr. Amelia for her encouragement and counsel. Standing at the entrance to the convent he wondered if Sr. Amelia would be glad to see him. A young novitiate answered his knock and ushered him in. With her eyes downcast she asked whom he wished to see. Politely he asked for Sister Amelia and was ushered into a small waiting room. Sitting quietly, he couldn't ignore the beautiful statue of the Blessed Mother smiling down on him. He bowed his head and silently begged her for forgiveness and guidance. Just sitting in this lovely room with the statue of the Blessed Mother gave him a peace he had not felt since that night with Anna. The serenity had calmed his aching heart.

When Sr. Amelia entered the room her face beamed, she was delighted to see Carman, and was impressed by his demeanor and dress. She was full of questions for him regarding his work and his plans for the future. After listening to Carman she asked what she could do to help. He finally told her he needed her help to get into night school at a college close by. Somewhere he could attend without travelling downtown. The only college Sr. Amelia could think of Fordham University.

"Would you like to go to Fordham," she asked?

"Sister dear, I would love to go to Fordham. You're aware of my finances; I could never afford the tuition."

"Don't be so sure Carman I have a few friends in high places who would be glad to help you in your endeavor to earn a degree, and in their endeavor to get to heaven. Have a little faith in Sister Amelia and with God's help we'll see what we can do."

"Oh Sister you are an Angel. What would I ever do without you? I believe you and God can do anything". With a kiss on sister's cheek Carman left the convent and breathed a sigh of relief. He was forever astounded in what that little nun was capable of doing.

It turned out that Sr. Amelia was able to get him into Fordham University as part time student tuition free. His only obligation was to go to mass once a week and pray for his benefactor, whoever he or she was. He resumed his schedule of work and school to the chagrin of the fair ladies of the Bronx. For one glorious but arduous semester Carman went to Fordham University. In retrospect it was one of the most memorable times of his life. He was constantly challenged to do more, master more, and become proficient in every course he had selected. It was during this time that he made a friend for life in Father Brown, his teacher, his mentor, his friend, but never his confessor. That would have been just a little too much for the dear Father to handle.

Unfortunately, that incredible time was very short lived. Working at Similetti's was just too close to the relentless and constant Anna. There was nowhere he could he turn that she was not there ready to be of assistance. Just when he thought he had outsmarted her she would return to the scene ready to do his bidding. She literally wore him down and he felt despicable for the way he treating her. Finally he asked her to dinner. Classes were over for a few weeks and he deserved a little respite. Anna had been so helpful to him all of the time he was working and going to school. He knew in all honesty that he could never have made it without her help in the office. His shameful behavior toward her prompted him to ask her out. It was a small gesture to salve his conscience and to thank her for her help and so Anna and Carman went to dinner.

It was an unforgettable evening and the first fun Carman had in a long time.

Incredibly this beautiful, slightly crazy young woman could make him so happy.

"Anna how can you be such a delight" said Carman earnestly.

"Carman please, I'm only delightful when I'm with you, or are you so blind, that you are not aware of my feelings for you?"

"Anna I try not to think about you. Do you really expect to have a relationship with me? I'm more than four years younger than you are and as poor as a church mouse. Not to mention the fact that you are actually engaged to Guardo.

There is, unfortunately, one more thing. I don't think I really love you. I can't say I don't find you attractive, and God help me, I wish we were making love this very minute. I just don't feel the way I should to make this a reasonable commitment. Age is something we could overcome. It's more than that Anna. I don't want to hurt you. I care for you. Why wouldn't I? I wish it was different but it isn't. I don't love you".

Carman put his face in his hands unable to meet Anna's loving gaze.

"Carman, I love you, and that's all that matters to me, even if I marry Guardo,

I'll always love you. That's just the way it is."

"Please, Anna think of what you are saying, you don't love me, you just like to make love,"

"Carman, don't be silly, I've never made love to Guardo, and I'm engaged to him.

What I feel for you is beyond physical, and it really scares me."

"Anna, you've never been afraid of anything in your whole life, you just have sex mixed up with making love. I really enjoy making love to you; I just don't love you. Loving someone is not a prerequisite for making love."

"Carman, you should write that down, it's so fitting. Loving someone is not a prerequisite for making love, I love it."

"You're not being practical Anna. Love is very important but lovemaking is just a release. I'm sure that if you happen to really love the person you're making love to, it's heaven."

"I know the feeling Carman, I sincerely do. I never realized how romantic you are. I wish you loved me but, I can live without it, Guardo loves me."

"Oh Anna, you're crazy but I like you so let's be friends and forget all this business about love, Ok?"

"Ok, Carman no more love talk, how about lovemaking?"

"Anna, lovemaking could be very dangerous now. You would mistake it for the real thing, or God forbid, you could get pregnant."

"Carman," she said laughingly, "we'll be very careful."

"You're hopeless Anna, what do you want for desert."

"You," she replied wistfully.

"Someday Carman, someday, you wait and see."

Carman called the waiter and ordered two pieces of cheese cake and coffee. After the waiter brought their dessert and coffee, Carman said,

"Enjoy Anna this is all I can give you."

"Just you wait and see", she said as she delved into the cake.

To Carman's surprise and relief they became good friends. They often went to the movies or for a bite to eat, with no further mention of love or love making.

Regrettably his guard began to crumble and he relaxed when he was with her.

Slowly and carefully like a good fisherman Anna hooked him and drew in the line without making a ripple on the water as only a woman in love can do.

Before long, Carman was eagerly waiting for Anna, completely enchanted by her and entirely blind to her madness. He wasn't in love with her. She fascinated him. He was just too young to know the difference.

Chapter Ten

1929

A tap at the door distracted Carman from his reverie. He slowly opened the door and was pleased to see his brother Steve.

"You probably won't believe me but I was just thinking about you, Come'sta," he asked?

"Ah, Carman I'm always tired, Pauline is always sick and the children, God bless them they never stop. What about you are you really going through with this tomorrow?"

"Si, do you still think this is the wrong thing for me to do?"

"Do you want an answer or a justification," replied Steve?

"Maybe both, Steve, what would you do under the same circumstances?"

His brother sighed heavily and replied "in my whole life Carman, I have never been in as much trouble as you have on any given day. I can't honestly give you an answer or a way out of this mess, but I will tell you that whatever you do tomorrow, no matter how I feel I'll stand by you. Who am I, to judge what you do? You're my little brother, and I will do whatever it takes to help you if all of this turns ugly."

"What would I do without you, Steve?"

"Carman, the only one I worry about is your little girl, this will break her heart."

Steve had not been able to stop thinking about his brother's daughter. Being a father himself he couldn't understand how Carman could even consider what he had already planned to do. "Somehow I will make it right for her too. Don't worry Steve; I'll do everything I can. If something really goes awry, will you take care of her," asked Carman.

"You know I will," answered Steve as he reassuringly put his hand on his brother's shoulder.

"God, Steve do you remember how beautiful Anna was then? I was just remembering how you tried to stop me from seeing her".

"If Papa couldn't stop you, what chance did I have? You want some coffee?"

"No I've had enough, go in the kitchen Mama made some not too long ago."

While Steve walked into the kitchen Carman remembered how Papa really understood what was going on then. He fervently wished that he had listened to his father then.

When Papa found out that Carman was seriously dating Anna, he took him aside and begged him to stop, telling him that Anna was not for him. He reminded him that not once had he ever given him the wrong advice. He said that Carman was much too young for this woman, and to please forgive him but he was sure that she was not quite right in the head. Papa also warned him about Anna's future husband Guardo. If he became aware of them going out, Carman might find himself in the East River.

"Listen to me, this woman can only bring you grief."

Carman promised that he would think about everything Papa had said. He could not see any harm in going to a movie or for some spaghetti with Anna. He knew that Anna was going to marry Guardo and he never intended anything more than friendship. He remembered telling his father to stop worrying.

His father had replied, "I'll stop worrying when you go back to school and have no time for this nonsense."

"Soon Papa, I'll go back soon," is what told his father.

Although he had the best of intentions it was unrealistic for him to imagine he could avoid Anna, while still working at Similetti's. His intentions were Honorable, but the magnetism between the two was constant. Anna came to his office several times a day on one pretense or another. It was a truly intolerable situation. She would inadvertently brush against him setting his mind on fire. She was completely aware of her affect on him and played it to the hilt. In sheer desperation he begged his brother to sign the papers necessary for him to join the Army. Papa had flatly refused to even address the situation. Steve reluctantly agreed on the one condition that Carman finish one more semester of College. Carman agreed and set a schedule for himself with absolutely no time available to see Anna away from Similetti's. He threw himself in bed every night too exhausted to even fantasize about her. Toward the end of the semester, Carman stayed late at the office to make use of the typewriter to finish some reports. Mama would pack him a cold supper and he would eat it with a tin of beer from the corner bar. One night as he put the finishing touches on his calculus equations content that everything was in order, he reached for his tin of beer and there Anna stood, glorious in the reflected moonlight. He caught his breath at the sight of her. Recovering from the jolt he laughed nervously and asked, "what are you doing here?"

"I thought you could use a little company, and I've missed seeing you. I've been very lonely."

"Come on I see you going out with Guardo. You two make a handsome couple," he added nervously.

"I know we do, but I'd much rather be with you. You know that."

Ignoring her reply, he asked, "when are you two getting married, you've been engaged forever?"

"You know I'm waiting for you," she answered as she looked at him with those unbelievably beautiful eyes.

"Madonna Mia, please help me," he prayed silently. He had more beer than usual tonight, to celebrate his last report. He was exhausted and she was so beautiful.

"Anna gently pushed Carman's hair out of his eyes as she coaxed him out of his chair. He stood looking at her beautiful face and her tiny little waist and her lovely breasts he swallowed, closed his eyes, and gave up the battle. He pulled her toward him, and holding her tightly he kissed her deeply. He searched her mouth with his tongue that she bit gently sending shivers up and down his spine.

She undid her blouse and offered him her naked breasts. Longingly he kissed her nipples gently at first and then bit her in his passion. Anna sighed softly and whispered "more, more." The sound of her voice halted his frenzy. He stood back looked at her in her disarray, and carefully began to undress her. She grabbed his head to her breasts and he was lost in the taste of her. Looking around for some place to lay down Carman seized a padded piano cover and threw it on the floor. Half undressed, they collapsed together and to Anna's delight he entered her. In the depths of passion he was unaware of the pain he caused her for she never uttered a word.

When it was over she said that he had hurt her, He was ashamed of his behavior but Anna told him she thought it was wonderful in spite of the pain.

But it wasn't what I wanted, he thought. How could I act like such an animal?

She seemed to read his mind and whispered in his ear "my animale."

My God, he thought, she really is crazy if she enjoys being hurt. How, in God's name do I get out of this? How could I have let this happen? Sure, now that I've had her I can ask "why?" Only a few minutes ago I would have sold my soul to make love to her.

As gently as he could, he got up from the floor and quickly dressed. He apologized again and again for his hurting her. The shame he felt was like a rock in the middle of his stomach. Anna couldn't understand what all the fuss was about. When Guardo hurt her he never said a word but just went on pleasing himself. She wished she could tell Carman but he thought that Guardo never touched her.

Walking home they decided to stop at the park. They sat and talked quietly into the night. In all of the time they had known each other they had never actually had a real conversation. They had never shared their thoughts about things that mattered to them. Without realizing what was happening to them their conversation flowed. Anna confessed that she was convinced that she loved Carman. Carman conversely argued categorically that what had been developed between the two was purely physical. Anna ultimately agreed, although she persisted that the emotions that they were experiencing exhibited more than desire. Carman eventually convinced Anna that love was not the emotion they were feeling. In the end they decided not see one another outside of Similetti's Emporium. He was certain that eventually their craving for one another would ebb. Carman took Anna home and spent most of the night walking the streets attempting to understand the physical pull Anna had for him. Finding no logical reason for his desire he returned home completely exhausted. He fell into bed and remained there in a deep sleep until well into the next day.

Mama was confused by Carman's behavior. No matter what time he came in, he rarely slept late. She quietly went into his room and gently felt his head to see if he was feverish. Cool to her touch, she decided to let him sleep.

Carman ultimately awoke feeling rejuvenated and ravenous. Observing the amount of food Carman consumed, Mama was assured that there was nothing wrong with Carman. "He works too hard," she told Papa, who willingly agreed with Mama, but suspected there was more going on than just exhaustion. Papa waited patiently hoping that Carman would come to him if he needed help, but he never did. There were some things he just couldn't talk to Papa about.

FATHER BROWN

Father Dismus Brown was a scholar of limited renown but heralded in the confines of Fordham University. He was respected and admired by his colleagues and treasured by his students. When every door on campus was closed to you, Father Brown could miraculously open them. If you needed a friend or a confessor he was there for you. Even if you were out of funds, he would lend you money. The word "no" did not appear in his vocabulary. He was a breath of fresh air on the University dessert. Everyone who came in contact with the priest was moved by his innate goodness. Still he was an enigma, and no one really knew him.

When you are in a state of concern you invariably turn inward neglecting to see what is directly in front of you. No one saw Father Dismus. They were too busy worrying about their own problems. They never saw how tired he looked or how thin he was. They just needed help, and if you needed help, you searched for Father Brown. Very early in life Dismus Brown discovered the joy you can receive helping people. It was something he did best and loved every minute of it. Except of course for the rare occasions that his council was inadequate and only God's intervention could save you. Then of course, the priest would pray earnestly on your behalf with miraculous success.

It was Father Brown's habit to take a walk after dinner around the grounds of Fordham University ending usually at the Chapel where he would spend some time in prayer and reflection. As he approached the Chapel he saw Carman sitting on the steps with his head down staring at the ground.

"Well Charlie, are you waiting for me now?" asked the priest startling Carman out of his contemplation.

"Father please, why do you always call me Charlie?"

"Can't help myself son, you're the spitting image of my dearly departed brother Charlie. The resemblance is remarkable."

"Tell me Father; was your brother by any chance Italian?"

"No son, he was as Irish as Patty's Pig, but he could have passed for an Italian. His hair was black as pitch, and eyes to match, a good looking boy he was, I can tell you."

"What happened to him Father?

"Well Charlie, he got a lassie in the family way and her brother didn't take too kindly to him and called him out. Oh, it was a terrible brawl; I'll tell you. In the end poor Charlie lay dead on the ground. He hit his head on the curb and that was it."

"Father, that's terrible, I'm so sorry".

"That's alright, Charlie me boy, it was a long time ago, but you remind me of him, and I loved him dearly."

"Now Charlie," asked the priest, "what can I do for you?"

"Well Father I could use a little advice".

"Speak up son, that's what I'm here for," the priest answered sitting down next to Carman.

With the ease that comes from being in the presence of someone you trust he told the priest all about Anna. Well, almost all about Anna. Father Brown was after all a priest. He also told him the most disturbing aspect of his future, his plan to join the Army to escape Anna. He also confided in the priest his hope to have a great adventure.

As was his custom Father Brown listened attentively, nodding his head and whispering "Go on Charlie" whenever Carman faltered in his verbalization of the unusual developments his young life had taken in just a few short months.

"How old are you now Charlie the priest asked?"

"I was sixteen a few months ago," he answered.

"Well boy, you're very young to be in college never mind the Army. I would prefer that you remain at Fordham and get your degree. You have a fine mind Charlie, a gift for numbers and prose, very unusual for a young man just sixteen. The Army is an exciting life when war is not on the horizon. But just now, the Army is a very dangerous place to be for a young man with so much in life to savor. So, take my advise dear boy and stay as far away from this tempting young woman as possible, or mark my words, you'll end up being a very young father. The world has enough warriors; it needs men with brains to bring this country to its destiny. Do you have the will power to avoid this young woman?" he asked softly.

"Not so far, Father" Carman answered truthfully.

"Knowing your weakness is half the battle, praying always helps. In my profession it's the primary weapon. Have you tried it," the priest asked?

"Actually Father, I haven't, it just doesn't seem right, I should be able to handle this myself." Carman replied.

"I do believe that Adam had the same misconception. I certainly don't have to tell you what happened to him. Charlie my son, I do believe you have met your match with this "Anna" of yours. We'll have to use every weapon at our disposal in order to escape the plans, I believe, she has for you."

"Ok, Father, where do we begin?" Carman asked.

"Let us stop in the Chapel Charlie, and see what the Lord has to say, since we won't know until we ask. Come on son."

With his arm around Carman's shoulder the priest guided him into the only sanctuary he'd ever known, his church. Together they knelt and prayed for guidance. The priest prayed as hard as he knew how. He knew too well the determination of a woman once she gets her mind set. He only hoped it wasn't too late to keep the boy out of her clutches. At least until he was a little older and wiser. This young lady Anna seemed like an adversary worthy of ardent prayer.

Carman left Father Brown calmer than he had been in months, determined to evade Anna at any cost. He was prepared to leave Similetti's if need be. Weeks went by and Anna made no attempt to see Carman. She never came near the store. Carman began to breathe easier certain that Father Brown's prayers were working.

1929

He wondered where Dismus Brown was tonight. He could especially use a little of his guidance right now, but Father Brown was probably chewing the fat with his cronies at the old priests' residence. He couldn't help but remember how that man could make up a story for any occasion. It was only recently that Carman became aware of how Father Brown's brother Charlie had indeed died.

It seemed that when Charles James Brown was barely fifteen and living on Webster Avenue in the Bronx, on one blustery very cold and windy night he decided to take his sled for a ride down Snake Hill, one of the longest hills in the Bronx. That hill ran neck and neck with the Fords street hill that was favored for roller-skating. When he arrived at the top of Snake Hill he had to wait his turn. It seemed every kid in the neighborhood had the same idea as Charlie. Finally his turn came and one of his friends came over to him to warn him about the ice at the bottom of the hill. Charlie thanked him and jumped onto his sled. The wind blowing in his face felt like pins piercing his skin, but the euphoria he felt as his speed increased made up for any discomfort. At the bottom of the hill there were stones and ashes scattered over the snow to help stop your sled from taking you into the traffic on Webster Avenue. Because of the wind and constant accumulation of snow the stones and ash were practically obliterated. When Charlie's ride came to an end his sled bounded right into the middle of the avenue where a trolley car was dropping off passengers. He tried desperately to veer his sled away from the trolley but with the speed of a missile he hit the car and was killed instantly. Not one bone was broken in his young body. The only evidence of the collision was a small bump on his forehead.

Father Brown said he was eighteen at the time of the accident and was the first member of the family to arrive at the scene.

Why he invented the exciting story of Charlie's demise was anybody's guess. Maybe in some way a truly dramatic story of a slain lover was somehow easier to tell. A bump on the head isn't considered lethal, even though in both stories it was only a bump on the head that killed his brother Charlie.

"I could use a good story to cover what I'm about to do. Nothing could be more dramatic than what I have planned," Carman thought. He tried valiantly to come up with another scheme but regrettably, no matter how hard he tried nothing would come to him. He knew he should be able to find another solution but his memories kept getting in the way with Anna as the precursor.

1914

It was well over a month before Anna appeared at Similetti's. Of course she picked a very dark Friday evening when everyone, save Carman, had gone home.

Carman was unaware of her presence in the office as he bent over his figures to finish his bookkeeping for the week. When he finally looked up from his work he was startled to see her gazing at him. She was a vision to behold. Anna had surpassed herself as she stood smiling at Carman wearing a black satin dress that clung to every curve in her voluptuous body. Her curly blond hair framed her beautiful face as it hung loose and wild down her back.

Carman gasped at the sight of her as he prayed silently for strength.

She leaned over casually exposing her breasts and taking his face in her hands kissed him deeply. He was overwhelmed with desire. With one sweep of his hand he removed all the paper work from his desk and lifted her in his arms kissing her roughly.

Anna whispered, "gently Carman, gently."

Recovering his senses he unbuttoned her dress. As it fell to the floor he was surprised to see that she was absolutely naked. Her body shimmered in the moonlight that came through the window. Carman stood back and admired her beauty. Just looking at her was almost enough, almost but not quite. He acquiesced and kissed her lightly, trailing his kiss down her body to her waiting breasts. She purred with delight managing to maneuver his head between her velvet legs where he brought her to the height of passion. He could not hold himself back any longer. Tearing at his clothes, he managed to enter her gently, moving slowly until she screamed "faster, faster." It was easy to fulfill her wish. Her cries of joy were unending but eventually he was spent. Too weak to move he stayed within her cursing himself for his lack of control. He could not believe that he was unable to resist her.

Anna delicately removed herself from beneath him and carefully put on her dress.

"Thank you Carman," was all she said and left as silently as she had arrived.

Carman walked to the small bathroom where he washed himself as best he could. It was only then that he realized he had made love to Anna unprotected. The far-reaching implications of his stupidity flashed quickly through his mind. "Impossible," he said aloud, and continued to dress hastily knowing he was late for his date with his brother and sister for spaghetti at Guardo's restaurant.

Entering the restaurant, Carman was acutely aware of the owner Guardo, who was engaged to Anna.

"Carman, how the hell are you? I haven't seen you here in a long time. So what's been going on?"

"If he only knew," thought Carman, "I'd be a dead man."

"Not a thing Guardo, not a thing, talk to you later, I'm late and I don't want to keep Steve and Dominica waiting." He answered calmly as he hurried to the back of the restaurant where his brother and sister patiently waited for him. He bent to kiss his sister and realized how lovely she was.

"Dominica, how come I haven't noticed how pretty you are?"

"Oh Carman, stop," she answered blushing, She was pleased to be told what she hoped was true.

"Steve, tell me is our sister not the most beautiful girl in the Bronx, and perhaps Manhattan."

"Carman, sit down, I'm starving," he replied. Completely aware of Carman's habit of being flamboyant whenever he didn't want to explain why he was late.

"So am I Steve so am I."

They gave their order to the waitress, Guardo's Mama. It was impossible not to notice the staggering beauty of this woman who was well past fifty. It was her magnificent eyes that hadn't aged. They were almost lavender. A color not often seen, especially in Italian woman

Steve told them about his big promotion in the Telephone Company. They were surprised as Steve rarely spoke about himself,

"Well, did you get a big raise?" asked Carman.

"Not too big, but enough money to help when the baby comes."

"What baby," they both asked?

"Didn't I tell you," replied Steve?

"We're lucky you told us you're married, so what about the baby," answered Carman?

"Well, we're having a baby in five months."

"Five months, why didn't you wait until it was two years old to tell us," complained Dominica? "Mama Mia, I'm going to be an Aunt."

"Have you told Mama and Papa," asked Carman?

"I'm going over there tonight, listen you guys; it wasn't that I didn't want to tell you. It's just that my Pauline isn't that strong and the doctor was afraid she might lose the baby, I wanted to be sure before I told you."

"Ah, Steve we didn't mean anything, right Dominica?"

84

"Right Carman, we're just so happy," she replied getting up to kiss her big brother.

It was at this precise moment that Carman decided to join the Army. Mama and Papa would be busy with the baby, and his going wouldn't upset them as much with the joy of a baby coming.

"Carman, what's the matter, you look so sad, you're not happy I'm going to be a father?"

"Happy, I'm ecstatic, I'm just dumbfounded; I can't believe you're going to be a father."

"Dear God, neither can I, Carman, neither can I."

"Don't look so worried, you'll make a wonderful father, you're a saint already, Carman teased".

"Compared to you Carman, anybody could be a Saint."

"Come on, am I really that bad?"

"Yup, answered Dominica," and I don't know half the things you're up to." "Not even seventeen and I've got a reputation; I guess its time to move on."

"Move where," asked Steve?

"The Army" said Carman.

"What, are you really crazy? We're practically at war with Germany and you want to join the Army," exclaimed Steve?

"No Carman, you can't go. I need you home," cried Dominica tears clouding her vision.

"Relax; the Army is a good place to be right now, full of adventure. We're not at war and now I can pick exactly where I want to go."

"And where exactly do you want to go," sighed Steve?

"The Cavalry," exclaimed Carman.

"You ride horses now," said Steve?

"Well not quite, but that's just the point I can join the Cavalry, learn to ride, and possibly get a commission."

"What kind of commission," replied Steve?

"It's a commission to be an officer."

"How many Italian officers you think are in the Army, huh," said Steve?

"Come on, I was born here, I'm a full blooded American, they can't refuse me if I qualify, and I really want this. I have two years to go before I have got my degree and unfortunately, circumstances make the Army look very appealing to me"

A look passed between brothers. Steve knew there was more to Carman's sudden interest in the Cavalry. He just didn't know what would cause him to put his college education on hold to join the Army.

"Ok, Ok, we'll talk about this some other time replied Steve, tonight we celebrate my becoming a father and dinner is on me."

"What, you're paying for dinner, you always pay for dinner. Why do you think Dominica and I never refuse to go out with you," Carman said laughing?

That's how the evening went with the three Duva children laughing, hugging and just glad to be together. Sometimes they were a little teary, but not that night. The news of Steve's baby was too good to spoil. They decided not to talk about Carman's joining the Army. Steve was certain he could talk him out of it and Dominica couldn't bear even thinking about it. As usual, they had a wonderful time together.

Although somewhat masked, Carman was startled by Mr. Similetti's reaction to his decision to enlist in the Army.

"A wise move," he replied to his plan," the situation being what it is, puts you at great risk. I would hate to see your future put in jeopardy by some unforeseen predicament. Honestly son, I will really miss you. Sadly, I have become dependent on your expertise with my books. To my knowledge, no one could have done a better job. I look forward to your return when you are a little older and perhaps wiser. My only concern is your putting your degree on hold. Have you given any thought of how this will affect your future?"

It was almost impossible for Carman to answer. He had naturally assumed that his entanglement with Anna was undiscovered. His shame and embarrassment echoed in his voice as he answered.

"Actually sir, his head bent in humiliation, I believe that if I don't join the Army now and leave for a while, I won't be able to continue my education in any case."

"Sadly, I agree with you. It's a pity that this situation has developed."

Realizing the boy's utter discomfort he added, "Don't be too hard on yourself. There's a new phrase I've just heard; 'It takes two to Tango.' When do you think you will be leaving?" he added softly.

"That will be up to my father. If he's willing to sign my induction papers I could leave within the week. Unfortunately, my plans to enlist will come as a complete surprise to him. I am certain his answer will most certainly be "no." But I must ask him first."

As they left the little upstairs office Mr. Similetti whispered to Carman,

"Your brother Anthony can sign for you."

"I know, but I must talk to Papa first. Maybe I can persuade him to sign."

"Do what you must Carman," he replied putting his arm around the young man feeling somehow responsible for his dilemma. He should have seen it coming. He could have stopped it before it began. He remembered how intrigued Anna was with the young boy when he first came to work for him. What a fool he had been not to recognize what was happening right in front of him. Thank God there wasn't any permanent damage to his Anna. This young man was strong and had his whole life ahead of him. The Army would make him into a man. It will probably be very good for him. Hopefully America's involvement is just talk. Anna's engagement to Guardo was finally looking very good to Similetti. It was time to start making the arrangements.

Walking down Melrose Avenue, Carman was completely oblivious to his surroundings. Consequently he stumbled over a little girl who had wandered away from her mother. He was halted in mid step as the mother screamed and scrambled to retrieve her little girl from his path.

"It's a start you gave me son, you barely missed me princess with those hefty feet of yours," said the obviously Irish mother.

"I'm sorry, lady I didn't mean to scare you, I don't know what I was thinking of. Can I pick her up," he asked. The woman nodded and, as he lifted the little girl she gave him a big smile. He was completely taken with her and in no time at all he had her laughing merrily with all the sounds he could manage to make, that usually delighted little children.

"You certainly have a way with children lad, my Marie doesn't usually take to strangers."

"Well she is one beautiful little girl. I bet that she will break a lot of young men's hearts when she grows up," said Carman as he gently set the little four year old down.

"I'll tell you lad, it takes a special combination to create such a beauty." the mother replied.

"And what exactly is that special combination?"

"Why it's Italian and Irish of course." she replied.

"Well I'll be, I never thought about that particular combination myself, around here Italians marry Italians, and the Irish marry Irish."

"True enough lad. Me husband and I have been banished by both our parents, but it's been worth it, just look as the beauties we've made."

Embarrassed by the woman's candor, he looked around and saw two handsome little boys and, of course, the little Marie.

"I must confess, my dear lady you are surrounded by your truth."

"That I am son, that I am, and good luck to you boy, you look like you could use a little cheering up. Just remember that nothing is ever as bad as it seems, take it from me."

"Goodnight and thank you," said Carman smiling as he continued down the avenue surprised to find that he was whistling.

"I do feel a heck of a lot better," he thought, "and nothing is as bad as it seems," he said to himself as he rounded the corner to his house.

Opening the door to his house, he heard he father call him.

"Is that you Carmino?"

"Yes Papa."

"I want to talk to you."

"Sure Papa, I'll be right there, I just want to get something to eat."

Suddenly he was starving. Still whistling he went into the kitchen, and there was Mama already making him a sandwich.

"Now that's what I call service Mama. I think about eating and you make the sandwich. Is it eggplant by any chance?"

"Yes, its eggplant."

"I don't know how I'm ever going to get used to taking care of myself."

"What do you mean, you going someplace?" she asked.

"Mama I can't live here forever, I'm 16 already."

"16 is still a boy," she replied.

"Come on Mama, you were married at 16."

"Sure, that was the old country, today I wouldn't marry until I was at least 22."

"Why 22, is that a special age," asked Carman?

"I like that number. I had two children by the time I was 22, and that was much too young."

"In that case I won't get married until I'm 22, how's that? I really think it's almost time for me to be on my own."

"Carman, what are you really talking about ah," asked Mama?

Just then Papa called from the parlor and Carman dashed out without having to answer his mother.

He walked into the parlor with a mouth full of eggplant and he almost choked at his father' first words.

"No, no army, that is my decision and that's all there is to it. Here have a drink of Papa's beer."

Shocked at the offer, Carman barely took a sip and handed the tin of beer back to his father. As long as he could remember Papa's beer was off limits. It was Carman's job to run and get a tin of beer for his father. Tin in hand, and ten cents in his pocket he would race to the beer garden. He never failed to take a sip of beer on his way home hoping he wouldn't be found out.

"Carman you barely had a sip, you used to drink more than that on your way home from the beer garden."

"How come you never said anything to me then?"

"Ah, what could I say you were always licking the foam off your mouth when you gave me the tin. A little beer couldn't hurt, but getting shot with a gun that could kill. No, the answer is no. You are too young to go into the army."

"Papa, I didn't ask yet, and what makes you think I want to join the army?"

"The whole beer garden knows you want to join the army, and Papa knows too, and the answer is no. No is my answer."

"Papa you have no idea why it's imperative for me to join the army now."

"What's imperative in Italian, I don't understand?"

"Important Papa, it's important for me to join the army now."

"It's important for me you don't join the army now."

"Please Papa, listen to me."

"No, you go in the army I never see you again. What's the matter you don't read the Papers, you don't know that in a couple years there's going to be a big war? Mark my words Carman.

"Papa, I'm not going into the army to fight, I'm going to seek adventure. America is not at war, its 1914. Great Britain declared war on Germany, America didn't."

"Use your head Carmino, if Great Britain declared war on Germany, how far behind is America? "

"Not for years Papa, by the time there is a war I will be out of the army."

"Carmino, if there is a war you will fight, there is no getting away from that, so be a good boy and go to work, go to school and become the engineer you always wanted to be.

"Papa, I'll be an engineer some day, but not now, it's important for me to get away."

"Dio mio, Carman, are you in trouble? That's no problem Carman, Papa has money saved. I'll send you away, someplace nice. Maybe to Italy, you'd like that Ah?"

"Papa, I can go to Italy for free if I join the army."

"Yeah, and come back in a pine box. No, I can't sign Carman, even if you were old enough to join, I would be against it. Now you are too young to make a decision like this. No, you can't go, and that is that."

"Ah Papa, I love you so much, I hate to disappoint you but I really have to go. I'll see Italy and maybe France and maybe Africa, who knows? Papa it's going to be wonderful, please try to understand."

"My son, I do understand, but you have to realize and understand why I cannot sign. How can your Papa send you into danger? It's not right; I could never sleep at night or draw a breath without thinking that I sent you into danger. I just cannot, your Papa cannot. If you must go, ask your brother to sign but don't tell your Mama, for she will kill both Anthony and me. I do not jest Carman, she will truly kill us. Make up a story, do what you must. Only there has got to be another way to avoid this woman."

Carman stared at his father in utter disbelief. Was it possible that the entire world knew of his entanglement with Anna?

Papa continued, "I meant it when I said I had the money to send you anywhere you want to go, and if it's not enough I'll borrow more. Am I not the best mason in New York City, Huh? You try, Carman, for Papa."

"I promise Papa, if there is another way, I will take it."

He picked up his half-eaten sandwich and went back to the kitchen. All of a sudden his appetite was gone. He sat staring off into space. No one understood. If he didn't get away now he would never get away from Anna. She had a hold on him he couldn't break. The only answer was to leave. The only place feasible was the army. Where could he get a job making enough money to support him? The army was the answer.

He got up from the table and poured himself a cup of coffee that was warming on the stove. He couldn't think about it anymore.

Carman spent the following two weeks desperately seeking a way out of his situation. Invariably, he could be found sitting in the park looking completely desolate feeding the gathering pigeons. In desperation he sought out his brother for support, acutely aware of the underlying need for Steve's signature on his induction papers. As he passed St. Francis Church he gazed longingly at the entrance, knowing the cool esoteric interior could salve his soul. Only inside the confines of his church did Carman feel really safe and able to confront the truth within him. He knelt in his favorite pew and looked up at the statue of the Sacred Heart of Jesus, depicting Christ with his heart bleeding onto His pure white robe as His eyes gazed lovingly at the world. Looking up at the statue Carman sighed and immediately felt at peace. Completely relaxed, he looked at his Jesus and silently prayed for direction. In less than a minute he uttered aloud "I know, I know" and laughed softly to himself.

The truth was that he really wanted to join the army and get away from everyone and have the adventure of a lifetime. He was so caught up in the news from abroad that he read everything printed on the war in Europe and Arabia. The headlines in the Times rang in his ears. England Declares War on Germany; British Ship Sunk; French Ships Defeat German; Belgium Attacked; 17,000,000 Men Engaged At War Of Eight Nations etc, etc. He wanted to be there not on Morris Park Avenue, he wanted to be in France and maybe Italy, wherever. He wanted to be a man and fight the great fight. All the books he had read of the Crusades and Arthur's Court were beyond his grasp. But this war could be his war and he was ready. Maybe not old enough but bold enough and tough enough and by God he was going.

The fact that he was scared to death that he would get Anna pregnant and have to marry her was also a consideration. He knew he could, if he really wanted to, have the will power to not make love to Anna. After all, he was in charge of his emotions, wasn't he? It was just the fact that Anna had some kind of hold on him that he couldn't seem to break. Just thinking about her would set his hormones racing. The Army was his way out, or something beyond his control would happen. Yes, he would definitely join. He literally ran out of the church determined to get his brother to sign his induction papers tonight or tomorrow for sure.

Suddenly he had an undeniable urge to see his friends. He was in desperate need to drink until his head spun, eat until his stomach ached and laugh until his sides split. That is exactly what Carman did the night before he joined the U.S. Cavalry on August 7, 1914.

Years later when the brothers talked of the "Old Times," Steve would always question Carman, "How did you get me to sign those papers?"

Carman would answer always the same, "the wine Steve, the wine," and both brothers would collapse in laughter.

Chapter Eleven

1914

The Army gave Carman two weeks to straighten out his affairs before he had to report to Fort Smith in New York State. It was barely time enough for Mama to stop crying. She managed to accuse every member of the family of betraying her and sending her "bambino" to war and certain death. The fact that the United States was not at war had no bearing on Mama's grief, for she was, in spite of her indifference to the English language, completely aware of the situation in Europe. No one bore the brunt of her wrath as much as her son Steve did. Enraged, she threw a kitchen knife at him, which whizzed past his head and landed in the kitchen wall. It remained impaled on the wall until it finally fell of its own accord the next day. This was the last outrageous deed from Mama until the day that Carman left home. She locked herself in her room surrounded by her numerous statues of the saints and prayed for a miracle to keep her son home. When none came she took it as a sign that God had His own plans and she must accept the inevitable.

Anna was shocked at the news of Carman's enlistment. Unable to see him at her father's store she was frantic. She must find a way to see Carman alone just one last time before he went away. Her hands were tied. She could not knock at his door and ask for him although the thought had crossed her mind. She was officially engaged to Guardo and could not jeopardize that relationship. She intended to marry Guardo and live a reasonably happy life. Certainly not as exciting a life with Carman could be but that was out of the question. He was only sixteen, talented in the ways of lovemaking, but still only a boy. Anna was determined to have one last encounter with Carman, something to think about after she married Guardo. It never occurred to her that Guardo might be more to her liking. After all, he did have a reputation as a ladies man. Anna never really took that rumor seriously. She refused to believe anyone could be unfaithful to her and so she dismissed it as pure gossip. There was only one way open to her and she used it. On Guardo's willing arm, she approached her mother and suggested that she give a small dinner party for Carman. Mrs. Similetti agreed immediately, as she was quite fond of the boy herself. She was disturbed that her husband was against the plan but dismissed his reluctance as sadness for Carman's leaving.

Mr. Similetti was also upset at Carman's joining the Army. He was very aware of the circumstances and blamed himself for helping the young man make this decision. On the other hand, Anna could have saved herself a lot of trouble since Carman attended his party with a pretty young girl from the neighborhood that never left his side. Anna never realized that he was afraid to be left alone with her and had prearranged a plan with his companion to stay close to him. The entire Duva family went to the party. Mrs. Similetti with Anna's unexpected help, made elaborate plans for the party. The food was catered from Guardo's restaurant and the wine was imported from Italy. The household staff outdid themselves carefully scrubbing and shining every nook and cranny. There was dancing in the main dining room with music provided by a well-known Italian orchestra. Anna convinced herself that all she had to do was get Carman to dance with her and everything else would fall into place. Carman feigned exhaustion when Anna begged him for a dance. She was beside herself with disappointment almost to the point of losing her famous temper. Carman mindful that Anna would spring some kind of trap for him considered dancing with her too close for comfort.

At one point in the evening, Anna managed to get close enough to him to whisper in his ear "I must see you alone."

Carman whispered back, "not on your life,"

She was stunned by his reply. She could not believe that he was not eager to be alone with her. Looking at him beseechingly, she asked innocently "Why?"

Carman could not ignore her pleadings and, taking her hand, he led her onto the balcony.

Surrounded by the smell of flowers from the garden and a million stars overhead he sat her down on a garden bench. Standing above her, not daring to sit down next to her, he explained as gently as he could how impossible the situation between them had become, and how in all fairness to both of them they had to avoid one another as much as possible. She was overwhelmed by his allegations and protested vehemently. Aware that he couldn't make her understand he left her on the balcony and returned to the party. Guardo who had been searching for her finally found her sitting on the balcony obviously crying.

"What is it Anna, did something happen?" he asked tenderly.

"No, no Guardo, I couldn't help myself. I was thinking of that poor boy Carman going into the army and it made me so sad."

"Anna, my poor baby, you are so sweet to feel sad for poor Carman."

He kissed her lightly on the lips and was startled by the passion she returned. He embraced her gently as she pressed her body close to his. He was confused and elated by her apparent change of attitude toward anything intimate. Amazed by her reaction to his kiss, he gently led her to the gazebo in the back of the garden. They sat and continued making love, until their longing engulfed them. Murmuring words of love and desire" Guardo clumsily entered her body and was amazed by her eagerness. Because his love for Anna was real, his feeling of joy was absolute.

The idea of making love to her before they were married was, up until now, inconceivable. Judging by her actions, he was inclined to believe it was perhaps not her first time. He swept the thought from his mind as she cried out in apparent pain. It was her innate ability to deceive that saved her from being exposed. The act was far less gratifying than she expected. It was more difficult feigning enjoyment than hiding her lack of innocence.

After it was over, poor Guardo was beyond remorse. He almost wept. Anna had a difficult time keeping composure. It was hard not to laugh at him. She managed to convince him that they were blameless. Guardo consumed with guilt wanted to believe her. Rearranging their clothing they hurried back to the party surprised to find that they had not been missed.

Anna knew then that Guardo could never fulfill her desire.

The day after the party Carman took a trolley car, and then a train, another trolley car, and another train to get to his destination at Whitehall Street. His mind was full of last night's drama, complete with Mama quietly crying in a corner of the Similetti's house, always conscious of propriety even though her pain was almost too much to bear. Papa sat next to her quietly holding her hand. Steve and Pauline lingered close by in case Mama needed them. Steve tried to coax Papa into drinking a glass of wine. He even found Mama's favorite sherry among the countless bottles of liquor they had at the party. They would have none of it.

"Mama please have something. You can't spend the next four years in mourning. Carman isn't dead. He's just going into the army. It will be a great adventure for him. I envy him," he added, "I wish I could go."

At that last statement Mama looked up and murmured in Italian, "Over my dead body, you go." Steve couldn't help but laugh at his mother and ignored the deadly look she gave him.

"Wait and see," he continued undaunted, "he'll be home after his training and you'll see how happy he is. Come on; please try to enjoy yourself. The Similetti's have gone to great expense to give this party for Carman. You'd think we were at a funeral."

"Sure," replied Mama, "they only want to make sure Carman stays away from that daughter of theirs. They'd give him a party just to get rid of him."

"Mama, Carman really wants to go, look how happy he is."

Mama looked up to see Carman dancing with the girl he brought to the party. Leaning over to Papa, forgetting how sad she was, she said,"Look Paulo, how nice they look together."

"Who looks nice together?" answered Papa staring into space.

"Carman does Papa. See how nice he looks dancing with that pretty girl. "

"Very nice Mama, maybe she can talk Carman out of this nonsense?"

"No sweetheart I don't think so. I think our Carman is really going into the army. Even though it breaks my heart to see him go, it's probably for the best, with that she devil around."

"Maybe you're right; maybe we have some nice wine, huh?"

Mama leaned over and gave Papa a kiss and agreed to have a nice glass of sherry and perhaps one of those pastries she noticed when she came in.

Steve realizing the change in his parent's attitude grabbed his wife Pauline for a dance and edged close to Carman.

"Carman, you ok?

"I'm fine Steve; I'm having a great time."

"Good, you still want to do this?"

"I still want to do this. Will you stop worrying about signing my papers? It's going to be the best time of my life."

"Sure, if you don't get killed."

"Don't worry, nothing is going to happen to me," replied Carman with more conviction than he felt. Carman danced, and ate, and shook hands with every one at the party. He seemed to be having the time of his life. Unfortunately, he spent the entire evening avoiding Anna. When he saw her and Guardo come in from the garden his heart stopped. He hadn't really seen her before. He was so busy evading her he hadn't noticed how beautiful she looked in a long green satin dress that seemed to cling to her body, and her hair piled on top of her head.

"Mama Mia" he quietly exclaimed. But it was more than her appearance. Anna radiated something directly to Carman. He averted her gaze and engaged his date Rosa in banal conversation. As the evening was drawing to an end, Carman began to breathe easier and found to his surprise that Rosa was not only pretty, but also was a very clever young lady. He was really enjoying himself with this pretty girl. With his head bent to capture every word Rosa whispered he didn't notice Anna coming closer.

"Have you no time for one dance with me Carman," she whispered breathlessly? "Of course he has time for a dance with you" chimed in Rosa, "but just a short one. I'll be watching, so keep your distance," she said as she winked at Carman.

With the look of doom on his face Carman led Anna to the dance floor and carefully kept his distance as they danced to an old, Italian waltz.

"You even dance well Carman. We should have done more dancing and less lovemaking," Anna whispered in his ear, sending chills up his spine.

"Mama Mia," replied Carman."

"Is something wrong Carman?" Anna asked as she snuggled close to him."

"Not a thing Anna," he said as he whisked her back to Guardo.

"Here she is Guardo, no worse for wear," he said.

"Come sit here Carman," beckoned Rosa.

"Thank you," Carman replied kissing her softly on her cheek."

"You're welcome Carman. That Anna is a rare one and you looked as if you needed some rescuing."

Holding Rosa's hand, Carman made the rounds to say goodnight to all his friends. Steve had promised to take Mama and Papa home. Mrs. Similetti blushed with pride as Carman kissed her cheek thanking her for all the trouble she had gone through to give him such a wonderful going away party. Mr. Similetti hugged the young man and wished him Godspeed. Just when he thought he was going to leave unscathed, Anna rushed up to him and gave him a kiss that set his head spinning. Luckily Rosa came to the rescue and unerringly whisked him out the door.

Once outside she remarked, "just how much rescuing are you going to need?"

"Whitehall Street, Whitehall Street next stop", shouted the conductor waking Carman. For the moment he couldn't remember where he was. Grabbing his small grip he leaped out of the train just as the doors were closing. He stood on the platform still a little dazed. Checking his watch he realized he had been asleep for over an hour. Taking a deep breath to clear his head, he strode purposely toward his destination, not looking left or right afraid he might turn around and head for home. Was he doing the right thing, he wondered? Maybe he should forget the whole thing. After all he hadn't signed anything yet. "Jesus, I'm scared shitless," he thought silently. Turning the corner he couldn't miss the sign that read, "Enter Here Induction Center." He squared his shoulders, said a fast Our Father, and went in. Men of all ages gathered in small clusters waiting. Some were smoking nervously, others were reading the newspaper and still others were standing perfectly still, as if mesmerized. One such young man caught Carman's eye, and with absolute joy he shouted,"Marty, Marty, is it really you?" Sure enough it was, and the two childhood friends grabbed one another laughing and joking and found their fear passing.

"I can't believe you're here, I had no idea you wanted to join the Army; I haven't seen you in years. Where have you been?" asked Carman.

"Unlike you I've been working my ass off, that's where I've been, down in the sewers laying pipes."

"You're kidding, in the sewer, what are you crazy?"

"Not exactly, I just wanted to make the most money I could in the shortest amount of time. But no matter how hard I worked, or how much I made it was never enough for my family. I decided I wasn't going to spend my whole life underground. I'd join the Army and see the world. What brought you here?" asked Marty.

"You'd never believe it, I barely believe it myself," answered Carman.

"Hey Carman, you know you can tell me anything. We may not have seen one another for a few years, but I think our stab at the priesthood has made us friends for life, he answered laughingly.

"I believe you Marty; I'd forgotten how easy it was to talk to you."

"Hey Carman, we go back a long way for two guys not even eighteen yet. Come on, let's sit down and get caught up on our lives. I've got stories you'd never believe," said Marty. The two young friends found an empty bench to sit on and they reminisced about their days at St. Simon's Seminary. They laughed and laughed until one of the Sergeants called their names and brought them back to reality.

They were marched into what resembled a clinic, and told to remove their clothes. Marty and Carman stood shaking in their long underwear as several doctors pinched, prodded, and pulled at their bodies checking for God knows what and totally ignoring their cries of indignation. At one point they were injected respectively with various anti-toxins to ward off any strange bacteria they might encounter in their travels. They were told they would probably feel sick for a few days, and they did. The army doctors were not aware that these two boys had been subjected to probably every living bacterium known to man. They were perhaps stronger and healthier than their counterparts from other rural areas of the country. Even if the Army knew, nothing could have saved them from being inoculated. After they had been carefully turned inside out the two friends stood side by side and proudly pledged their lives to their country and were inducted into the US Cavalry. They were ecstatic with their luck. There was a very good chance that they could have been inducted into the infantry.

"How did we do it?" they asked one another jumping up and down like the two kids they were.

It seemed that a young sergeant had mistaken information that all Italians were horsemen, just like American cowboys. He had read a book about Teddy Roosevelt's "Rough Riders" which mentioned that some of Roosevelt's men were descendents of Italian landowners. What better place to send these young Italian recruits than the Cavalry?

No matter, the boys were thrilled with their fortune. Not only were they in the Cavalry, they were together and that was by far the best thing that could have happened to them.

Unceremoniously, they were loaded on trains heading for Fort Smith, somewhere in New York State. Neither boy wondered or cared exactly where he was going. They were in the Cavalry and they couldn't be happier. The smiles on their faces remained in place until they met their first horse.

Although the ride to Fort Smith was long and slow, most of the men on the train were grateful for the chance to sleep. Few of them, if any, had any sleep for the week before enlistment. With parties and good-byes to friends and family, the idea of sleep escaped most of them. If they had been fortunate enough to get some sleep, the trepidation and anxiety of joining the Army caused many a fitful rest at best. When the young officer checked on his new recruits, he found them all sleeping peacefully, unaware of what lay ahead for them.

The sun was barely over the horizon when the military train came to a halt, waking Carman and Marty with a start. They jumped up toppling over bags and parcels crowding the aisles of the train. A young sergeant stuck his head into their train and yelled, "Alright men, up and out and don't leave anything behind, you'll never see it again, move it, move it."

Scrambling to pick up their belongings, nervously laughing at their awkwardness, the boys staggered off the train into the early morning light. Another sergeant, seemingly appearing out of nowhere began barking orders, which they all tried valiantly to follow. One young man actually fell on his face in the dirt. His companions picked him up and they all walked the short distance to the camp. The area around the train station resembled a painting of Middle America with farms dotting the roadside, green pastures with horses and cows grazing, and birds flying overhead. It was a comforting sight to see smoke rising from the farm house chimneys. The sky was bright blue and the air was fresh and fragrant with the smell of summer. Most of the young men walking along had never been out of a city. They were amazed at the beautiful countryside within New York State. They called to one another, "look at the horses, and look at the cows." "Wow, where's the farmers daughters?" yelled one of the recruits. As if on cue, three lovely young girls came walking down the road leading a young donkey laden with milk cans, heading for the train station.

"Alright men, look sharp, no shenanigans, eyes straight ahead", and the small band stood tall and marched tall, looking neither left nor right. The girls were delighted and giggled shamelessly.

"Carman," whispered Marty "did you wink at the middle one?"

"What middle one?" answered Carman?

"The pretty one," answered Marty

"I didn't even see her; I kept my eyes straight ahead," laughed Carman.

"Well she certainly saw you. She stood still watching you until we passed."

"Yeah right Marty, all these guys and she picks me out. Give me a break."

"Carman you'll never change, you never see it, the ladies just love you," answered Marty.

"Hey, keep it under your hat, I don't need ladies, a lady got me here. I just want to be a good soldier and make me mother proud."

"Now you're Irish too?"

"Well you are, why not? That reminds me; I asked the Sergeant Major when I signed in to change my first name."

"Change your first name, what are you talking about?" asked Marty.

"I thought I'd like to be called Charles instead of Carman. He put my name down as Charles Carman Duva, real American huh Marty?"

"Yeah Carman, pardon me, Charles. Hey it does sound more American, but I like Charlie better. It suits you."

"That's what my friend Father Brown always said; in fact he's been calling me Charlie for years. I think it'll bring me luck," answered Carman hopefully. For the next few years and whenever it suited Carman's purpose, he called himself Charles. Carman wrote to Father Brown and told him of his name change. The priest wrote back completely delighted.

Little did Carman realize how important a new name could be?

The young recruits marched into the camp and their faces fell in disappointment. Instead of barracks, there were shabby tents. The horses that were grazing in the field looked as if they were rejects from the vendors on Canal Street, in New York City. They stood immobile with their eyes riveted on the scene, unable to look away or even speak.

Carman was the first to utter, "Dio Mio."

Moved by the overwhelming silence the young sergeant shouted, "It's not as bad as it looks."

"Right," whispered Marty, "its worse."

"Come on men, let's head for the Reception Center," yelled the sergeant as they wearily followed him to a shack behind the tents.

"Wow a real Reception Center," murmured Marty," what next?"

The young recruits approached the sad little building with their heads bowed so low they looked like a troop of midgets. They entered the building and were shocked at the cleanliness and order all around them. Unconsciously they stood taller moved by their surroundings.

"Attention" shouted the sergeant as an even younger Colonel entered from another room.

"Welcome men my name is Colonel Armstrong. When you see me, wherever you are, I expect you to salute. Got it?"

Receiving no answer he repeated "got it?" a little louder. He stared at them disdainfully waiting for an answer."

"Sergeant," he shouted.

"Yes Sir," the sergeant replied.

"Are these men deaf, by any chance?" asked the Colonel.

"Not to my knowledge, Sir."

"Then why don't they answer, are they plain stupid?"

"I don't think so Sir; they're just recruits, Sir."

"Would you be kind enough sergeant, to instruct these "recruits" in the proper manner to answer a senior officer?"

"Yes Sir."

"Alright men, when you are asked a question by a senior member of this outfit, which I believe at this moment includes the horses you passed on your way in here, you are supposed to say two little words, and they are, "Yes Sir. Now let me hear you say it."

The sad little band of would be soldiers whispered, "Yes Sir."

"Louder please," replied the sergeant.

"Yes Sir," they replied a little louder.

"Louder," shouted the sergeant,"I want them to hear you in Albany."

"Yes Sir" they shouted, finally reaching the crescendo required.

"Thank you sergeant," the Colonel said as he moved in front of the men, "as I was saying, whenever you see a Senior Officer you salute. Got it?"

"Yes Sir," shouted the recruits

"I do believe you've got a good group here sergeant. They learn fast."

"Alright men, Sergeant Cassetti will take over now. From today on until you are full fledged Cavalry, the sergeant will tell you when to eat, when you can sleep and what you can dream. He will be your instructor, your priest, your rabbi and your mother. When he tells you to jump, you will jump. When he tells you to breathe, you will breathe. In exactly twelve weeks you will be Men of the Cavalry. Or I'll know the reason why. Just remember one fact men, I may be young but I'm mean as hell."

"Yes Sir," they replied wondering just how mean this guy was.

"Good," said the Colonel as he strode off to his office.

"Men, we're here to make you fighting men and the first thing you will need is a haircut. After that you will get uniforms, but first, you will be assigned your tents where you can drop off your belongings. Don't waste any time because after you see your tents we'll go to the mess hall and have some breakfast.

They hardly glanced inside the tents and were ready for the short walk to the mess hall for breakfast. Carman and Marty were assigned to the same tent with two other young men from New York City. They lined up outside of the mess hall, the first of hundreds of lines they would wait on for the next four years. The mess hall was actually one giant tent that looked as if it were long as a city block.

The smell of the coffee combined with the smell of bacon and eggs on the grill wafted to the starving recruits as they quickened their gait to the confines of the mess hall. Once inside, the aromas were mesmerizing. Carman finally reached the head of the line and gratefully accepted anything they put on his plate whether he recognized it or not. He couldn't remember ever being this hungry in his entire life. One strange glob after another was laden on his tin plate, which he acknowledged giddily. When at last seated next to Marty, with his mouth full with what he assumed were eggs smiled joyfully at his friend who was just as content with the food as he was. Both of them smiled knowingly at the absurdity of their happiness. They were so young and it was such a uniquely different experience for them. They were eager for the riddle of army life to unfold and grasped at the mystery that awaited them.

After breakfast they were shown the latrines, an engineering phenomenon of army life. With obvious urgency they were ushered into the barber's tent. The look of astonished incredulity reflected on their faces as they left the tonsorial. It could have been hysterically funny, but no one was laughing. If their mothers had been there they would have wept.

Carman was surprised to discover that his ears stuck out. Marty on the other hand, looked incredibly like a pyramid. After the shock wore off, both of them fell down laughing until their sides ached. The coupe de grace arrived as they received their uniforms. Both boys just seventeen and not quite inhabiting a man's physique were issued regulation fatigues that would have dwarfed John L. Sullivan.

Completely devastated by their appearance, they reluctantly crept outside their tents for formation. Delighted at the sight of their counterparts, not one soldier felt out of place. As if by design, the entire platoon resembled boys in their father's clothes. Sergeant Cassetti unfathomed by their appearance addressed his men as if they were dressed as the King's Guards. Tripping over their uniforms they marched to the parade ground for their first taste of army drills.

That night, every recruit slept the sleep of the young, unworried by the day's events, unaware of their surroundings, and completely, unequivocally, and dead to the world.

The blare of a trumpet shattered their peaceful retreat, and with little enthusiasm they lined up outside of their tents for another day of torture, torment, and pure hell. But that was the army, and if these young men were going to take part in an inevitable war, they had to be prepared, primed and readied for any eventuality. After only six weeks, their ill-fitting uniforms began to flatter the new torsos they had acquired. Where there had been flab or just skin and bone, muscle appeared. Their previously scalped heads were now covered with neatly trimmed hair. They looked marvelous.

Sergeant Cassetti was proud of his men and they in turn were proud of themselves. Now came the hard part; teaching them how to ride a horse. Most of them had never seen a horse until they arrived at the camp. In the past six weeks they learned how to care for a horse. They especially learned how to clean out a stable, which was a prerequisite for sitting a horse in the army. They would not just learn to ride. They would become equestrians of the first Order of Kings.

Before they could become horsemen, they had to learn the fundamentals of mounting and dismounting, and the various riding styles using proper signals to control and direct the movements of the horse. Learning to mount a horse using the several separate acts that are executed in one continuous movement took complete concentration. This was something that came instinctively to Carman but was severely lacking in Marty. Carman took to horseback riding like a duck to water. He loved the animals and they sensed it. When he mounted any horse they became one in motion and movement. Regal was the word that came to mind watching him gallop, trot or walk his horse. He was never far from the stables and his pockets were invariably stuffed with sugar cubes or apples pilfered from the mess.

Carman spent hours instructing his friend, Marty.

"Ok, stand beside the left shoulder of your horse, facing his backside, while you hold your reins in your left hand. Not the right hand. Please Marty stop looking around, nobody is watching you. They're too busy falling off their mounts."

"Gimme a break Charlie, my grandfather wasn't a Padrone like yours. He didn't ride all day checking his vineyards. He just drank the wine your grandfather made."

"Maybe you're right. I never rode a horse until I came here. It could be inherited, like drinking. Perchance you did a little drinking last night, which makes it just a little difficult, if not impossible, for you to mount your steed. Let's not make this too arduous. Just focus that's all, try and just focus."

"Now with your right hand twist the stirrup toward you and insert your left foot in it. Good, now place your right hand on the cantle and pull yourself up. Try transferring your weight to your left foot and both of your hands. Now, remove your right hand from the cantle and swing your right leg up and across."

Finally after countless attempts, Marty was able to get up on the horse. Carman yelled "Jesus, you did it. What a pro."

Marty sat tall in the saddle, proud as a peacock. Carman didn't dare let Marty dismount. He was so happy to get him up on the horse; he decided to leave him there awhile. As long as Marty was relaxed and calm in the saddle he could also show him how to be gentle with his horse and not heavy-handed, which could injure a horse's sensitive mouth. Teaching Marty to ride was another matter altogether. Carman became so skilled as a teacher it that he was assigned to instruct others, which he didn't mind at all. Marty, on the other hand, became his prized student.

1929

"My God, how many cigars have I smoked tonight?" he said looking at the almost empty humidor. He wished that he could sleep. He was so tired.

Carman could not believe that thinking of the past could take so much energy. He sat watching the falling snow remembering the happiest two years of his life in the Cavalry. How army life suited him. Hard work and lack of distraction on the base gave him time to ride and to read. He remembered that in that short space of time he actually grew two inches and gained thirty pounds, most of it muscle. His body was changing from that of a slim young boy to the body of a young man. In his whole life he would never again be in such splendid condition in mind as well as body. Little did they realize that most of the riding they would do, would be at Fort Smith.

They were trained to fight on horseback, as distinguished from the mounted infantrymen, who used horses for rapid transportation between engagements. Infantrymen fought on foot with most of their time served in the trenches. Throughout history the Cavalry was esteemed for their expeditiousness and mobility. In combat they were used for reconnaissance, delaying actions, raiding parties and harassing the enemy troops.

Fortunately for Carman and his friend Marty, they were completely unaware that they were now in a modern army where the Cavalry and mounted infantry would be replaced. Cavalry soldiers, using tanks, armored cars and other mechanized gear would obliterate the usefulness of the horse soldier. Horse Cavalry was used only to a limited extent in World War One. The glorious painting by Frederick Remington of the "Cavalry Charge On The Southern Plains" which had been instrumental in Carman's longing to be in the Cavalry, was past and never to be seen again.

The appearance of a rifle with a repeating device, in the latter half of the nineteenth century, was the most serious blow to the importance of Cavalry warfare. Charging cavalrymen were susceptible targets for armed troops with automatic weapons. Gone were the days of Teddy Roosevelt's "Rough Riders."

"Thank goodness, Marty and I were not aware of the coming end to the Cavalry after working so hard to become horse soldiers."

1914

After eight grueling weeks of basic training, they were given furlough to go home. Shouts of glee could be heard in Albany when the recruits were told of their unusual luck. Normally they would be required to finish ten weeks of training before they were allowed to return home on leave. No one knew why. They were permitted to go home and they couldn't care less, why?

Marty and Carman took extra pains with their uniforms to look just right for the folks at home. They had filled out considerably in only eight weeks, and looked great in their jodhpurs and high brown leather boots. The boots, definitely not army issue, were somehow acquired by Marty. Carman was afraid to ask where he got them. Carman had to stuff cotton in the toe of the boots to make them fit. Size was a small price to pay for such elegant boots, origin unknown. There was absolutely no one more pleased with their appearance than themselves. They stepped off the train in New York City ready to conquer the world. The trolley ride to the Bronx was more then they could hope for. Practically every young lady who saw them was positively dazzled. The flirting that went on for that short journey home was shameless.

"There's something about a uniform, hey Charlie," winked Marty.

"There sure is," replied Carman as they laughed and jostled each other all the way home. The same way they did when they were in Sister Amelia's eighth grade class. They left the barracks as men and within five minutes of being in New York, they were just kids again.

They jumped off the trolley, promising to meet later that night. Each one took off running for home. Racing up the stairs to his house, Carman could hear Mama singing in the kitchen. He stopped at the head of the stairs to listen as tears formed in his eyes; the joy of Mama's singing filled his heart. He couldn't wait more than half a minute. He burst into the kitchen shouting, "I'm home."

At the sound of her son's voice ringing in her ears Mama turned, clutched her chest, and took in the sight of her son. "Mama Mia you're beautiful," she cried. She grabbed and kissed him calling, "come everybody, Carman is home."

Dominica was the first to answer her mother's call. She came flying into the kitchen. "Oh Carmino, I can't believe you're really home. Papa, Papa come, it's Carman. He's home."

Papa came running into the kitchen and clutched his son in a bear hug so tight, that Carman could barely breathe. Papa finally let go of Carman and stood back to get a good look at him. "Good, you look good. I was afraid they were starving you. But, you look good." Papa took out his handkerchief and dabbed at his eyes, wiping away tears of joy.

"Talk about looking good. Papa you look wonderful. What has Mama been feeding you?"

"What Mama always feeds me spaghetti, what else?

"Dominica let me take a good look at you. If it's possible you are even prettier than when I left," said Carman.

Blushing, she replied,"get out of here; if I didn't know better I'd swear you were Irish with that "Blarney" you throw around."

"You know I'm right," Carman replied," I bet the boys are lined up around the block, to go out with you.

"Well a few come around," she answered shyly.

"Papa, have you had to fight off all boys trying to date our Dominica?"

"Only one, I really want to get rid of. Your little sister thinks she is in love with that barber, Paul Victore.

"I know him Papa. He seems like a nice enough guy. He's got plenty of money. He inherited a fortune from his father."

"Do you know where that fortune came from?" asked Papa.

"No where?"

"Enough now, we talk later. We have a lot to talk about ok?"

"Of course Papa," Carman said hugging his father. Carman could not miss the misery in his little sister's eyes. He winked at her reassuringly.

After dinner, when the commotion of his homecoming had subsided, Carman knocked on his little sister's door.

Opening the door she said, "Come in, and please sit on the bed and listen."

Carman sat quietly on the bed and listened as Dominica between sobs, told him the story of her love for Paul, the barber. When she finished Carman put his arm around her and said "what's the problem? You love

Paul and he love you. What's wrong with that?

"Absolutely nothing, not one little thing, except —"

"Except what, come on, there's got to be something. Papa wouldn't be so upset. What? He has a wife?" Carman said jokingly.

"How did you know? Does everyone know, oh my God?"

"Easy Dominica, easy, I was just joking. I had no idea. How old is this guy anyway?"

"He's thirty," she answered in a whisper.

"You're not even sixteen yet and he's thirty. Forget it. He's an old man already. Does he have any children?"

"No, there are no children."

"What does his wife have to say about this?"

"Nothing, she doesn't even know. She probably wouldn't understand if she were told," answered Dominica.

"Ok, said Carman. What's the rest of the story?

"Well Carman she's in a sanitarium."

"A sanitarium?" answered Carman.

"Oh Carman the poor woman went crazy after she lost her baby during childbirth. She's been in St. Michael's Sanitarium for ten years.

Incredible thought Carman, wondering what he should say to her.

He began slowly. "Please listen to me. You are only fifteen years old. No matter how romantic you think being in love with a married man is. It isn't. It's really just an affair. You don't want that, and I'm sure Paul doesn't want that for you. You haven't gone to bed with him, have you?"

"Oh Carman, of course not, I'm a good girl. I could never go to bed with a man I wasn't married to. You know that."

"Yeah, I know that. There is only one thing for you to do. You have to say goodbye to Paul."

"Say good-bye, are you crazy? I love him. He needs me."

"No, my dear little sister, he doesn't need you, and you certainly don't need him. I'll make a bargain with you. You start to go out with boys closer to your age. Only the one's you think you might like, and when I come back from basic training, if you still feel the same way about this old man. I'll see what I can do."

"Carman, do you really think Paul is an old man?"

"He's an old man Dominica, take my word for it. If his wife has been in a sanitarium for ten years, and this guy is still married to her and not fooling around, he's an old man. Has he tried to make love to you?"

"Of course not Carman, he is very proper."

"Not proper Dominica, just old. Do what I ask. If you still feel the same when I come home again, I promise I'll see what can be done. But you've got to start going out with boys your age, ok?"

"Ok, I'll do what you ask."

"How would you like to go out with my friend Marty?"

"Carman, I haven't seen Marty since I was a little girl and he used to pull my pig tails."

"You'll probably see him tonight. If you like what you see, I'll set it up. Is that alright with you?" asked Carman.

"Well I have to see if I like him first. I don't go out with just anybody," she answered.

"Ok, you let me know. I'm meeting him now anyway. See you later, he said and gave Dominica a kiss on the cheek as he left her room. Passing the kitchen he called to his mother to let her know he was going out to meet his friend Marty.

"Sure Carman, you go out with Marty, but don't go near that Anna. All the time you've been away, she's been coming around and asking about you. You stay away from her. She's a bad one. She's not good in the head, Carman."

"Don't worry Mama," he answered. I have no intention of seeing Anna.

He ran down the stairs into the street. A picture of Anna stayed in his mind. Mama mia, see Anna, that's all I need. Seeing Anna is the last thing I want to do. I don't know what it is about her, but every time I see her, the only thing I can think of, is taking her to bed. God help me, it happens every time. Forget it Carman, he told himself. One of the reasons you joined the army was to get away from Anna. Mama is right. There is something really strange about her, and what about me? There's definitely something wrong with me. I have absolutely no control, when she's around me. I better find Marty. We'll go down town and have some fun.

Walking through the neighborhood he was glad that nothing had changed. He felt like a lifetime since he was home. In reality it had only been eight short weeks. The sights and sounds of home were everywhere. In the smell of cooking coming from the restaurant on the corner to the overpowering aroma of fish from the market. Everything made him feel safe and secure. An experience he would not have again for a very long time. Unaware of what fate had in store for him, he thought that wonderful feeling would last forever. Why not, he was young and strong and not too bad looking? What more could he ask for? He found himself whistling. Something he did when he really felt good.

He was so caught up in this feeling of euphoria that he almost knocked Anna down as she stepped out of a doorway. She had been patiently waiting. Hoping to get a glimpse of him and had just given up, and she had decided to finally go home.

"My God, where did you come from," he exclaimed amazed by Anna's sudden appearance.

"Oh Carman, I never expected to see you. I was just visiting a friend. My mind was miles away. Did I startle you?"

"Yeah, a little," he answered.

"Your uniform becomes you," she said recovering from the shock of seeing him again.

"Thank you, I guess I should have changed. I didn't think of it until just now. You get used to wearing a uniform, I guess. Well I've got to go. Good seeing you."

He didn't know what he was saying. He only knew he had to get away from her imploring, unbelievably gorgeous eyes. Never mind the rest of her. Escape was the only word running through his mind. I've got to get away from her. With concerted effort, he gently pushed her aside and literally ran down the avenue in search of his friend. Luckily, he didn't have far to run. Marty was walking toward him with a confused look on his face, wondering why Carman was running so hard.

"Whoa Carman, take it easy. You'll have a heart attack. Who the hell is chasing you?"

"Jesus Marty, thank God you're here. You won't believe it. I just ran into Anna and I wanted to make love to her right there on the street. I must be losing my mind."

"Nah, you're not losing your mind. You just haven't had a, well you just, actually Carman I think we both could use a little feminine companionship. What do you say, we find ourselves a couple of lookers?"

"Good idea Marty, where do we start?"

"I think perhaps the Blue Grotto is the place for us. As I recall," Marty continued, "it was the last place I got you know what."

Never having been to the Blue Grotto, I'll take your word for it. In fact it sounds like the place we should stay for a couple of days," answered Carman.

"You got any money on you Carman. Cause if we get lucky, it might cost us a few bucks."

"It just so happens Marty that my Papa forced fifty bucks on me, and I'm more than willing to share the wealth."

"I do appreciate your readiness to help a deprived friend. On to the Blue Grotto," replied Marty.

Arm in arm they headed down town to the famous Blue Grotto.

1929

He sat slowly smoking his cigar. Remembering the unqualified joy he experienced that night, so many years ago. Together with his friend Marty they savored the ecstasy of uninhibited sex. Well, at least fifty dollars worth. Through all the turbulent years he experienced, the exquisite pleasure of that night never lost its luster. Even now he could smile at the pure magic of that night. Is it possible, he thought, there are certain things that never lose their splendor? I guess there are.

In retrospect, he realized it was the last night of his freedom. From that day, to this, he's had the feeling that he was in purgatory.

If only I had stayed with Marty in that wonderful Blue Grotto. I wouldn't be leaving purgatory and walking directly into hell tomorrow.

Let's see I left Marty about two a.m. That's where my life took a turn as if I had a proclivity for catastrophe.

Wearily Carman left the Blue Grotto, tired but satiated with compensated love in forms he didn't know existed, but was eager to experience. He was surprised at the amount of money he still had, and was encouraged to consider a return trip back to the Blue Grotto at least once before he had to return to camp. Consumed by the night's exertions, he barely managed to climb up the stairs and fall unconscious on his bed. He slept fourteen hours straight.

His mother, apprehensive of what she might find and expecting the worst, crept into his room and softly called his name. In answer, Carman groaned and she sighed in relief. She recognized the ravages of drink, and she suspected that he undoubtedly had a little something else, which she refused to name even to herself.

"Come Carman," she called, would you spend your leave in bed?" She smiled at her choice of words because in bed, was where he probably got so exhausted. It is time for a mother to quietly disappear, she thought. Her son's room was not the place for an old woman's imaginings. She quietly closed the door and went about her day not thinking of her young soldier son sleeping off the last evenings' activities.

Carman stirred at the sound of his door closing and was confused by the wonderful feeling of wellness that engulfed his entire body, filling his mind with peace and rapture. Why didn't he have a hangover, he wondered? Unable to bear the confines of his bed he leaped up and headed for the bathroom. Luckily there was plenty of hot water for a leisurely scrubbing and perhaps a little sanitizing after last nights' adventures. By the time he emerged form his bath his skin was puckered, but he was invigorated and starving. A meal for a king was waiting for him in the kitchen. God bless my Mama he thought, as he sat down to the best food in the world.

He left home with the intention of seeing Father Paul to tell him all about boot camp. He headed for the trolley when unfortunately; he met Anna standing on the corner dressed to the teeth in white. As he approached her she smiled sweetly. God damn it, she looks like an angel, thought Carman as he slowly walked to his fate.

"Anna, is it my imagination or have you been stalking me, "he asked sarcastically trying desperately to hide the beating of his heart as the blood rushed to his face causing him to blush unceremoniously. He was embarrassed by his ironic reaction to this startling beauty. He tried to focus on anything to distract his senses from the Neanderthal response Anna's presence induced. Carman took a deep breath, and made the mistake of all his predecessors when he thought, I can handle this.

"Carman, how can you be so mean to me after what we've been to one another? I don't intend to seduce you, if that's what you're thinking. I just want us to be friends and perhaps share a meal together and just talk. We certainly don't have to make love every time we meet. That part of our relationship is over, as far as I'm concerned. Do you agree?" she whispered as she looked up at him with those so innocent, eyes.

"Actually, that's exactly what I was thinking when I saw you," he replied praying that his manhood wasn't making a fool of him as he tried in vain to keep his body at ease.

"Good," she replied adding "maybe we could have a quiet dinner tonight at Pinto's, if that's alright with you. Or do you think I might rape you in a public restaurant?"

"Don't be ridiculous," he replied. Of course we can have dinner, but it will have to be tomorrow night. I have plans for tonight."

"No problem Carman tomorrow is fine. See you at seven at Pinto's." With the most innocent gesture she kissed Carman lightly and gently massaged his lips with her sweet little tongue.

Watching her walking down the avenue he murmured over and over "Jesus, Jesus, no way can I have dinner with her. I must be crazy. Forget it. I'm not going, he thought as he got on the trolley car, happy to be on his way to see his friend and mentor, Father Paul.

When he finally got to Fordham University and knocked at Father Paul's door, he was greeted by the maid who told him that the good Father had been called away to give the last rites to a dear friend. Carman thanked the maid and turned away wearily, disappointed that the priest was not there to give him the strength to avoid Anna.

He returned to the neighborhood in search of Marty. It never occurred to him that Marty was still at the Blue Grotto. He started his search going from one neighborhood haunt to another, finally stopping at Guardo's for a sandwich. Entering the little bistro, he didn't notice Anna sitting demurely picking at a salad. Anna looked up and loudly yelled, "Carman."

Carman stood stock still ready to retreat when Guardo emerged from the kitchen to investigate Anna's scream.

"Are you alright Anna?" he asked.

"Forgive me Guardo I just didn't expect to see Carman here."

Looking up Guardo called, "Carman, how nice. Come sit with my beauty and me and have a nice bowl of macaroni. He walked over to Carman and propelled him next to Anna and then sat down himself.

"So tell me," Guardo continued,"how is the army treating you? You look terrific. Doesn't he Anna? Look at him, doesn't he look terrific?"

"He looks really good," answered Anna, amused at Carman's discomfort.

"My, my you look as if you grew a couple of inches too," said Guardo.

"Yeah, could be Guardo. I haven't measured myself since I've been home," he answered laughing, as he gained some control.

"Carman, maybe you can talk some sense into my beauty's head. She keeps putting off our wedding date."

Carman answered truthfully, "You really should get married Anna. There's no better man for you than Guardo."

"I intend to get married Carman, and you'll be the first to know when I definitely decide who to marry."

"What is this you're saying? When you decide whom you will marry. I thought I was the one you're marrying," interrupted Guardo.

"Of course you are, Guardo. I meant to say when I marry Guardo, of course."

"Gee Anna, it's nice that you want to let me know when you're marrying Guardo, but the truth is, I'll be leaving for Vera Cruz after I finish basic training so I guess I'll miss your wedding."

"Oh Carman," replied Anna touching his hand, "that's too bad. It positively won't be the same without you."

"So what have you decided to eat?" asked Guardo.

"I must be coming down with something. All of a sudden I've lost my appetite. I better head home." Carman said his good-byes and left.

He walked home in a daze. Seeing Anna again was too much for him. He'd have to do something or he was doomed. Is it possible he was in love with her? She just touched my hand and I was on fire. What does it mean? I can't escape her she makes my senses reel. Of course we could all move to Brooklyn. There are lots of Italians there but Mama would never move. There has got to be an answer to this dilemma. Then again, he thought, maybe I am in love with her. What's not to love? She's gorgeous, and her Papa is very rich. So she's four years older than I am.

It wouldn't matter at all if it were the other way around. Of course she's nuts. That's something I won't be able to deal with. Mama also thinks she's not quite right, and Mama never exaggerates. Even Papa says she's a loony. Okay, I've got to be practical, but I can't stop thinking about her. Making love to her is the closest thing to heaven I've experienced so far and she's gorgeous and rich. Now on the other hand, she's really nuts. Other than that she's almost perfect. Yup, there's only one way out, I've got to get out of here. Tomorrow I'll go see Father Paul and have him put me up for a few days until I report back to camp. With his mind made up he walked home with a much lighter step and whistled all the way. He opened the door to his house and was stunned to find the house dark except for a small light in the kitchen. He could smell the sweet aroma of Mama's cooking and the underlying ever present, scent of fresh coffee, but not a soul was home. He called softly, and one by one opened the doors to all the rooms. He found the house in perfect order but no Mama, no Papa and no Dominica.

"Hey, where is everybody?" he shouted.

He finally went into the kitchen and noticed a note on the table. He read it quickly and breathed a sigh of relief. The entire family was at his brother's house waiting for his sister-in-law Pauline to give birth to her first child.

There was a table setting waiting for him and a pot of spaghetti on the stove. He ate his dinner and decided to take a short nap before joining the rest of the Duva's. This thing with Anna had him exhausted. He walked to his room, loosened his tie, covered himself with a shawl and was asleep almost before he hit the pillow.

He was sound asleep when a hand shook him gently. He opened his eyes to see Anna peacefully sitting on his bed.

"Christ, where the hell did you come from? What are you doing here?" he shouted as he jumped to his feet knocking Anna to the floor.

"Mama Mia Anna, what are you doing here?" he repeated as he lifted her from the floor where she had fallen with a thud.

"Carman please, I had to see you alone," she murmured.

"How did you get in?" he asked "Carman please," answered Anna incredibly "does your Mama ever lock the door? I bet you don't even own a key, right? And everyone knows your entire family is waiting for your sister-in-law to have her baby. So I thought I would come and see you."

"In my bedroom?" he asked amazed by her actions.

"Carman please, she purred as she slowly unbuttoned her blouse revealing a lacey camisole.

"Please Anna, you've got to stop'" he said as he held her hands to stop her from continuing.

She released her hands from his grip and wrapped her arms around his neck and looked beseechingly into his eyes. She unbuttoned his shirt and kissed him gently while removing her camisole. The feel of her warm body touching his was too much for Carman to resist. He was consumed by desire, craving to possess her. He smothered her with kisses.

Anna grasped his thick hair and whispered, "piano, piano, Carman" as she led him to his bed and he gently took her. She smiled knowingly for she had finally won.

After they made love and lay in each others arms, Anna said, "again Carman, again." "Anna please, I can't." he replied.

She jumped up and started to scream, "You can't or you won't. Now, I want you now." The more Carman tried to calm her, the more frenzied she became. "Please Anna" he pleaded as he rocked her in his arms soothing her until she was quiet. He prayed God help me I love this mad woman.

Fearing that someone would discover them, he persuaded Anna to dress. He walked her home trying to keep her calm. Arriving home, she began to hit her head against the door. Gently at first but harder and harder until her head started to bleed. Carman didn't know what to do. He pulled her away from the door and held her firmly. As soon as he relaxed his grip on her she continued to bang her head against the door. The door opened and her mother appeared, immediately cooing, "Easy

Anna, no more child, no more." Anna, in complete oblivion, stared at her mother.

"Come my darling, everything is alright, and thank you Carman," whispered Mrs. Similetti as she took her daughter into the house and silently shut the door leaving Carman completely baffled. What the hell happened thought Carman as he walked to his brother's house?

It wasn't until the early morning hours of the next day that Carman had a chance to think about Anna and what had happened the night before. He and Steve were sitting together smoking cigars basking in the delight of a new baby in the family. The thought of Anna invaded his mind. He couldn't help wonder how responsible he was for her bizarre behavior the night before. All of a sudden the wonderful feeling he had was gone, replaced by a feeling of doom and remorse.

"Hey Carman what's the matter, you don't look too happy? You're finally an uncle and you look like you lost your best friend. What's going on?"

'Nothing not a thing, I couldn't be more pleased with that beautiful nephew of mine. Maybe someday I'll be lucky enough to have a son like him.

My problem has nothing to do with you."

"Your problems have always been my problems, Carman. Tell me what's worrying you?" asked Steve.

"It's O.K., I can handle it. Everything will work out, "he replied hearing the doubt in his own voice.

"Come on, tell me. You know by now nothing you say can shock me."

Before he realized what was happening, he was confiding in his brother.

"Well Steve, here goes." He told him the story of what had happened the night before. It sounded even more incredible today.

When he finished, Steve sat speechless. Finally after what seemed hours to Carman, he exclaimed.

"Mama mia, right in your room?"

"Right in my room," quipped Carman, "right in my room."

"I'll be damned, why doesn't anything like that happen to me?" mourned Steven. "Not even in my dreams."

"You don't understand Steve, she's crazy."

"Hey Carman, you can't have everything," replied Steve.

"I need help, and you think it was some kind of party."

"No Carman, I just have a hard time believing it. Christ, I was a virgin when I married Pauline. Here you are seventeen and you've got a woman coming to your room for God's sake."

"You're forgetting something very important Steve. One small adjective, a crazy woman came to my room."

"Here we go. I've got the answer. You've got to get away from here before more women start lining up at your door," replied Steve laughing hysterically

At the sight of his brother who was somber most of the time, doubled up with laughter, Carman could not help but join in.

At this precise moment Papa came out on the porch with a jug of red wine, he said came from Callucci's cellar.

"Here I thought I'd bring you two something to celebrate with and you started without me."

"No, no Papa. We could really use some wine. Come have a cigar with us and we'll drink to the new baby. What is his name going to be?"

"Paul, after Papa of course," answered Steve.

"That's good Anthony, I mean Steve. Thank you. You make me very happy, said Papa.

"You're welcome Papa. It is an honor to name my son after you," Steve answered hugging his father.

During the night of drinking and celebrating little Paul's birth, Carman was able to put any thought of Anna, out of his mind. After several cups of coffee and a good breakfast, the thought of Anna resurfaced. Why worry, he asked himself? He was heading back to camp tomorrow and wouldn't see Anna until his next furlough. By that time she would be happily married. I'm well out of it, he thought. As soon as he could locate Marty, who had mysteriously disappeared, they would make preparations to return to camp. He was anxious to find out for sure where they were actually going. Rumors were everywhere at camp on the day they left. It was anyone's guess where they were going.

It wasn't until late that evening Carman found Marty still at the Blue Grotto wrapped around a woman of indistinct age or ancestry. Although it was difficult to persuade Marty to leave the Blue Grotto, Carman finally convinced him and took him home to Mama to sober him up. She gave him a concoction of ingredients that could kill you with just the smell. Marty was so far gone he didn't know enough to refuse the drink. Miraculously, after sleeping only a few hours, he was sober enough to get on the train with Carman to return to camp. Poor Marty didn't know where he was going until they finally got off the train.

After settling down in their barracks, they joined the chow line. It was there that they learned exactly where they were being sent. They were not going to the banks of the Seine River. They were not going to the Europe at all. They were going to Arizona. They would be trained and then sent to Cuba to a possible uprising in Oriente Province.

"Where is Oriente Province, Marty whispered painfully, unaware of the potion that had been forced down his throat?

"I don't know exactly. It has to be somewhere in Cuba," replied Carman. "Not to worry, we're going to Arizona first. Maybe we'll get to see the Grand Canyon. Good, huh. What do you think?"

"I think if I don't get something to drink, I'll die. My throat is killing me. I feel like I drank motor oil. I don't care where they send us as long as I get some juice."

"I'll get you some Marty. You'll feel better tomorrow, and then we'll make plans. You'll see, Arizona will be wonderful."

Arizona is wonderful, in winter or early spring. Unfortunately, the platoon arrived in mid August when the heat is unbearable. After a few days in the hot sun, half the outfit was in sick bay and the other half were waiting to get in.

Most of the platoon was sent to Tempe, Arizona. Luckily, Marty and Carman were sent to Flagstaff where it was twenty degrees cooler, to a place called Walnut Canyon National Park. Since Arizona had become the forty-eighth state in 1912, national parks were springing up everywhere. What they were supposed to be doing there was anybody's guess. At least the boys were on horseback most of the day and they learned to track and hunt in the barren desert.

Almost every weekend they would travel to the Grand Canyon to witness the mile deep gorge sculptured by the Colorado River. The views were spectacular but their favorite was the vista from the north rim. By the time they left Arizona to go back to the base they were more like cowboys and less like soldiers. In fact, they decided that after their hitch in the army they would come back to Arizona to buy a ranch and live there for the rest of their lives. Even the unbearable heat at Tempe could not change their minds. Their first choice to locate their ranch was near the town of Sedona. They spent hours talking and planning, forgetting they were only going to be there a short while. Like tourists before and after them they fell in love with the beautiful mountains and other landscapes of Arizona. When told that they had to go back to New York and wait for their orders, their dreams of a new life began to vanish. Saddened at the thought of the difficulty of attaining such a dream they vowed that someday they would come back and try to make a home in Arizona. All too soon they were sent back to New York to wait for their orders.

Long lazy days awaited them as they cleaned innumerable stalls and brushed countless horses until their hands were raw.

Whenever Carman was free of work, he would ride his horse to the outskirts of the camp. Returning from one of his rides, he saw

Marty frantically waving at him. Reaching his friend he couldn't help but notice the strained look on Marty's face.

"What's wrong?" he asked, fearing the worst.

"Get down Carman, the Captain wants to see you," Marty answered.

"Is it my family?" asked Carman unnerved by the look of doom on Marty's face.

"No, they're alright Carman, but something is really wrong. I saw Anna and her father in the Captains office. You better go see what's happening.

"What the hell are they doing here? Marty, do me a favor and take care of my horse, O.K.?"

"Sure Carman, no problem," said Marty taking the reins from his friend.

Completely bewildered, Carman entered the Captains' office. He stopped at the clerks' desk and was told to sit down and that the Captain would see him in a few minutes.

Carman sat there with his mind racing trying to figure out what was going on. Finally he was ushered into the Captains' office. As the door opened he saw Anna and her father seated at the Captains' desk. Carman saluted and stood at attention until the Captain gave the command, "at ease soldier, take a chair." Carman sat down in a chair close to the Captains desk.

"There seems to be a little problem here, which I hope you can rectify, said the Captain. "It seems," he went on, "that this young lady and her father have traveled here with a request that you marry this young lady."

"Excuse me sir, did you say marry?"

"Yes I did soldier. I believe, under the circumstances it would be the only option you have."

"Excuse me sir, but why exactly would I have to marry Miss Similetti? I'm too young to get married."

"No son, you're not," answered the Captain. "Miss Similetti is in the family way, and..."

Before the Captain could finish, Anna started to scream and cry hysterically, talking incoherently. Her father, try as he might, could do nothing to stop the screaming. After several minutes, to everyone's amazement, she suddenly stopped crying and screaming and sat perfectly still in her chair.

The quiet was deafening. Carman was the first to speak.

"Sir, I firmly believe that I am not the father of Miss Similetti's child. She is, after all engaged to another man."

"Is this true Mr. Similetti?" asked the Captain.

"Yes Captain, this is true. But my daughter insists that Carman has fathered her child."

"What proof do you have, Mr. Similetti?"

"The word of my daughter and on that Captain I would stake my life." Why, I ask you, would she come all the way up here to claim that Carman is the father, if indeed her fiancé is responsible? I know for a fact, her fiancé would marry her immediately, if he were the father. In fact he is waiting at home convinced that this is some kind of a game that Anna is playing just to make him jealous."

"Well, is it girl?" asked the Captain.

Lifting her beautiful tear stained face to the Captain, Anna between sobs, managed to convince him that Carman was young as he is, responsible for her pregnancy.

Unfortunately for Carman the Captain said, "Soldier, you will marry this young lady this afternoon in my office or I'll know the reason why."

He called in the company clerk and instructed him to call the nearest Justice of the Peace and have him come directly there.

"Sir," pleaded Carman. I can't marry this lady. She's almost five years older than I am. Don't I need some kind of written permission from my parents or somebody, to marry her? I had to get written permission to join the army because I was too young.

Don't I need my parents' permission to get married? How do I know that I am actually the father of her baby?"

"Young man," answered the Captain angrily, "I happen to be in charge here. You will marry this poor girl today, and that will be the end of it. Do you understand me?"

"No sir, I don't understand," said Carman.

A short time later a Justice of the Peace was performing the ceremony and Carman Duva was married to Anna Similetti.

As soon as the ceremony was over the Captain told Carman to return to the barracks. "Sergeant Duva, what you do after your enlistment is up to you, but this young lady is now free of ridicule and can have her baby without fear of embarrassment. Do you understand?"

"Yes sir, I understand," replied Carman but he really didn't. Slowly he left the Captains office and returned to his barracks.

"Carman, what happened? You've been gone for hours. I thought you were in the brig."

"If only that were true," Carman answered. "The brig is a sweet place to be after what I've been through,"

"What happened?" his friend asked bewildered.

"I got married," replied Carman.

"Oh sure, you got married. What are you crazy, you can't get married. You're too young."

"Not in the Army Marty, not in the army."

As Carman related the events of the afternoon, Marty stood unbelieving, shaking his head no.

"This can't be happening Carman, can it?"

"God Marty, it seems to have happened already. Not only am I married but I'm also going to be a father. Can you believe that?"

Marty handed Carman a bottle of whiskey and the two of them drank well into the night. The next day Carman lost his one stripe for unbecoming behavior. During his career in the army, Carman earned and lost his stripes many times. Once he was even a sergeant. When he left the service at the end of the war, he had several medals but no stripes. He was still just a private.

Several days later Carman sat down to write a letter to his family. He was still unable to believe the events that had taken place. One minute he was a happy carefree seventeen-year old. The next he was a married man with a baby on the way. "Married to Anna", he kept repeating over and over again until he thought he would lose his mind. What can I say to them, he thought as he stared at the empty sheet of paper. How can I explain when I don't understand myself? I'm not a fool, I'm always careful. What could have happened? I can't be the father. "God I'm married," he whispered.

This can't possibly be happening to me. I'm just a boy; I'm not a man. I can't be a father. I have trouble enough just being a son.

What can I write? What can I say to them? I can't. I have no excuse."

Maybe I can stay in the army forever. I'll just keep re-enlisting and when I'm away Anna will fall in love with somebody else a real man, not a boy like me. Hell, I've got my whole life ahead of me. This is no time for responsibilities. I'm just a kid, ask my brother Steve, he knows.

"Please stop talking to yourself," said Marty. "We'll find a way out of this mess. It looks like we're going to war anyway. Maybe we'll be killed. What are you so upset about? You didn't marry Anna in church. You can get a divorce, or an annulment or whatever. It's no real marriage without a priest, right?"

"You're right. It was just a Justice of the Peace. It wasn't even a minister. It's probably not even a marriage. At least not in the eyes of the Church. What am I worrying about? I'll write Father Paul and see what he says. Maybe I can get out of this before my enlistment is up. Marty, you're a life saver."

"Good, now maybe we can work at getting your stripe back. Your shirt looks empty without it," answered his friend.

Smiling broadly, Carman put his arm around his friends' shoulders as they walked to the mess hall to see if they could get something to eat. All of a sudden he was ravenous. In fact, he couldn't remember when he had eaten last.

Their orders came the very next day. They were going to Santa Cruz.

"Santa Cruz," said Carman, "Why the hell are we going to Santa Cruz? I thought we were going to Cuba.

"Who cares?" answered Marty. "It's nice and warm there and the woman are beautiful."

"Jesus, I don't know Marty. You and I seem to walk in dog shit in this man's army."

Carman could not have been more astute in his assessment of their luck so far. It would have been fortunate if they indeed had been sent to Santa Cruz. As it turned out they were to become a part of Pershings' expedition into Mexico in pursuit of the bandit Pancho Villa.

Before they left, Carman wrote his brother Steve.

Dear Steve,

I'm writing to you in hopes that you can explain to Mama and Papa about my marriage to Anna. The first thing you have to tell them is that I was not, I repeat, I was not married by a priest. That information alone will, I hope, lessen the impact of this so-called marriage. You've got too assure them that this entire marriage affair, was not my idea. Not in this lifetime would I consider marrying that crazy girl, Anna. You and I know she's not all there. You also know that I have on more than one occasion, slept with her. I'm not proud of this but you know me, I'm always careful. In fact you're the one who brain washed me, remember? I know you were still a virgin when you got married, but you have always watched over me and you were, thank God, very persuasive in your attention to detail concerning my sleeping with the opposite gender.

O.K., so you know I was careful, then how the hell could I get Anna pregnant, huh? Please, dear brother, just reassure Mama and Papa that as soon as I am out of the army I will straighten out this whole mess. I was coerced into marrying her. If I didn't I would have been dishonorably discharged. So Steve, please make it sound simple to Mama and Papa. It's no big deal. It's something that I can handle when I come home. Tell them I'm sure it's not my baby. She's probably not even pregnant. You know how crazy she is. Tell them I'm sorry if I hurt them. Tell them I love them.

Give my love to Pauline and kiss my beautiful nephew for me. I almost forgot. Please tell Dominica everything will be fine. I don't want her to worry. I'll be home before you know it and I will take care of everything.

Your brother Carman

Steve sent a letter almost by return mail. It read:

Dear Carman,

All is well. Mama and Papa are not upset about Anna. They only worry about you. I assured them that you are fine, so you better be. I am here to help you, not to worry. When you get home we'll take on the Similetti's. Mama is on a prayer brigade, so we have heaven on our side. Pauline sends her love and me too. Take care little brother, you're just a kid. Don't worry your big brother will help you out. Dominica sends her love too. She's going to write to you herself.

Love Steve

There was, of course, one letter Carman dreaded to write. His only consolation was that he would be the first person to inform his mentor, Father Brown of his marriage. With great trepidation, he wrote:

Dear Father,

I'm sorry to have to disappoint you again. It seems that in my naivete I have left a young woman in a family way. Believe me Father when I tell you that I never intended to disobey God's law. Unfortunately, I seem to be ruled more by my body and less by my mind or heart. I am sure you understand this more than I do. I have great difficulty coming to terms with what I have done. Although I did have a physical relationship with the young woman, Anna, who you probably remember my telling you about, I have a hard time believing that I am the father of her unborn child.

O.K. Father, hold on to your hat. I was literally forced to marry Anna by my Captain. Luckily it was not in church but by a Justice of the Peace. In my mind this constitutes no marriage at all. In the eyes of the United States Government, I am indeed married. I can imagine how disappointed you are in me, but please believe that I am even more disappointed in myself. I've gone to confession so you can stop worrying on that account.

Please pray for me, Father. Not for me to come home safely for I believe God has already made those arrangements, but so that I can accept this responsibility. Because if Anna's baby is mine, I will never be able to abandon the child:

Charlie

A sweet note arrived from Dominica, which read:

Carman, I don't care what anybody says. You didn't do it, so there. Please come home soon.

Love you,
Dominica

Everyone who needed to be told was told. Everyone went on with their lives expecting only good things to happen. Such is human nature. Except of course Anna, who sent the following letter to Carman:

Dearest Carman,

I miss you so much and our little angel, who is resting just below my heart, anxiously awaits your return. You can't imagine just how much I miss you. You are the best lover I've ever had.

Your wife

After Carman received Anna's letter he didn't sleep for several nights. With all that was happening around him he eventually forgot her and everyone else when he and Marty were hand picked to be part of a small band of soldiers under the command of Pershing to go to Mexico to capture Pancho Villa. Before they crossed the border into Mexico, neither one of them had ever heard of Pancho Villa. Now as they lay exhausted gazing at the Sierra Madre Del Sur, a maze of volcanic mountains, they would not trade places with anyone for their bone weary quest was the most exciting adventure they had ever had.

"Hey Marty, where do you think Pancho is hiding today?" asked Carman.

"You know Charlie, I don't give a shit. As far as I'm concerned if I never see him will be time enough for me. I hear the guy is a real madman."

Even Marty had started calling Carman Charlie, as did everyone in their small band.

"Did you know", continued Marty, "that he crossed the border at the Rio Grande and attacked Columbus, New Mexico? He killed seven American soldiers and at least twelve civilians before he plundered the town."

"Yup, I know," replied Carman.

"What do you mean yup? What are you a cowhand or something?"

"Nope I'm just a tired ole polecat, partner."

"Lay off Charlie. You know how I hate that kind of talk."

"Marty, did you ever notice how the rest of the soldiers eye us whenever we talk?"

"Yeah, what does that mean anyway?" asked Marty.

"Well I believe we have what they would call "New York accents."

"That doesn't bother me," answered Marty adding, "as long as they don't call me "Wop and imitate me too. What a laugh and we're both born here. Imagine my poor brother Steve, he was born in the old country and if you listen to him talk you can hear that Italian accent. But Steve has some punch; they wouldn't tease him for long either."

Just then they heard the sound of a bugle which meant that they were again on the run. They were supposedly heading for Bolson de Mapimi in the Valley of Anahuor. At least there the land was fairly flat and it was an easier ride for both horse and horseman. All afternoon they searched the plains with not one glimpse of Pancho Villa, or any of his band.

That evening as they gathered back at camp for a hot meal and some sought after rest, John Joseph Pershing himself addressed his small contingent of soldiers.

"Well men, we only have a few more days to locate this Villa fellow and then it's back to the states for us. Let's see what we can stir up tomorrow. You boys get some rest now. You've been riding hard for over two weeks, maybe we'll get lucky."

"Yes sir, they answered in unison." They were in awe of Pershing as he was a magnificent specimen of a soldier. Every man was proud to serve under him. Any order was followed to the letter for the man was a born leader. Pershing became a Major General after this campaign.

They lay shivering in their flimsy tent, ice cold after sweating in the blazing sun all afternoon. Completely exhausted Carman whispered to Marty, "What's that crawling over there in the corner?"

"Jesus, it's a snake," yelled Marty as the two of them scrambled out of their tent and headed for the campfire.

"That's it Charlie, no more sleeping in a tent for me. From now on I sleep in the open by the fire. Snakes don't like the heat and Christ If I see one more snake I'll have a heart attack."

"You and me Marty you and me," answered Carman almost asleep as the two of them snuggled close to the fire.

In the morning the sun was hot in the sky as they ate the unbelievable chow that cook had rustled up for them. With such a small group of soldiers, they all ate the same chow Pershing was served. Some things that were served to them were unrecognizable by a pair used to only Italian cooking. It didn't matter to them for whatever it was tasted too delicious to care about. There were no complaints from this bunch of soldiers.

His name was Mathew O'Malley, but everyone called him Mat. Except for the few fearless souls who called him "Fat Mat" in halted tones, when they were completely convinced that he was not in the vicinity

The man was enormous. He had to weigh well over three hundred pounds of pure muscle. The monicker "Fat Man" did him an injustice, for there wasn't an ounce of fat on him. If providence had been kinder, Mat's heart would have mirrored his girth, but Mat's heart was missing. Any semblance of feelings good or bad was non-existent. What was beating in his chest was just an organ to pump blood. The only emotion Mat exhibited was hate which for reasons unknown to him, came and went without justification. The only human emotion he displayed was for his horse, which was the biggest animal the army could find. It resembled a Clydesdale in size, but was gentle as a lamb and answered to the name "Baby." If you wanted safety, you stayed as close to Mat as possible. The sight of Mat on his horse coming at you was awesome and one hundred percent intimidating. He was the perfect comrade in arms.

Regrettably Mat O'Malley, for reasons beyond his understanding, hated Charlie Duva. Possibly the fact that Charlie was tall thin not bad looking and well liked by his comrades, could have jolted Mat's psyche. Whatever the motivation,

Charlie avoided Mat like the plague. For whatever Charlie, alias Carman, was or wasn't, he was no man's fool.

Hours on end, Charlie and Marty would talk about this phenomenon.

"I swear," said Charlie to his friend, "when that guy looks at me my legs turn to jelly. This has never happened to me in my life. You remember Al from the neighborhood? He was as big as a house but I could take him in a fight. This guy Mat is a Golem."

"What the hell is a Golem?' replied Marty.

"It's a mythical monster made of stone," answered Charlie.

"Yeah, yeah, that's him alright.

"What the hell am I gonna do. Every time I pass the ape he literally growls," said Charlie.

"Get outta here really?"

"Really," said Charlie, "this guy could give you instant diarrhea. I've got to find a way to take the guy, or make him my friend."

"Come on Charlie, this guy's got no friends, unless you include his horse.

"Aha," replied Charlie. "I forgot about the horse. There's got to be an angle there. Let me think about this."

On long cool nights as he lay sleepless in his tent, Charlie felt that time was running out.

Apart from Mat O'Malley, army life seemed to agree with Charlie. Looking for Pancho Villa was exciting in its own way. In reality they caught sight of him only once. Though the search continued day after day, they could never catch him. The rumor was that they would move out of Mexico any day. With this in mind, Charlie's caution was laid aside and he unconsciously bumped into Mat O'Malley. A seemingly inadvertent bump, but the sound of it echoed through the entire camp. Mat O'Malley effortlessly lifted Charlie into the air and threw him head first into a pile of manure. Dazed but undaunted he got up and charged "Fat Mat". For a moment the men in his outfit stood motionless, unbelieving. A cheer arose from the incredulous Cavalrymen, as they threw Charlie back at Mat every time he was hurled into the air. The only thought running through Charlie's mind was, somebody stop this slaughter. This guy is killing me. A shot rang out and everyone stood still, except of course Charlie who actually collapsed at Mat O'Malley's feet, as he never heard the shot.

John Joseph Pershing stood there, gun in hand and ordered some men to bring Charlie into his tent where he had a medic put him back together again Miraculously Charlie had no broken bones. He just hurt all over his entire body. The first visitor in Pershings' tent was no other than Mat O'Malley. He crept in, and as soon as Charlie saw him he tried to drag his painful body off the cot, but failed miserably.

"Take it easy Sonny, I ain't gonna hurt you none. That was some fight we had out there, wasn't it?" said Mat shaking his giant head up and down.

"Yeah," squeaked Charlie barely able to move his poor mouth.

"I gotta hand it to you Sonny, you got some balls to try and take me on. I appreciate stuff like that," replied Mat adding," from now on Sonny, you and me are gonna be friends. I ain't never had a friend. There's been no one to stand up to me. A man needs someone to do that, an equal you know?"

"Yeah," sighed Charlie, yeah that was some fight I almost gave you," as he gently passed out.

In a few days Carman was back on his feet and to everyone's surprise he seemed to have inherited a bodyguard who was none other than the notorious Mathew O'Malley. Marty, Mat and Charlie went everywhere together. You would see the three of them walking to and from mess, with Marty walking cautiously next to Carman, afraid to get in Mat's way. After a while, the three of them just being together seemed very natural. Eventually, some of Marty's courage resurfaced and in spite of his fear, he too occasionally walked next to Mat. Mat would continually ask Charlie if he was really his buddy, and so Charlie started calling him Buddy and the name stuck. Carman never exhibited any fear of Buddy; his giant companion. He realized the big guy was here to stay. Buddy knew instinctively, that if he wanted to call Charlie friend, he had to accept Marty as a friend too. This arrangement, though awkward at first, became second nature. Mat took great satisfaction in being called Buddy. The big oaf absolutely grinned every time Charlie called him.

"The poor bastard never had a friend. Now he had two, plus of course, his horse," confided Marty to Charlie, "and I'm beginning to like it."

To see this mammoth on horseback, riding behind two fairly skinny boys was unquestionably comical. Not one soldier in their little band would dare laugh. No one had the guts. When Pershing saw the little group ride by one day he grinned from ear to ear, glad that Charlie had convinced him that the fight indeed had been fair and that Mat had not meant to harm him.

"After all Sir," Carman argued,"he didn't break anything."

Pancho Villa could not be found, therefore the troops were ordered to make one last sweep for any sighting. Suddenly, as if from nowhere, a rattler appeared on the path frightening Charlie's horse and throwing him directly in the path of the venomous snake. Quick as a flash Buddy bent down from his mount and with one hand scooped Charlie up and delicately held him aloft till they were clear of the angry rattler.

"Holy shit," whispered Charlie as he was gently lowered to the ground. "Buddy, how the hell did you do that?"

"It was no trouble at all. You surely are a skinny fella, aren't ya Charlie?"

"Thank God I am, Bud, I'd be wrapped up for lunch for that rattler," he said brushing himself off.

"Thanks Bud, you absolutely saved my life."

"Anytime Charlie, anytime."

News of the near calamity spread through the small band of soldiers and Buddy was touted as a hero, which was very curious for him. Buddy was conditioned to being the heavy. He never aspired to being a paladin. In fact, he took great comfort in being feared. He was accustomed to seeing the dread in men's eyes whenever he appeared on the scene. Buddy was not sure he could take to this adulation.

"Well, I'll give it a try and see if it's works out. If not, I can always break a couple of heads," he thought.

Try as he might, Buddy was all too quick with his hands and Charlie spent a good deal of his time sparring with Buddy to keep his hands off the "guilty son of a bitch", that just happened to pass in Buddy's sunlight. It became almost a full time job. Until one fateful day Charlie turned to Buddy and reluctantly stated, "Buddy you big ape I'm exhausted trying to keep you from smashing every guy who crosses your path. From now on Bud, you take your chances. I can't protect the whole company, got it?"

"Gee Charlie, little fella," replied Buddy, I never realized how hard it's been on you so from now on I'll just blast only the really rotten guys."

"Ok, sure Bud, Ok," nodded Charlie. His job as interloper became less tiresome. Buddy was true to his word, he just bopped the rotten ones. And Charlie just stood by and watched, although if he was making the call there'd certainly be fewer men lying on the ground after Buddy walked through. Finally, to everyone's relief it was time to say adios to Mexico. Pershing was made Major General and his punitive expedition into Mexico came to a halt. The exhausted contingent returned to America, first by rail, then by open truck, and finally on foot. The three caballeros trudged through the camp and made their way to their tent collapsing on their cots. Coming home had been more arduous than the entire Mexican adventure. They were unaware that rumors of Mexico's alignment with Germany in the Great War that was raging in Europe, was a reason for their return to the States. The three young comrades in arms were unaware of how close war loomed in front of them. They were just glad to be back and hoped for a leave to go home and see their families.

After only a few days, their wish was granted and the three friends made plans on their long train ride home. It was Charlie's idea to bring Buddy home to his yet unseen, new home with Anna. He had hastily written her a letter telling her of his plan to bring Buddy home on leave. It had never occurred to Charlie that there would be any problems. After all, he had brought many a stranger home to Mama for a clean bed and a bowl of spaghetti. He could not imagine Anna having any reservation about Buddy. If the house they had been given by her father was half as big as Anna described in her last letter, Buddy could disappear in the house and not be in anyone's way. It had been three months since the hasty marriage and surprisingly, he has remained true to Anna. He had made a pact with himself that no matter what happened he would be a good father and the best husband Anna could imagine. The fact that he had to marry Anna and was still not quite eighteen was not a factor in his calculations. He would return to school, work very hard and get his engineering degree and make a life for Anna and the baby. He was a realist and knew that his involvement with Anna was as much his fault as hers. He could not deny his physical attraction to her and hoped he could fall in love with her one day. Well, you can't have everything. No use looking back or ahead. His future was sealed and he was determined to do the right thing.

Marty could not believe that Charlie avoided any feminine companionship while in Mexico. It was just not natural, and he was impressed by Charlie's stoicism. Marty, on the other hand, got a terrible case of the crabs while in Mexico and kicked himself for being eighteen and hornier than he would ever be in his entire life. "Aside from the crabs,

Charlie didn't know what he missed," thought Marty, as he powdered for the thousandth time his private parts with some God forsaken remedy that was Army issue.

Charlie knew exactly what he was missing. It was a strange crew of three that disembarked from the train. There was one soldier seemingly older than his years, and another unable to stand still for more than a few seconds due to an uncontrollable urge to scratch himself in a much forbidden area. And last but definitely not least, one giant of a man whose mere size caused strangers to make room for him as he casually walked through a crowd

Chapter Twelve

It was not unusual for people to stare at Buddy when he appeared on the scene and today was no exception. Perfect strangers stared, unable to disguise their shock at the size of this young soldier. Carman heard a man whisper to his wife, "We have nothing to worry about if this young man is on our side." Carman looked at Buddy and couldn't help but nod in agreement.

This is one hell of a giant I'm bringing home I can't imagine what reaction Anna will have, he thought. He didn't have long to wait as he saw her approaching carefully, unable to take her eyes off Buddy.

"You look wonderful," he said as he kissed his startled wife.

"Oh Carman, I'm so happy you're home. Hold me tight, I can't believe you're here," she whispered as she hugged him, unwilling to let him go.

"Please tell me this giant monster isn't you're friend?" she continued.

"Ah, but he is. Don't be frightened sweetheart, he won't hurt you," Carman said as he turned to Buddy and said, "This is my Anna, Buddy".

"Whoa Carman, you said she was beautiful, you didn't say she was gorgeous," Buddy exclaimed as he picked Anna up and swung her in the air.

"Easy Buddy, that's a little mother you're holding there. Handle with care," said Carman.

"Sorry little lady", I didn't mean to scare you but you're such a little thing, I forget my own strength," he said as he gently put her down.

"No harm done Buddy, let's get you two home, you must be starving," said Anna.

Carman delighted by Anna's behavior with Buddy breathed a sigh of relief. He had called Mama earlier just in case Anna was reluctant to welcome Buddy into their home, but to his amazement, Anna seemed enchanted. Carman was euphoric. Anna never failed to amaze him.

Marty was whisked away by his family as he shouted to Carman that he would see him as soon as he could get away. Anna leading her two soldiers walked swiftly to a waiting carriage and the three of them headed home.

Carman felt strange walking into his new home. He looked around in amazement.

"Carman, don't look so bewildered," said Anna. "I will lead you carefully through the house so that you will feel at home here as you would at your Mama's. Come Buddy let's find a lovely room for you and have cook make us all something to eat. Carman you go down the hall to your right and find the kitchen. Tell cook to make us something to eat. Anything you think you want and something special for Buddy."

Carman walked slowly down a beautifully decorated hall. His feet seemed to sink into the thick carpet. There was an unmistakable new wood scent, synonymous with new houses, prevailing. Suddenly the aroma of freshly cooked tomato sauce reached him and he knew he was heading in the right direction to the kitchen. Walking through the kitchen door he was amazed at the size of the room.

My God, he thought, you could fit almost our whole apartment in this kitchen. There were pots and pans in every size and shape hanging on long chains from the ceiling. Countertops seen only in magazines or in a woman's imagination lined the walls. In the center was an island of sinks. Against one wall there were at least three stoves. He stood wondering just how many stoves they needed to cook here. Mama mia, what a place. If we ever go broke, we can open a restaurant. You could cook for an Army in here, he thought as he walked around the kitchen, touching the cabinets, amazed at the texture and gleam of the wood. This wood belongs in a church, not a kitchen. Whew, how the hell am I ever going to belong here?

He was startled by the appearance of a young woman coming out of the pantry.

"Oh excuse me sir I didn't know anyone was here," she said not daring to look up. Aware the master of the house was coming today, she never expected to find him in the kitchen.

Recognizing the maid, Carman gasped in amazement, "Madelyn?"

Looking up she cried, "Carman, my God, what are you doing here, you must leave, if that little bitch sees you I'm out on my ear and you, well God help you."

"Madelyn," answered Carman still surprised to find her in his kitchen, "I'm married to that little bitch."

"Oh Carman, you poor thing, you married her? God help you Carman, God help you," she whispered.

"Madelyn please," he said as he realized Madelyn was dead serious. Looking at her he was startled by her appearance. He remembered her being pretty, but now she was truly an Irish beauty.

Whoa, Carman stop he suddenly reminded himself, remember you're married to the lady she refers to as the little bitch. This girl can mean nothing to you, absolutely nada. Recovering from his surprise he said, "I'm sorry my Anna strikes you as a little bitch, maybe you don't know her well enough yet?"

"I know her only too well Carman. I'm sorry you're the one she hooked."

"What are you talking about hooked," he answered.

"The story is all over the neighborhood, even in the Irish section, how your little bride got you to marry her."

"Unfortunately it's all true Madelyn, but I married her for better or worse. You don't know the entire story. I think you should give Anna a fair shake. Sometimes what you see is not the real person."

"Poor Carman, you just don't know. She's a little touched, if you get my drift," answered Madelyn.

"Oh I know she's different but come on Madelyn "touched" give me a break"

"You poor fool, run don't walk. Get yourself out of here fast. Have the marriage annulled; you can't possibly stay here Carman you just don't know".

"Madelyn please, don't you think you're over reacting? I never remember you having such an over zealous imagination, you've always been so clear headed, so down to earth".

Listening to Carman go on and on, she realized that no matter what she told him he would never believe her. Unfortunately he'd just have to witness the madness of Anna to believe it. If she didn't need this job so desperately she would have left in a minute. Fortunately Madelyn learned how to deal with Anna, just stay out of her way. If caught unaware just keep nodding your head in the affirmative, no matter how asinine.

"Ok Carman you win. Maybe she'll improve with you home, we'll see. Now get out of my kitchen."

"Get out, I followed the smell of sauce all the way to the kitchen and you want me to get out, just give me a hunk of bread, and if you don't mind I'll sample your sauce."

"All right, you're the big boss here help yourself," she answered.

Carman couldn't help but smack his lips. This sauce was just like Mama's.

"Where did you learn to cook Italian and just like my Mama? Well almost like Mama?"

"Even Irish girls can cook, you just have to give us a chance," she laughed.

"Now please get out of here so I can finish making dinner."

"Ok, Ok Madelyn, I'm out of here, he replied."

He walked from room to room, floor to floor taking in the beauty of the house. He'd like to think of it as his home but when would he be able to afford a place like this. Not in this lifetime he imagined. Who knows if I'll live through the war that's inevitable? I'm seventeen and I live in a veritable mansion with a raving lunatic. Maybe departing from this lush life is the best way to go. Not kicking the bucket, but disappearing after my stretch in the Army. If it weren't for my family, I'd disappear now. What am I losing my marbles too, what a crazy idea. I'm going to be a father and this baby will be the most important person in my life. Enough of this nonsense, I know Anna is a little crazy. I've seen her in action. Let's pray the kid takes after me. Please God, don't let my baby be like Anna, please.

Wandering aimlessly with his head down Carman almost collided with Buddy coming out of his room.

"How you doing pal, everything Ok," exclaimed Carman.

"I can't believe this place," replied Buddy, "it's like living in a palace. I never realized you were so wealthy you pal."

"Wealthy, Buddy I couldn't afford the towels in your bathroom. All this stuff belongs to my wife," Carman answered as he clasped Buddy's arm and they walked down the stairs to dinner.

Carman and Buddy were still laughing at some inane joke from the barracks when they entered the dining room. Carman stood immobile. He could not believe the ornate glittering vastness of the room. The dining table was large enough to sit twenty people easily. There were candles lit everywhere, on mantels, breakfronts, sideboards, everywhere. There was staff of four young maids standing at attention waiting to serve dinner. Carman and Buddy stood waiting not knowing where or if to sit in this palatial setting.

Anna realizing their discomfort said, "come Carman sit next to me, and Buddy sit at the end."

"Excuse me Anna but Buddy won't be able to hear a word we say way down at the other end of the table," said Carman with a broad smile.

"Wipe that smirk off your mouth and sit where I tell you, or you don't eat," cried Anna waving her hands dramatically indicating that Buddy sit where she told him.

Carman still amused by Anna, not realizing how serious she was added. "Come on Anna, Buddy is a guest in our house, our first guest, let's not be ridiculous."

"You call me ridiculous, you are in this house not one hour and you dare to call me ridiculous, out," she screamed, "get out of my house now."

"This is madness Anna. Be quiet and sit there like a good girl," replied Carman gesturing to Buddy to sit down next to him. "Not another word Anna or I'll send you to your room." Watching carefully as Anna sat down he asked, "Is everybody comfortable?"

Anna nodded her head shyly and Buddy said, "Sure Pal."

"Good, now will you please serve dinner" he said to the staff standing like statues unable to move. "Please, I don't know your names yet, but I would appreciate your serving dinner now."

Silently the four young maids entered the kitchen and dinner was served. Anna chatted away with Carman and Buddy seemingly unaware of what had just happened. When they had finished eating she complimented the staff with a few words of praise and asked one of the serving girls to ask the cook to come into the dinning room. When Madelyn entered, she stood with her eyes downcast not knowing what to expect from Anna.

"Very good cook," was all Anna said and dismissed her.

"Let us have coffee in the drawing room," said Anna as she left the table and entered the room on the right of the dining room.

Buddy and Carman got up from the table and walked out the door to the hall making a dash for the front door. They stood on the stoop looked at one another and started to laugh uncontrollably until they could barely stand up.

Finally catching his breath Carman said, "Do you believe what just happened? I don't know why I'm laughing. I'm married to that crazy woman in there."

"Charlie, that had to be the craziest dinner I was ever at. That poor wife of yours needs help pal. What's even crazier we stayed there and ate that dinner?"

"No, that wasn't crazy Buddy we were starving. We haven't eaten anything since yesterday. Anyway that's why I stayed. I tasted that macaroni sauce earlier in the kitchen and I wasn't about to let any crazy woman ruin my dinner."

"Charlie my boy I think we'd better get out of here before that woman comes out looking for us."

"You go Buddy, take a right turn at the corner and walk about three blocks west; you'll see a big sign that reads "Guido's Restaurant. I'm sure you'll find Marty there. I've got to go in and see what the hell is going on around here. I'll make sure the servants leave the front door open for you. I'll see you at breakfast, said Carman as he reluctantly entered his wife's house. He took a deep breath and marched into the drawing room. There was Anna sitting huddled up on one of the couches crying softly into a lace handkerchief. Instead of admonishing her he was moved by her genuine despair.

As gently as he could he asked her why she had behaved so abominably to his friend and why the histrionics. Anna could barely speak she was so upset. Finally Carman sat down and held her in his arms until the weeping subsided.

"Can you tell me now what is going on?" he asked.

Fighting to speak without crying again she dabbed at her eyes to wipe away the tears and said, "It's just that I love you."

"I don't think you know what love is Anna. I came home to you to try and start a new life together so that when the baby comes we would be a real family. I try to understand your mood changes but I'm at a loss to understand why you can change so rapidly. It isn't fair to someone like Buddy to be so downright mean. You act as if you were really out of touch with reality. If this marriage is going to work you've got to try and behave normally." Carman talked on and on about the commitment he had made to her and their baby and how much he wanted them to have a life together. He even told her about being true to their marriage vows. Which even in Anna's depression seemed to make a very big impression? The anger he felt gave way to compassion and he found himself kissing her tears away. Anna could barely restrain her joy at his tenderness. She tried to explain to him how difficult it was for her to share him with anyone. He got her to promise that in the future she would try to behave in a more enlightened manner. Finally after all the ridiculous antics had been explained away and laughter replaced Anna tears, it was time for bed. Gently Carman carried her up to their room and they spent the night making love.

Chapter Thirteen

1929

Carman stared at the blinding snow covering the city. It transformed all the ugly, unsightly, unattractive repulsiveness of the city into a beautiful wonderland. Somehow he equated the transformation of the city by the glorious snow to Anna's beauty which hid her madness under her loveliness. He realized now how incomprehensible Anna was to him at seventeen. Her actions mirrored her poor tortured mind, but he never really saw it.

He only saw the shell.

At the time, he couldn't understand why her family accepted his hasty marriage to Anna without objection. They never reproached him for taking advantage of their daughter. He was especially bewildered by her mother's approval. He knew she thought he lacked any status in the community, not to mention his personal poverty.

So convinced of his own appeal to people in general, and with a seventeen year olds' mentality, it never occurred to him that he was being manipulated by the entire Similetti family.

Carman stifled a laugh as he envisioned himself as the Similetti's pictured him a meaningless son of an Italian emigrant; a stupid boy waiting to be used and that's exactly what he was.

The only time he ever showed any resentment to the entire affair was by the way Anna treated his friend Buddy. The poor man certainly didn't deserve the behavior he got from Anna. It wasn't until I took him to Mama was Buddy able to feel comfortable and welcome.

On the other hand, I wasn't so lucky. Anna's wrath and cunning were her favorable attributes, which she used freely to keep me in control. Fortunately for Anna, her madness was easily hidden from a self-proclaimed man of the world that unfortunately, was just a boy.

She had lied about her pregnancy and was determined to make it legitimate. I never questioned her incredible appetite for sex. I supposed, as other young boys before me, that I was just irresistible. I remember asking if so much lovemaking was good for the baby and Anna replying, "It's the best thing in the world for a baby."

The lovemaking continued until I could barely stand up. Anna reluctantly surrendered. Just to make sure her plan was successful she paid a welcome visit to Guardo. The poor bastard never knew what hit him. After knocking at his door and shyly begging him to let her in for a few minutes, she had him under the covers and ready to make love. Her plan to conceive a child was successful. She never gave a thought about which one had fathered her child. She didn't know or care. Miraculously during her pregnancy, she was completely rational. She manifested such ordinary behavior that her parents were considering having the marriage annulled and finding a more suitable husband for Anna. Almost immediately after the birth of her daughter, she reverted back to her madness and spent almost a year in a private sanitarium. Ah but I'm getting ahead of myself back to the big war.

It wasn't until Carman returned to Camp Smith that the actuality of World War I finally materialized with the sinking of the British Lusitania. He and his buddies were young and anxious to prove they were men. The reality of war did not set in until they were in the trenches in France. Now they were eager to get to Europe, the sooner the better.

Camp Smith was bursting with new recruits along with a few sailors who had re-enlisted into the Cavalry for a second hitch. One of the new arrivals was a young sailor called Candy Pellicano, who immediately latched onto Carman, Marty and Buddy. Buddy's size and manner didn't bother him. He saw directly that Buddy would definitely be an asset. The three buddies became four and waited patiently for their orders to move out. The long wait made Carman do some real soul searching. It was something he had never done and was long overdue. He came to the decision that as soon as he returned home, if he ever did get home, he would get his marriage annulled. The more he thought about Anna's erratic behavior, the more determined he was to put an end to the farce. He was also resolute in his goal to get custody of his child. He could not in all conscious leave the child in her custody. Although completely inept in the face of mental illness, he knew there was something definitely wrong with Anna. Never having encountered anyone else with mental illness, he was reluctant to make any unqualified guess to what exactly was wrong with Anna. The word crazy kept jumping into his mind and it frightened him. He had no idea what the consequences of her affliction would mean.

There was one sure thing he was aware of. A story his mother would tell about her poor brother being caught in a marriage to a deranged woman who was confined in an asylum. Because of her condition he was never able to get an annulment from the church. Although his wife remained institutionalized, he was unable to remarry in the eyes of the church until the poor woman died twenty years later. He was determined that before Anna was certified insane he had to get the marriage annulled. Carman persisted in tormenting himself with images of Anna's vacillating behavior.

Because the camp was so overcrowded, it was decided that the men who were assigned to ships for embarkation were given weekend passes. Reluctantly, Carman went home to Anna's house determined to discover what precisely was wrong with his wife. He was armed with resolve. Whatever it was he would face it and somehow either get help for Anna, or if everything else failed he would try to get his marriage dissolved. Somehow he had to get the baby to a safe place away from Anna until he was sure of his wife's mental condition. He was seventeen and believed there was no obstacle he could not beat. Unfortunately, the subtleties of mental illness were unknown to him.

And so, when Carman entered Anna's house, and was greeted by every man's dream of the perfect wife, he was completely misled. She stood before him with open arms, radiant with the glow of impending motherhood. Her angelic appearance and manner left Carman speechless. She literally gushed with good health and a semblance of joy. The most important asset she demonstrated was complete sanity. Gently he was led to the kitchen where all his favorite foods were laid out. Anna carefully laid a napkin on his lap and sat across from him literally beaming with love. The gleam of the pots and pans hanging from the ceiling and the sweet smell of sauce simmering on the stove filled him with the warmth of his Mama's kitchen. He tried to find his voice but was so overcome by relief at the sight of his wife he was unable to speak. After a meal fit for a king, he was led willingly upstairs to their room where she allowed him to make magnificent love to her. For the entire weekend there was absolutely no trace of any imbalance in Anna's behavior. He was certain all was well and grateful for the undeniable change that had taken place in Anna. He returned to Camp Smith spent of his qualms about Anna and sad that he had to leave her. But he was only seventeen.

Any thoughts of Anna good or bad were obliterated by the urgency of his Lieutenant to pack up his men. They were finally going overseas to Europe or wherever. A sea journey was definitely on the agenda. Although a Sergeant, Carman was not privy to any orders, he just made sure the men in his squad were ready as ordered by the Lieutenant. Miraculously after their Mexican adventure, all three buddies became Sergeants and they took their responsibilities very seriously this time. Buddy had little difficulty keeping his men in line. One look would terrorize them into submission. Fortunately, Carman had a way about him that lent itself to using authority.

It was Marty who had the most difficulty. He was still thunderstruck that he had actually made Sergeant. It took him awhile but eventually, like most men, he enjoyed giving orders and having them carried out.

They left Camp Smith on a train loaded with men occupying every available space, with some of them hanging on for dear life in the small space between cars. Mercifully, it was a short ride to New York City where they were herded onto a waiting merchant ship. The men were caught up in the excitement of actually being sent overseas and couldn't wait for the ship to leave port. Like all things in the military they had to wait for their journey to begin.

From the beginning, life aboard ship was horrendous with nowhere to go or hide or even to vomit in peace, which he remembered doing quite frequently. It was a full three days before he could hold plain water down. After that test of endurance for himself and a lot of his men, came the unrelenting boredom.

Unfortunately Carman chose arm-wrestling as an alternative to ennui. He became champion of his squad and went on to greater glory challenging any contender. He was still too young and inexperienced to realize he wasn't invincible. That there could be someone who could not only beat him and harm him; this was not a factor in his calculations. Then, that day came when he was not only beaten, but also left with a broken wrist. He could never again challenge anyone. A somehow meaningless development, but terminally an excellent lesson was learned, and if nothing else, Carman was a quick study. He never again fell into the trap of superiority. Happily he fell upon some books and was contentedly lost for the rest of the arduous excursion in someone else's fantasy. There were always regular jousts with his staunch comrades Buddy and Marty who took to the sea like sailors with nary a burp.

The seemingly endless journey terminated and the weary squad of men disembarked to a destination unknown to the entire company. They queued up and waited interminably for someone to order them somewhere, anywhere. At last they were given an order to march. After several miles they came to a camp with hundreds of tents awaiting their arrival. The feel of ground beneath his feet was enough to boost Carman's morale and he led his squad with panache to their assigned quarters. It was three whole days before it was rumored that they were in France. Where in France exactly, no one knew but they were in France and that was enough for them. The spirit of romance and adventure was waiting for them, but they couldn't go anywhere. With virtually nothing to do but wait they took to singing some barrack songs like Mademoiselle from Armatures Parley Vous and that old favorite called My Cockeyed Consumpted Sara Jane. They sang for hours on end with each man changing the chorus to rowdy approval if it was more risqué than the last one. It was a while before the absence of horses started to worry Carman. When they first arrived he was told they were grazing in fields several miles from camp. But who was taking care of his horse, and was she being fed properly and brushed to the high sheen she was used to?

"Come on Lieutenant," begged Carman, "what field? Give me a lead and I'll find them, I just want to see them."

"Give me a break, I don't know where they are either," he answered. "I'm beginning to suspect they've been taken somewhere else. We may be traveling by foot from now on."

"What do you mean?" Carman replied nervously. "Are we somehow becoming infantry?"

"Jesus Charlie, I sure as hell hope not, it just doesn't make sense for the horses to be billeted somewhere else," he answered bewildered. "As soon as I know I'll clue you in. Not to worry Charlie, we're all in the same boat. The army always takes very good care of its livestock. Your horse is probably eating better than we are. Go back to your men and stop tormenting yourself. Enjoy the time we have left. I believe we're going to see combat very soon, don't quote me, it's just a feeling I have. Keep it just between us, Ok?" He patted Carman on the back and sent him on his way.

Christ combat, maybe we're at war already. "Not now, Lord please," he prayed," give me some time to see Paris first."

1929

Not only were our horses missing we didn't even know what country we were in. It was a week before we realized that we were in England and not France. We were amazed that the local farmers could speak English so well. We were on the coast of England not the outskirts of Paris. Just as the disappointment started to set in we were herded on to a transport boat. Clutching to anything we could grab onto we were navigated across the English Channel, in what we referred to as "the ride through hell". How any of us survived that trip only God knows.

1914

"You know Buddy, if the Army keeps this up and there really is a war coming, we'll be dead by the time we get there."

"Take it easy Carman, we'll be in Paris soon and we'll forget this shit. We're gonna be surrounded by the most beautiful woman in the world."

"Jesus, I hope so Bud, before I die, I want to wake up wrapped in the arms of a French girl."

"And you a married man Carman, shame on you," he answered.

"What married, the license isn't valid in Europe. I've been in this man's Army over a year, and married or not I'm gonna have a French girl." And he did. He had several French girls, and French women and even one Moroccan who he claimed, knew more about love making than the entire American Army. Fortunately for them in his heart he truly loved them all.

Their base camp consisted of row after row of tents with several, constantly busy mess halls. Thankfully the latrines were scattered behind and far away from the sleeping quarters. They were easy to find. The distinctive aroma would guide you even in the black of night should nature call. The men shifted from tent to tent playing cards drinking confiscated wine. Fortunes were won and lost at the turn of a card. No one seemed to care. The war was real and money had little value to them. The optimistic few, who hoarded their winnings and survived the war, came back home rich men. Most of the young soldiers didn't care about tomorrow. They weren't sure they'd live past next week. They were uneasy and nervous waiting, always waiting for something. Waiting is the plague of the Army. It wasn't until their horses arrived that the men seemed to relax a bit. For them to go into combat without a horse was unthinkable in the Cavalry.

Once the camp was running smoothly, passes were issued. All they had to do was find a way to get to Paris. Carman, Buddy and Marty traveled by foot, by cart, and finally by train, but they got there, only to spend their entire leave in a brothel located a block and a half from Notre Dame. They would often regret that they had never seen the inside of the cathedral. They never regretted their visit to the "Palace of Dreams."

The three buddies found the brothel by pure accident. They were in route for Notre Dame. In fact they could see it spirals shinning in the sunlight a few blocks away across the Seine River. As they passed a house on St. Michelle's Square, a beautiful oriental girl beckoned them with a smile and the soft words spoken in English, "Pleese come in boyce."

Could they not answer her delicate call? At breakneck speed, pushing one another away from the door they finally entered. The scent of exotic perfume filled their senses. The walls of the foyer were draped in various colors of shiny satin, nothing garish but definitely appealing.

They were ushered into a giant living room where scantily clad, very young ladies were lounging on red velvet couches of different shapes and sizes. They could barely keep their eyes on one girl because they were all so beautiful. It was almost impossible to hone in on one. They stood there like three kids in a candy store with a pocketful of money. They didn't believe their eyes. Eventually one of the young ladies asked them to follow her as the other girls looked on with amused laughing eyes. They were taken up a magnificent winding staircase and ushered into the most lavishly furnished boudoir they had ever seen. In the middle of the room lying on several lace pillows on an enormously large bed, was a woman of unimaginable beauty. The walls of the room were painted stark white. The bed was white, the carpet was white the lace curtains were white and the lovely lady has gorgeous white hair cascading down her back. She was dressed in a flimsy red lace negligee that barely covered her gorgeous body. She beckoned them to come closer. Hesitatingly at first the three young men inched closer as she spoke to them in the sweetest strains of French they had ever heard. They had no idea what she was saying but somehow knew exactly what she meant.

Her voice was like velvet soft as a kitten. "Closer," she murmured breathlessly. Slowly, as if in a dream the three comrades moved even closer. In perfect English she whispered, "you my superb Adonis," pointing her delicate finger at Buddy, "you stay with me and my two sweet angels you go with Mimi." Buddy stood transfixed unable to move a muscle as the white haired goddess rose to put her arms around Buddy's neck.

Willingly he crept onto her bed and was consumed by her kisses. Reluctantly Carman and Marty followed Mimi out of the room as they listened to the obvious sounds of pleasure coming from the bed. They were led into a room with walls covered in various shades of purple gauze. They walked on thick carpeting with an oriental design in shade of the palest pink. Against one wall three barely clothed female musicians played softly on stringed instruments. Mimi led them to enormously large satin pillows, which engulfed them in their softness and delicate aroma of spring flowers.

Carman whispered to Marty, "I don't know what's coming, but at this point I really don't care."

Marty's only response was, "yeah."

The music wafted over them as the three musicians played so softly it almost lulled them to sleep. From behind one of the curtains a seemingly tall young girl dressed in the same gauze that decorated the walls began to dance. She was serene and completely composed. They were mesmerized and totally fascinated by her movements. As the music heightened, her body began to gyrate as veil after veil fell from her ravenous body. Carman's eyes were riveted on her as she danced. She seemed unable to control her movements, as the music became a thunderous ear piercing sound. Carman was completely unaware of the entrance of a tiny, delicately endowed Egyptian beauty that had sat unceremoniously on Marty's lap and began kissing and massaging him in places Marty never connected with eroticism. As the music swelled, so did his manhood. He didn't know why, nor did he care.

Carman was completely spellbound by the dancer and stood unmoving as she finished her dance with only one sheer veil covering her tall generously endowed body. Her raven head was bowed in submission as Carman gently took her hand as she led him to a sparsely furnished room with an enormous bed. It was in this bed that Carman spent the first two days of his leave. He managed to visit almost every room in the establishment until he realized that his funds were diminishing and he really did want to see some of Paris. In reality, the boys just had too much sex and wisely decided, for the sake of their immortal souls; they had better leave "The Palace of Dreams" before they died from sheer exhaustion.

Haltingly they left promising to return before their leave was over. The three young soldiers left with half their buttons undone, their boots badly wrapped. They were unshaven but clean as they had been bathed every day and sometimes twice a day. Stumbling down Plaza

St. Michel Avenue arm in arm, holding one another up, laughing uproariously, they went in search of a cheap room so that they could at last get some well deserved sleep.

Marty noticed a small hotel with a sign that read Hotel Vous in small black letters.

"What do you think guys," he asked pointing to the sign. They all shrugged and headed for the small door to the hotel. They walked into a tiny reception room and Mary asked the young woman at the desk in Italian if they had a small cheap room for the three of them. Smiling the sight of three very young, very weary young soldiers she answered "Why yes, I think we can arrange for a room the three of you, please follow me. As she led them up two flights of stairs they seemed completely unaware that the young French woman had answered them in English had understood Marty's Italian and was quietly singing a German song. Some other time perhaps they could be impressed by her skill at language. For now they could barely make the stairs. She had seen many soldiers stumble into her little hotel exhausted from, she imagined, any nearby brothel. She did not judge them. She was after all French.

When they reached the third floor she walked down a narrow hall-way and stopped at what looked like the door to an attic. As she opened the door, all the boys could see were three lovely beds waiting to be slept in. She handed Marty a key, and he nodded to her gratefully.

"There is a bathroom at the end of the hall with a large tub, if you're interested.

"Maybe later," answered Carman. She looked at Carman for the first time and caught her breath. After he closed the door, she stood for a few seconds outside the door wondering what it was about the young disheveled American soldier that attracted her. With a sigh, she walked swiftly down the stairs puzzled by her own reactions.

The three friends literally dived into the beds. Half of Buddy's ample body seemed to be hanging off his bed. He didn't seem to mind. The room was very clean and very small. A bureau with a mirror was squeezed between two of the beds. The other bed seemed to be in front of a closet. They didn't care if the room was clean or dirty, small or large, or whether it had a closet or not. They were sound asleep within a few minutes.

Carman awoke first, trying to remember where they were. Rubbing his eyes he went down the hall in search of a bathroom. He was surprised to find the room much larger than their bedroom, with a tub big enough for the three of them and towels enough for a week. Taking off his shirt, he went in search of his knapsack sure that he had left it at the Palace. Back at their room he was surprised that the three knapsacks were lying in a corner. He rescued his and tip toed back into the bathroom. After a shave and bath he emerged expecting to find his friends awake, but here they lay just as he had left them.

Suddenly he was ravenously hungry and went in search of food. It was obviously very early in the morning, so he crept down the stairs and followed the aroma of fresh brewed coffee and bread baking coming from across the street at a small cafe. He sat at one of the tables and speaking in his mothers' Italian dialect he managed to get some wonderful croissants and jam with piping hot coffee, poured together with hot milk. It tasted just the way Mama made it.

It wasn't until he had devoured three croissants and three cups of coffee that he noticed a young woman staring at him from a table in the back of the cafe. She looked at him as if she knew him. Looking at her she seemed familiar so he politely nodded and paid the bill with some difficulty. He had no idea of the exchange rate and was determined to find out before his next meal, as his resources were very low.

Carman breathed the fresh spring air and began to walk aimlessly through the city. He was fascinated by its charm. This early in the morning he was uninhibited by passing crowds. The cobblestone streets and the appearance of horse drawn fruit and vegetable wagons made him feel at home.

Beautiful cathedrals with unique architecture were everywhere, as if every building was a museum. Cherry blossom trees were in bloom throughout the city. As he passed one café after other young men in white aprons were lining up small tables right on the sidewalks. Woman began to appear carrying baskets of flowers and almost on cue the entire city came to life. He knew at once that he would always love this city. It was Paris, and he was really here.

Amazingly he found his way back to the little hotel and was surprised to find his friends still asleep.

"Come on you guys wake up, we're in Paris for God's sake, do you want to sleep your lives away, come on get up times a wasting."

"Please I beg you, just let me sleep. I don't care where we are. Do you have any idea how lucky we are to be sleeping in real beds? Don't you realize this will probably be the last time we do? At least not until the end of this war," pleaded Marty.

"Give me a break. We'll be dead a long time. You can sleep all you want then, now get up, furthermore who said we're at war. It's just a rumor. Do you think with blokes like us in the Army, they would consider going to war? Come on, could we three win a war, any war. Maybe a war against the ladies of the Palace, but with them we wouldn't want to win. Don't worry about the war. Let's just see Paris, what'll say, huh."

"Ok Charlie we're with you," said Buddy throwing Marty out of bed and dragging him down the hall into the bathroom.

"Get a load of this bathroom. I think I'll sleep here tonight, said Buddy as he threw Marty out the door.

Wow now this is what I call heaven, he sighed locking the door. Immediately he burst into song.

Marty returning to their room asked, "God Carman listen to that voice, they'll throw us out if you don't go down there and shut him up."

"Don't worry; did you ever see anyone throw Buddy out?"

"You're right, what was I thinking. Ok what do you want to see first?"

"Everything Marty, just about everything, but I don't have much money. You got any?

"Sure Carman, you know me I always have some stashed. That is if our sweet little tricks didn't rob it. Hold on let me look."

Carman watched incredulously as Marty pulled several hundred-dollar bills from the lining of his uniform.

"Where the hell did you get that money? You're unbelievable. I haven't seen that much cash since I left Similetti's."

"Actually Carman, I won it in a crap game aboard ship, when you were heaving over the side of the ship."

"You're kidding me?

"Honest to God Carman, that's where I got it. In all my life, I never had such luck. I've been afraid to spend it, like it wasn't real. But Carman we're in Paris and all this dough is gonna take you me and Buddy to heaven."

"I hope not Marty, just to the Folies Bergere and a few underground bars, and maybe a good restaurant."

"Anywhere you want to go Carman, but please shut that palooka up, and get him out of the bathroom, I really gotta go."

"No problem Marty."

Carman walked down the hall and knocked at the door, "Ok Buddy out, now."

"On my way pal, I'm on my way," Buddy sang out.

For the next three days they saw everything there was to see in Paris. On the last day they invited the concierge from the hotel to join them. With her help they saw a side of Paris only the French see. They dined in a small elegant restaurant. The atmosphere was delightfully quaint, the food delectable and the waiters friendly. After dinner they went to a real underground tavern where Adagio dancers flung one another all over the dance floor. They hugged and kissed Lola goodbye as her eyes glistened with tears. She kissed them warmly and promised to pray for their safe return to Paris

At least Lola finally understood why her heart stopped every time she saw Carman. She had a good old-fashioned crush on a younger man. Given time she was sure she could have made him her lover. After all, she was sure she hadn't lost any of her charms. She was only thirty years old and convinced that although Carman never made any advances to her she had on occasion caught him looking at her longingly. Too bad, all she needed was a little more time. Oh well maybe he'll be back. If not there were plenty of Frenchmen waiting in line.

World War I began on July 28, 1914. The United States did not enter the war until April 6, 1917. Carman had been in the cavalry for two years and had made sergeant three times. Each time he lost his stripes was always connected to some woman and each time he vowed it would never happen again. His friends Marty and Buddy never lost their stripes and remained sergeants throughout the war. Carman was so accustomed to losing his stripes he took the ordeal for granted. Fortunately when President Wilson declared war on Germany, he had just become sergeant again. His stripes enabled him to stay and fight along with his friends. The three comrades faced the horror of modern trench warfare together.

Their combat began in Marne, where the Germans had pushed the allies. A mere 40 miles form Paris. It was hard for them to believe they were so close to Paris and yet they seemed a million miles away living in mud filled trenches. The American troops managed to stiffen the allied line until it ceased to bend.

On May 28th they captured the town of Cantigny from the Germans.

Wearily Carman, Buddy and Marty trudged through muddy fields' red with the blood from their squads searching for survivors. Grateful to be alive they were changed forever by their ordeal. One long dreary night when the fighting had momentarily abated the three dirty shivering friends sat around a small forbidden fire trying to dry off.

"Jesus Charlie, I'll never be warm again," murmured Buddy.

"After this war is over we're all going to take a trip to Sicily. I'm telling you Bud it's always warm there. We'll loll on the beaches surrounded by beautiful Italian girls. Just think of that Buddy and your blood will warm up in no time."

"Even you can't dream up anything to warm me up Charlie. I've never been as tired in my whole life. Not even after we left the "Paradise" in Paris was I as bone weary as I am now."

"There you go Buddy, remember that French girl who did the dance of the seven veils? Whoa, that'll warm you. How about that gorgeous blond who fell in love with you at first sight? You think about her."

"Charlie if it wasn't for that beautiful blond I would have frozen to death yesterday."

The three friends in their misery could not help but laugh spontaneously. Here they were cold wet, and hungry afraid this could be their last day alive and laughing uproariously.

Well why not thought Carman, they were alive weren't they? Countless men lay scattered all over. There were some of them in ditches and all of them waiting to be identified. At least they had each other.

They heard the sound of trucks arriving and were told to board their men. Huddled together, bouncing against a place to rest and cleans up, and dry out. Their squads were put under the command of a brilliant French strategist Ferdinand Foch. He was also in command of the entire new American troops who arrived at the rate of a quarter million a month.

Their rest and warmth was over. Under the command of Marshall Foch, the American troops near Verdum and the Argonne Forest wiped out the German salient of St. Michele, which for four years had withstood the allied forces. It was here that Carman got back the stripes he had lost in Marne when he mistakenly took to bed the commanding officer's wife.

The three comrades faced the enemy together and with Buddy's help managed to stay alive. It was 1918 and they were still in the field fighting. During September, October and November of 1918 they were involved with the Argonne-Muse drive. Approximately 1,200,000 American soldiers forming 21 divisions fought 40 divisions of Germans.

The battleground was the impenetrable Argonne Forest. They were part of this insuperable drive, which pushed the Germans until they reached the Sudan. Marshal Foch testified that "the American soldiers are superb." The three buddies couldn't agree more as they celebrated in a deep trench drinking confiscated wine and singing at the top of their voices. Suddenly without any provocation Buddy threw himself on top of Carman and Marty crushing them under his weight. Simultaneously the loudest explosion they had ever heard erupted. Carman lay unconscious under Buddy's lifeless body. Marty had miraculously been hurled unharmed twenty feet away. With the help of three men they managed to lift Buddy's body. Marty stood in shock to see Carman unconscious but breathing. He gently lifted his friend's head and cradled him in his arms as he cried softly.

Carman didn't regain consciousness for two days and Marty never left his side. He slept on the floor next to his cot waiting for him to wake up. He wanted to be with Carman when he woke up and realized that Buddy had died saving them.

1929

Tears fell freely as Carman recalled the utter agony he felt so long ago. Some things are too hard to remember he thought, as he blew his nose in the soft white handkerchief Mama insisted he carry. All this reverie will kill me. Those days in the army were the most gratifying days of my life. Knowing Buddy changed my whole perspective on life. After he was killed I was no longer a boy.

My God, it was a dreadful war. I'll never forget the cries of men lying in darkened trenches begging for someone to come. There was blood everywhere. They had no medicine, no bandages no anything. At last medical trucks began to arrive; nurses and doctors didn't know which way to run. The one screaming the loudest was helped first. It was the brave ones Carman remembered most, the soldiers who stifled their screams, too brave to cry out. Until the day he died

Carman cried out in his sleep for someone to help him care for his men who lay dying.

Ah Buddy if you were here today I wouldn't be in this predicament. The war taught me many things, how to be a man, how to loose someone you love, how to stand helpless in a field of blood but no one can teach you to die. He realized that as he stood on a field in Marne in France in 1918.

1918

After the Armistice they were given extensive leave with extra pay. Carman and Marty found their way to Sicily and lay on the beach with beautiful Italian girls and thought of Buddy. They were sure he could see them from heaven and was enjoying their holiday with them. Neither man wanted to return home; Carman had no desire to go back to Anna, even though he longed to see his baby girl. It seemed wrong for him to go home just yet. He felt there was something he had to do before he went home. What it was he couldn't say but even after they returned to their company Buddy and Carman gave up their space on ship after ship unable to leave France.

Eventually they were forced to return home and reluctantly they said farewell to their adopted country and set off for America. Luckily their term in the Army wasn't over and they had to return to Camp Smith to await further orders. They both refused leave and wandered aimlessly around the camp. One sunny summer afternoon a visitor to the camp arrived unannounced and because of his rank was allowed to wander the Camp freely. The visitor came upon his casualties sitting under a tree deep in conversation. He quietly approached shading his eyes from the sun clearing his voice to get their attention. As Carman looked up he saw his old friend Father Paul gazing down on them with a serene benevolent smile on his face.

"Father, or should I say Monsignor how did you find us, asked Carman?

"I have friends in high places boys, now what is this about not wanting to come home?"

"How did you find out" asked Carman still amazed at his appearance.

"Actually Carman it was your Mama who called me, and I was only too glad to get out of the city for a day to come and see for myself what was holding you boys here. Let's talk." And they did for several hours. Their horror stories poured out to their priest as he sat holding back his own tears. The Priest's heart was breaking as he to listened to their tale of war. They are so young to have lived through so much, he thought. What can I say to them, he prayed silently as Carman and Marty laid their souls bare.

When they were finished the young veterans of war were openly crying unaware of their grief. It was in the telling with no holds barred that they were able to unburden themselves of the horrors they had seen. The priest stood and held both boys in his arms until their sobbing stopped. No magical words were spoken just the presence of their priest was enough to start the healing process to begin.

"Come on boys, it's time we three went home." With his arms around each young soldier's back, they walked to the Captain's office for passes home.

Carman and Marty looked like children wearing their fathers' uniforms. Who would suspect that they were seasoned soldiers veterans of the "Great War.?" They had both lost a considerable amount of weight but they were as hard as rock to the touch. They were hard as a rock on the inside too. They had not only lost a friend but they had lost all their illusions and the one thing they could never retrieve again, their youth.

Father Paul left them to make their final journey home alone. When they reached Marty's corner they instinctively embraced, hoping to get strength from one another.

"I'll meet you later at Guardo's, Ok," whispered Carman.

"Ok Carman, I'll be there, don't forget." answered Marty.

"Don't worry I'll be there," said Carman as he stood watching his friend climb the stairs to his house. He turned to look at Carman one more time before he knocked on the door. Carman gave him a wave and turned away.

It was time to go it alone for awhile. Instead of going home Carman decided to walk the neighborhood but as he strolled aimlessly he realized that sooner or later he was bound to meet someone he knew and he was not quite ready to renew any acquaintances yet. He silently slipped down an alley and continued on his way home undetected, using his old short cut.

He opened the door to his mother's house without making a sound and was startled to see her standing there just waiting for him. She rushed to her son and hugged and kissed him until he cried for mercy.

"Mama please I can't breathe," he whispered.

"Oh Carman, I thought I would never see you again, I can't believe you're home. Come let me look at you. Mama mia you look like a skeleton. Are you sick Carman, tell me? You look so frail, like a little boy."

"No Mama, I'm not sick I just haven't had anything good to eat since I left."

"Ok, now you come and eat. I have everything you like waiting for you; macaroni, eggplant, sausage and peppers, stuffed mushrooms, and of course antipasto with aleach, ok?"

"But Mama how did you know I was coming home?"

"Please Carman, could you say no to a Priest and a Monsignor on top of that? I only send the best when I want action. I couldn't wait for you to make up your mind to come home."

"How did you know I would come here first and not go directly to my wife?"

"Please Carman, first your Mama fixes you up and then you can go see that - "she devil.""

"Mama, thank God you never change. First I'll have a little bite to eat and then I must go see my baby."

He sat at his mother's table and managed to devour almost everything she patiently served to him. Along with the food she heard the brutal story of his lost friend and with her eyes brimming with tears she hugged her son and whispered the soothing words only a mother can say as she wiped the tomato sauce from her son's lips and the tears from his eyes.

He left his mother's house with a full stomach and a lighter heart.

He walked toward Anna's house and his little girl, with his mind filled with apprehension.

Who would greet him at the door? The beautiful sweet Anna or that mad woman she sometimes became. He thought he should go check on Marty to see if he was all right, but he knew he would have to go home sooner or later. Besides he was almost certain his friend was fine. He could go back to Mama's. He never asked her anything about the family. He had no idea of what was happening. He should have asked. He should have done a lot of things, but the one thing he had to do now was face up to his responsibilities. There was no place to hide. He had to go home to Anna whoever she might be today.

Using his old key to open his front door, he wasn't surprised to find that the key wouldn't turn. He was startled when suddenly the door opened seemingly on its own. When no one appeared in the doorway he stepped into his house calling his wife's name in a hushed tone not wanting to frighten her. He roamed from room to room and finally opened the door to the nursery. He tip toed over to the crib and looked down at his baby daughter as she slept nestled deep into a fluffy mattress surrounded by lacy pink pillows and blankets. He could not believe her startling beauty. Her hair was as black as coal and surrounded her sweet pink cheeks in delicate ringlets. He was delighted to see the clef in her chin, which stamped her unquestionably as his daughter. He smiled broadly at the sight of her unaware that he was crying. At that moment his heart was so full of love for this baby, he knew that no matter what Anna was, or would become, he could never abandon this precious child.

Contemplating the nursery he mused that a princess could not have slept in a loftier chamber. The walls were decorated with tiny animals of every species smiling happily right at him. Deep lush carpet surrounded his shoes colored in the palest pink he could ever imagine. The windows were shuttered in white wood with gauze cascading down the windows and over the ceiling. The effect seemed to create the illusion of lofty pink clouds. The crib and chest were all in white and the same tiny animals that smiled from the walls were carved uniquely into the wood. He crept out of the room and gently shut the door almost knocking over a young woman dressed in white, which Carman assumed, was the child's nurse.

"Forgive me, I am so sorry I hope I didn't hurt you, said Carman."

"No matter sir, but may I ask just who you are and what you were doing in Carmina's room?"

"Actually I am the baby's father."

"Forgive me sir, I was told to expect you but you look so young to be Carmina's father."

"Carmina, you say, not bad, not bad."

"Didn't you know her name sir?"

"Actually no I didn't," whispered Carman.

"Now I wonder if you would be kind enough to show me where I could find my wife."

"Well sir, it's hard to say, one never knows where the mistress might be, but you could try the music room, it's just around the corner."

"Thank you I will," he said as her turned the corner. He took a few steps when a door opened and Anna flew out at him, causing him to stand transfixed and gaping as she flung herself into his arms sobbing and speaking incoherently. He held her gently in his arms caressing her tangled, mattered hair. He could feel her bones through the silk robe she was wearing. Out of the corner of his eye he saw a blur of white as he was shoved to the ground as Anna was dragged from his arms.

"Hold it; just hold it he yelled jumping to his feet. You let her go this minute or I'll hit you right in the jaw, so help me God woman or not."

But this extremely strong and very ugly woman held her ground and as Carman started toward her a voice rang out, "stop, stop Ingrid it is her husband."

Carmina's nurse rushed toward them pleading over and over, "it's her husband, it's her husband."

Realization finally struck and the very strong very ugly nurse put Anna down and gave Carman an astonishing smile that actually transformed her face to almost pleasant.

Carman put his arm around Anna and beckoned the nurse to follow. He led his wife back into her room and sat her gently on a lounge. He instructed the nurse to bathe and wash Anna's hair as he held her limp hands in his own. The vacant look in her eyes as she gazed into space caused a chill to run down his back. The nurse took Anna by the hand a led her into the bathroom. Carman called through the closed door that he would be in the study downstairs if Ingrid needed him.

As soon as he closed the door of the study, he headed for the liquor cabinet. He could not remember needing a drink this badly. After two stiff whiskeys he made himself a high ball and sat quietly on an enormous leather couch contemplating his future. No matter how he tried to rationalize his predicament it always came out the same. He was totally trapped. From now on he realized he would be staying here. Somewhere there must be someone who could help Anna. He'd just have to find the right doctor. How could he possibly leave Carmina with that poor woman he had married? Finally, the drinks took effect and he seemed to calm down. Eventually the nurse Ingrid knocked softly at the door. He asked her to come in and for two hours he listened to the almost unbelievable account of his wife's behavior.

1929

I would have thought it was impossible to walk into madness and calmly make a home there. It wasn't complex or mysterious. I just did it. At the time it seemed to be the singular course to choose. Of course naivete is no excuse for stupidity. It's the only excuse I have, and that was my undoing.

After spending four years in the army and losing my friend, you would imagine I might have gained some perception of how much I was sacrificing. I had my life but I had lost my sense of self-preservation. I should have fled. I should have gone anywhere until I regained my reasoning. I could have gotten an annulment easily. I should have saved myself. But I didn't. It seemed at the time that the ravings of a mad woman were a small price to pay for my daughter. Mentally and physically I was absolutely insensate. I still had difficulty believing I had made it back alive. I should have escaped at any cost. I know now what I should have done. It's a damn shame I didn't know it then.

1915

Carman was hardly home a week when Anna insisted they be married again in a Polish church. Why she insisted on a Polish wedding completely baffled him. It seemed to be a preposterous request. Although he was very patient with Anna he couldn't get a straight answer from her. Finally it was discovered that Anna's mother was Polish. A fact she had concealed all these years expecting reprisals from her husband and his family.

Anna got it into her head that she must set the record straight. She would marry Carman in a Polish Church where her mother should have had her nuptials.

Carman was almost convinced to go through with the second wedding until he spoke to Mama. His mother refused to go to the wedding.

When he asked her "why?" she answered that the Polish church was not catholic.

He told her she was being ridiculous. Her answer to that was she wasn't going and neither should he.

"I don't want to get excommunicated," she added.

"How can you get excommunicated if it's a Catholic Church? Please Mama, I want you to come."

"You already had a wedding. One is enough. In fact that one was too much. Carman you cannot marry that crazy one in a church, you will be stuck with her forever."

"I'm stuck with her now Mama, we have a baby remember?"

"One wedding is enough; the baby has your name. Why does she need two weddings? Listen to your Mama; if you marry her in that Polish Church you will never be free of her. Do you really believe the church will let you dissolve a marriage? Never! If you marry a crazy one it's even worse. There are people who knew how to get a marriage dissolved. A little money in the right hands and poof, you're free. But you marry a crazy one in church you're stuck for life. There is no turning back. All the money in the world can't buy your freedom. You want that huh. I don't think so. You are still too young to know. You think all of this will pass and that maniac you're married to will wake up some morning and be perfectly sane. It will never happen. She likes being crazy. She plays the game too well. Please Carman, I could not stop you from getting her pregnant, and I am proud of you for marrying her and giving your daughter a name. But once is enough. A justice of the peace is fine with the law. God only recognizes a wedding when; a priest blesses it. Let Anna hang from the chandelier if it makes her happy, but please in the name of God, don't marry her in church."

He knew his mother had spoken the truth. The church would never recognize a divorce if he married Anna in church. In spite of all his mother's pleadings, and his own determination, Anna got her way.

In point of fact he did fight a valiant war with Anna and her mother. Sadly she had best ammunition in the world, his baby daughter. The moment Carman saw her there was no turning back, whatever it took he would do it for her. His happiness was not a matter of contention.

She was the only person who filled his life with some serenity. When his dreams of the war woke him up in the middle of the night he would go to Carmina's room and sit by her crib watching her sleep. She was his only solace.

When Anna threatened to run away with the baby so that he would never see either one of them again, he was relatively unmoved. Only when Anna subtlety intimated how easy Carmina could be harmed, did he break.

The wedding plans resumed. What difference did it make how many times he married Anna? He was stuck for life. He realized how far Anna was willing to go to keep him. He never had a chance. She pulled the strings and he danced. She may have been crazy but clever enough to appreciate how important Carmina was. She knew beyond a doubt that he would never put Carmina's safety in jeopardy.

Unable to find a job, Carman was a captive in his home listening to the ravings of his wife. He was at wits end when a letter arrived from the Telephone Company asking him to appear for an interview at his earliest convenience. All he had to do was make a call and set up an appointment, which he did minutes after reading the letter. He made the appointment for the following day and set out to make the best possible impression on the interviewer. He desperately was in need of a hair cut. Consequently he went to his favorite barber, his brother. Fortunately Steve was at home and delighted to see Carman alone. It had been very difficult trying to talk to his brother in Anna's presence.

For no apparent reason, Anna appeared to be fearful of Steve. His influence over Carman frightened her. Visits to one another's home became tedious and often comedic as the brothers talked in their own dialect trying to communicate without Anna's interruptions and unreasonable interpretation of their conversation. It was generally impossible and the brothers were forced to just exchange trivialities, rather than run the risk of Anna's interruptions and probing. It was a delightful experience when Steve and Carman could speak freely.

After the usual kissing and hugging of Steve's family, the brothers went to the back porch, where the haircutting would commence.

Carman sat in the only straight back chair on the porch, which was the designated barber chair. His brother artfully draped an old tablecloth, which was the official barber cover, over Carman and waited for Carman's instructions. Which usually started, "don't take too much off."

"Ok, little brother let's have all the news. Are you going for that long awaited interview"?

"How'd you know?"

"Come on Carman you only come here for a haircut if there's a wedding or a funeral. You're not getting married again are you?" Steve asked with apprehension.

"No, thank God, the marriage has been postponed for at least a month. As you suspected, I'm going for an interview for repairman tomorrow and I desperately need your help. What exactly should I say and not say?"

"Well, at least you know the drill, first you nod your head and smile but not too much smiling you don't want them to think you're an idiot. The most important question you have to answer is your parentage."

"Verifiably, I believe I won't have a problem," Carman answered with a big smile.

"What do you mean verifiably?" Steve answered

"Well, do you remember how much trouble you had getting into the Telephone Company because we're Italian?

"Yeah, said Steve.

"When I enlisted in the Army I remembered how you had to lie, so when I filled in the birthplace of Mama and Papa I made Mama French and Papa Spanish. Now I'm a legal non-Italian."

"You didn't".

"I sure as hell did, and I have to bring my enlistment papers with me"

"Carman, I always said you were a smart ass."

"Gee thanks Steve that makes me feel good all over."

"Ok kid, how do you want your hair."

"Take off as little as possible."

"No kidding answered Steve, no kidding."

As Steve clipped Carman talked. By the end of the haircut, Steve was earnestly worried about his brother.

"What are you going to do about Anna," he asked

"There's not much I can do. I'm trying to delay the second wedding in church as long as possible. Keeping her pacified isn't easy. You have no idea what it's like living with her. If it weren't for Carmina I would have been long gone. She's more than crazy Steve, I swear she's possessed."

"Jesus Carman if she is truly possessed, maybe we can get her exorcised"

"Stop kidding Steve be serious, I'm boxed into a corner here."

"I am serious Carman, it goes on all the time in church, and you know how hysterical Italians get when they think the devil is involved."

"Ah, Steve cut it out, I need help."

"I'm serious Carman, we'll get her exorcised."

"Nothing is that simple. Anna is certainly crazy, and because she is, her sense of reality is warped. She doesn't distinguish between good and evil. Unfortunately she chooses evil most of the time. That doesn't make her possessed. I wish it did, and then I'd have something to look forward to. No, she's not possessed but she should be committed before something terrible happens. There must be something that can be done for her. There are times when she is absolutely sane. You can't imagine what it's like to watch her drift in and out of madness. But it's out of the question. Her parents would never stand for it. With their political pull I'd be the one they put in the asylum not Anna."

Steve asked, "They honestly believe the situation with Anna has improved since I've been home. I can't imagine how bad it was before.

The sight of Anna the first time I saw her was bizarre. No one would believe me. She was walking through the house raving. She hadn't bathed or changed her clothes for weeks. Her nurses were content to just appease her. They seemed to be frightened by her. They were being paid extremely well for doing absolutely nothing. All of that has changed since I came home. They keep her scrupulously clean and busy all day now. With me here they're more afraid of losing their jobs than Anna. My father-in-law keeps my bank account full for all her expenses.

He's very generous. But I can't spend his money on myself. I need this job at the Telephone Company, to get away from the house and to feel like a man again. No matter how imperfect my life is now, I'm the one who made Anna pregnant and I'm the one who married her."

"No you're not, how do you know you're Carmina's father. If Anna slept with you, she probably also slept with Guardo. She was engaged to him remember? It could be his child not yours."

"Steve, that little girl looks just like me," said Carman emphatically.

"Yeah, did you ever notice how much you and Guardo resemble one another. I'm not kidding Carman I never thought you were Carmina's father. I just thought that you were really in love with Anna and let it go at that. Now I positively wonder."

"Steve, it doesn't make any difference now. I love that little girl and I know in my heart that she is mine. Besides, I couldn't prove otherwise. Come on let's have a beer and enjoy the sunset. You've got the best view in town. The two brothers sat watching the beautiful sunset and drank their beer. They were too weary from talk to come up with any solutions. Content to be with each other, they enjoyed the wonders of the universe seen from Steve's porch in the back of a little house in the Bronx.

Chapter Fourteen

No one could doubt that the young man waiting to be interviewed was qualified for the job, whatever it was. He was tall, well dressed and handsome. If his interview had been conducted by a woman he would have been a shoo-in but as luck would have it the interview was conducted by a man. As it turned out the gentleman who finally had the authority to hire him was very impressed by the young man's war record and was willing to accept his unusual parentage even though he was convinced that he was hiring an Italian. Thus, Carman got the job right on the spot and was to report for work the very next day.

No one could have been happier. He danced down the street to the consternation of busy office workers on their lunch hour. Positively nothing could break his spirit. His first stop was at his mother's and as soon as she opened the door he picked her up and danced her around the house.

"Carman please, are you crazy, put me down," she squealed?

"Not today Mama, today I keep you up in the air until you cry Uncle."

"What are you, really patz? What is this Uncle business? Carman I'm gonna give you such a shot that your head will fly off," she yelled.

"No you won't Mama," he said laughingly as he put her down, "I just got a wonderful job at the Telephone Company, and tonight you and me celebrate. Tonight, we go to Guardo's for dinner, what do you say."

"I say sure," his mother answered giggling. "Tonight I put on my good dress.

And, we go. Me and my son are going out to celebrate."

"You bet Mama, tonight we celebrate."

After much hugging and kissing and laughing Mrs. Juanna Duva and her son Carman went out to dinner. It was the first time and not a soul could tell which one was the proudest, the mother or the son.

1929

Carman sat sleeping in his chair. His mind was at peace for a little while away from the memories that had led him to this night. His mother looked in on him and covered him with an afghan. The wind was still howling outside, and the snow continued to fall.

When would this night end, thought Mama? Sleep would not come to her knowing what her son had planned for tomorrow. There was no way to stop him. What had happened to the happy days when life was simple and her children content? Since Papa died her whole world seemed to fall apart.

Her sweet Dominica was trapped in a marriage of mutual hate and mistrust. Anthony's poor wife was always sick with some ailment or another. God bless him, he never complains, he prays. Seemingly, Anthony had grown closer to God with every adversity that befell him. Who knows why? He must be a saint. Well at least Anthony is content with his lot in life. Ah, but Carman is making a terrible mistake. What can he be thinking? Maybe he'll sleep, at least for a little while.

It seems like only yesterday that he took me out to celebrate his new job at the Telephone Company. That was a wonderful night. I remember we went to Guardo's for dinner. I was so proud of my young son and yet concerned for him married to that poor Anna. Everything else seemed to be working out for him. I remember how shocked Carman was when he saw the inside of Guardo's restaurant. It had been completely renovated since he last entered its doors.

Guardo welcomed them with open arms, lifting Mama in the air making her squeal with joy. Admittedly, Guardo had been devastated when Anna married Carman. He was in love with her and believed that she loved him. They had been engaged for almost a year. He presumed he was the father of her baby. He was amazed that Anna married Carman and not him. Now, Anna was in and out of a mental hospital and Guardo considered himself lucky and sincerely felt sorry for Carman. He himself hadn't done too badly. He married the owner of the butcher shop's daughter, Angelina, and to his amazement found himself very happy. True, she was not as beautiful as Anna but she had a level head on her shoulders and adored Guardo. He was a contented man and he owed it all to Carman.

One of the first things Carman did when he returned home was to search out Guardo and explain to him why he married Anna. Guardo held him off saying, "not to worry Carman, it all worked out."

For Guardo it certainly did. His father-in-law was a wealthy man and was more than generous to his daughter and her husband.

Carman could not extinguish the guilt he still felt. Given the circumstances he had no choice. Because Guardo knew Anna so well, he never really blamed Carman. He refused to give Carman a check that night. Mama reasoned that free food and wine for the rest of Carman's life would be a small price to pay to be free of Anna.

1929

Carman woke with a start, "Mama what are you doing up? It's three o'clock in the morning; you've got to look good tomorrow."

"Don't worry about me Carman, why don't you go to bed? Sitting up all night isn't going to change things, come on, go to bed,"

"I can't Mama," Carman sighed, "I'm looking for an answer and reviewing one's life can't hurt. Who knows, maybe I'll come up with something. It's not necessary for you to stay up all night too. I'll need someone alert tomorrow morning. Maybe you can dig out my car from the snow, huh, what do you say?"

"Carman I say goodnight, that's what I say. Please try to get some sleep."

"I will Mama I will."

But he couldn't stop remembering.

When Carman finally got home from his dinner with Mama, Anna was asleep and he was grateful. He never knew how Anna would react to anything. His new job could make her ecstatic or grossly morose and he was just too exhausted to cope tonight. After checking that Carmina was sound asleep, he crept silently into bed and set his alarm clock for his first days' work since leaving the Army. He was content, certain that things would get better since they couldn't possibly get worse.

Suddenly the alarm went off and Carman jumped up with a start, knocking over the lamp with a loud crash.

"What a way to get up" he said straightening out the lamp as he headed for the shower which he had installed his first week home. It wasn't until he came out of the shower that he realized Anna was not in bed. This was not a good sign.

"Where the hell is she," he murmured.

"Anna," he called, as he hurried along the hall. He looked in on Carmina and she was fast asleep. He carefully closed her door not wanting to wake her. It was barely six o'clock. "Where was that woman? Anna where the hell are you?"

Giving up his search he went back to the bedroom, and hastily dressed. After making a thorough search of the top floor, he ran down the stairs and searched every room, but Anna was no where to be found. As he neared the kitchen he could smell coffee perking, and he heart stopped racing. "She must be in the kitchen." When he opened the door, the kitchen was empty and the coffee was boiling over. Carman turned off the coffee, wiped up the mess and poured himself a cup.

"Where the hell is she, he again murmured and walked over to the window. There in the garden was Anna, happily cutting roses from her precious bushes. That she was still in her nightgown, and barefoot, prompted Carman to go out and get her.

"Come on honey" he coaxed, urging her into the house. She came willingly and he carefully removed the roses from her hands and sat her down putting his jacket around her shoulders to warm her. He made her a cup of sweet coffee and persuaded her to drink. She seemed to come out of her reverie and was startled to find herself in the kitchen, drinking coffee with her husband.

"Carman," she whispered, "how did I get here?"

She looked so frightened and desolate that Carman decided to make it as reasonable as possible. He told her that she obviously got up to make him coffee for his first days' work and decided to cut some roses for the table as the coffee was being brewed.

"Oh," Anna replied happy that there was an explanation for her being there because the last thing she could remember was going to bed last night. As she sipped her coffee she looked up at Carman suspiciously and asked, "What work?"

"Why, my new job at the Telephone Company. You remember I went there yesterday."

"But I didn't know you got the job. You came home after I went to bed last night."

"It doesn't matter Anna, I got the job and tonight we'll celebrate. I'll tell you all about it tonight when I come home."

"Ok, Carman, we'll celebrate. That sounds good. I'll tell the cook to make your favorite macaroni," and Anna walked away happy as a lark.

"Whew, that was close. I thought for a minute she would have one of her episodes and I would have to restrain her and call the doctor. Actually this was much easier. It doesn't take much, just a little imagination and I can keep her on an even keel. Not bad Carman. He went whistling out the door to his new job at the Telephone Company.

Carman reported to the repairman's division as he had been told the previous day. He was a little apprehensive and then realized how ridiculous it was to be anxious; after all, he just fought a war. There was nothing on this earth that could ever scare him again after that. He took a deep breath and walked in. His head high his step firm and ready for any eventuality. What he saw first were several men drinking coffee, obviously waiting for someone or something. That someone or something entered from a side door and all conversation stopped. You could hear a pin drop as the men seemed to stand at attention. It was then that he saw the reason for this kind of response. Although the man who entered was of average weight and height he had an air about him that was all business and no shenanigans.

"Ok men step up and get your assignments. Any new men stand back and wait until I've given out the work orders for today." In a matter of minutes he had handed out work schedules to every man there except Carman.

"Ok Pat you stay back a minute. I'm going to have a new recruit for you.

"I guess your name is Charles Duval, right."

"Yes sir," said Carman a little shocked at his new name. God bless the army for changing my name.

"Ok, young man I'm going to hand you over to Pat McGinty. He'll teach you the ropes. You pay very close attention to this man; he's one of the best."

Carman stuck out his hand to shake Pat's and was pleased to see a big grin on the guys' face.

"That's a good sign, "thought Carman.

"Come on Charlie, I'll teach you everything I know and then some. So you were in the Cavalry they tell me."

Carman nodded yes.

"Well meself was a foot soldier, and I'm dying to find out how the hell you got to ride a horse. Me feet will never be the same. I swear boy I must have walked 5,000 miles before I got of the army. Did you have coffee now?

Carman nodded no.

"No, we'll get you a cup and then we'll be off to fix all the broken wires and telephones in New York City. How does that sound Boy?"

"It sounds fine" laughed Carman charmed by a brogue you could cut with a knife.

After his first day's work Carman came home full of stories and just aching to tell someone. It was a positively fascinating day and who would believe a character like Pat McGinty. No one would believe the name, never mind the man. Just the way Pat said "I" talian was enough to send Carman or as he was now known, as Charlie into hysterics. In his neighborhood no one would believe this guy. What a day, what a great day!

When he got home it was quiet and no one was around except the governess who informed him that Anna took Carmina to her mother's house and was staying the night. Dinner was waiting for him in the kitchen if he intended to stay home.

Wearily he walked to the kitchen; sorry for once that Anna wasn't around to listen to his stories. Sometimes she would react and ask reasonable questions. They would even on occasion laugh together. These times were rare and Carman treasured them. They gave him hope that Anna would someday get well. Unfortunately, she generally stared at him completely oblivious to what was happening around her. He preferred that state to the histrionics she would often display screaming, ranting and sometimes actually hurting herself and anyone near her. That was what Carman feared most. It was at these times that he had to force himself not run away but to stay and handle the situation. Anna would only react to him. No one else could calm her at least long enough for the doctor to arrive and give her a sedative. Sighing he walked to the kitchen thinking at least I'm assured some peace and even a goodnight's sleep.

He was shocked to see Madelyn waiting to serve him in the kitchen. He had almost forgotten that she worked here. Life at home was so chaotic that it was unusual for their paths to cross. She was a sight for sore eyes standing over the stove stirring whatever.

"Madelyn, you're just the person I need to talk to tonight. How are you?"

Turning to answer Carman her face lit up with delight. Although Carman rarely saw her, Madelyn was keenly aware of Carman whenever he was in the house and watched him whenever she could without being detected.

"And what exactly did you want to talk about," she answered laughing softly.

"My God Madelyn, just the sound of your laughter makes me feel better."

"Well that's good," she answered, "now come and sit down to your dinner and I'll be happy to listen to whatever you have to say."

Carman sat and ate and talked and talked, telling Madelyn all about the famous Pat McGinty who Madelyn just happened to know, being Irish too, and living in the same Irish neighborhood. It seemed that Pat McGinty was a legend in his own time. Time just flew by while Carman talked and Madelyn cleaned up the kitchen and listened closely to his stories.

"Come sit down with me Madelyn; at least have a cup of coffee with me"

Madelyn set two cups of coffee down and sat and listened and prayed he'd never stop talking. But then he did, and Madelyn calmly got up from her chair and sat on Carman's lap and kissed him tenderly.

"Madelyn," he whispered hoarsely.

"Just kiss me Carman," she calmly replied.

And he did, over and over again. On her lips, on her neck and finally opening her blouse and tenderly kissed her breasts. He was overwhelmed with a passion he had not experienced for a very long time. Madelyn clung to him longingly, whispering his name over and over again.

"Come, come with me," she murmured as she led him up the backstairs to her tiny room that was just big enough for a small bed and a table. It was all they needed.

Slowly he undressed her, caressing and kissing each part of her body he exposed until she begged him to take her. He entered her slowly fearing his passion would overtake him. He began to move, tantalizing her with his deliberate unhurried movement, trying to savor the exquisite feelings bursting through his body.

"Faster, faster," she cried.

Unable to hold back any longer, Carman complied, and the earth moved.

They lay exhausted locked in each other's arms and drifted off to sleep. Carman awoke first, startled to find himself still wrapped around Madelyn. Unwilling to break the bond between them he steeled himself and gently disentangled his body from hers. It was several minutes before he could muster enough reserve to dress and leave.

This was what should have been happening with Anna, not the frenzied groping or the madness that engulfed him as he made love to her. This simple quiet ecstasy of rejoicing in the bliss of one another that happened with Madelyn filled his heart. Accustomed to living with Anna in mutual hostility had warped his soul. It had been a long time since he felt rapture and it filled him with loss and sadness at what his life had become. He doubted his feeling for Madelyn was love. Instead, he felt fondness and unmistakable gratitude. He was thankful to Madelyn for reminding him of what could be, not a replacement of what was. Carman was bound to Anna because of their little daughter. He had just forgotten how sweet life could feel. He looked tenderly at Madelyn as she lay sleeping and he bent and kissed her cheek, careful not to wake her. Silently he left her tiny room and crept down the stairs to his own room. As he approached his room he had the uncomfortable feeling that someone was watching him. He turned suddenly, but saw no one. Chalking the feeling up to the guilt he was feeling, he opened the door to an empty room and fell on his bed fully dressed and slept blissfully.

1929

That first encounter with Madelyn after I married was the first happiness I had, aside from Carmina, since I had come home from the Army. What a romantic fool I was, thought Carman, as he tried in vain to make some sense out of what was going to happen tomorrow. It was probably the biggest turning point in my life and I didn't even know it then. Madelyn, how well I remember her. She gave me her love so freely and I just used her to give my life some meaning. I don't even remember feeling guilty except for the first time. I should have, but it was such a delightful interlude in a morbid uneventful existence. How well I remember.

The next morning Carman awoke to the sound of quiet snoring. He was amazed to see Anna asleep at his side. "My God, when did she come home? I never heard her. It must have been early this morning. Talk about close calls; imagine if I had stayed the night with Madelyn. God help me, I'd probably be a dead man now. He knew he was right; Anna would kill him if she caught him in bed with Madelyn. No regrets, no second thoughts, action was Anna's mainstay. She would have picked up anything in her reach and crowned him with it. Carman knew he should take his little adventure more seriously but he just couldn't. Living with Anna had made the outrageous ordinary, the ordinary mundane. He wasn't nervous or in the least bit scared although he did consider what would happen to Madelyn hoping she was as fast on her feet as he had become.

Luckily, the entire household was ignorant of the bizarre behavior that transpired in their bedroom. He was eternally grateful for the thick walls that provided privacy for some of Anna's knocked down, dragged out fights with him. Especially when he avoided, as best he could, the barrage of missiles aimed at his head. Her behavior was not determined by anything substantial. She would "lose it" for no apparent reason. Imagine, thought Carman, if she had a reason.

Ultimately he calmed her down without getting injured. To his credit, he never laid a hand on Anna no matter how maniacal she became.

Carman headed for the shower, determined to abandon this train of thought, at least for the time being and get to work. His new job and Pat McGinty pervaded his thoughts. It was time to get back to the real world.

Carman avoided Madelyn as much as possible after their one glorious evening together. Unfortunately, his new job was more physical than he expected. Climbing poles was exhausting work. Not exactly what he had in mind but the mastery of this undertaking brought him pleasure. In a small space of time he was able to climb with the best of them and his body reflected the added exercise. He was at his physical peak. Woefully it took a lot of energy to keep up the pace that was expected of him. As a result, every evening he returned home ate dinner and went directly to bed. There was no time or desire to repeat his rendezvous with Madelyn. Incredibly, during this time Anna behaved in a remarkable manner and was responsible for his home life being reasonably carefree. She seemed to understand that all of his energies were spent at work and he could not withstand any outbursts. Unusually tranquil, Anna provided a haven for Carman to recoup. He was too exhausted to realize her transformation.

It wasn't long before Carman's body became accustomed to the added stress of his very physical job. Unhappily, as exhaustion left his body, desire returned. He refused to give into his feelings and lose the harmony that lay over his home with Anna, and so he overcame his feelings. Anna sensed his need and became a willing partner. Carman could not believe what was happening. His wife became a loving woman, his home was filled with peace and most important his little girl was laughing and was happy.

Was it possible Anna was miraculously cured? He prayed it was true. As time passed it seemed that his prayers were answered.

Both Carman and Carmina reveled in Anna's lucidity. Carman literally danced on air and life was sweet. He could not believe what had happened. He told everyone within hearing distance how happy he was.

His mother laughed and danced with him when he came to visit, sharing his joy. Although she suspected the reason for Anna's change, she didn't have the heart to tell her son. She prayed fervently that Anna's transformation would endure. Sadly, the Lord had other plans. The reason for Anna miraculous recovery became evident, as she was pregnant with her second child. Carman had not been a witness to her behavior at the time she carried Carmina and refused to believe that she would revert back to madness after the baby was born, as she did with the arrival of Carmina. They were, for once, truly a happy little family. Her parents were elated at Anna's transformation and became frequent visitors, hoping that this time her recovery would last. The little family went to Mama's for a family dinner with Steve and his large brood of children. Dominica and her reticent husband also joined in the festivities to the delight of the entire family.

Carman was convinced that this transformation of Anna's would beyond doubt, last. He went to see Father Paul to tell him of Anna's metamorphosis. As usual his friend and priest tried to share in Carman's delight but he was skeptical. Aware of Anna's schizophrenia this phenomenon of wellness during pregnancy was unknown to him. As gently as possible he cautioned Carman not to take this transformation too seriously but to enjoy it for what it was a respite. Father Paul knew his words were falling on deaf ears as he appealed to Carman's common sense.

Ultimately Carman seemingly acquiesced. It was so hard to face the reality of his situation. Try as he might, he could not give up all hope. The priest hugged his young friend and begged him to return if things took a bad turn. Carman left with some of his joy diminished, unable to believe that Anna could relapse to her old self.

That evening Anna sought Carman out for a quiet talk. No one had considered what was happening to her. Her mind, which was usually filled with delusion distortions and paranoia, was absolutely clear. Taking his hand she led him into the sitting room and sat down across from him so that she could look directly into his face. She spoke in a whisper as her tears spilled down her cheeks. "I cannot believe how happy I have been feeling. My mind is so clear I can not believe it. I lie in wait for my demons to return and wreck havoc. Do you have any idea of my torment? The madness takes hold of me, and I am lost. Please Carman hold me tight and don't let it come again."

Taking her in his arms Carman told her that he never loved anyone the way he loved her now. "Now you are the real Anna and I will fight to keep you. I cannot bear to think of life without you, now that I have really found you. You hold on, my darling. You are holding on not only for me but also for Carmina. The three of us will fight these demons together and we will win. We cannot lose you again."

Tears were running down both their cheeks as they held each other as if the world was coming to an end, and it was. Two weeks later Anna lost the baby. Her behavior became so bizarre that Carman was forced to put her away in a sanitarium where all of their dreams died.

1929

Carman sat remembering, fresh tears ran down his face. How could he do what he planned tomorrow, how? Remnants of that wonderful time with Anna still invaded his heart. How could his life have taken such a turn? Would it have changed the universe to let Anna have her sanity?

"Why God, why?" he cried silently into the night.

When Anna did come home it was a complete stranger who entered their home. Gone were the loving and happy wife and mother. Gone too, was the mad woman who walked the halls searching for her lost mind. In place Anna, a small thin pale woman with empty eyes walked into their home. Carman gently took her to her room and put her carefully to bed, as she seemed utterly exhausted. Whatever they had done in the hospital to "cure" her had left her bereft of memory and emotion. She fell asleep almost immediately without a word. Carman bent and kissed her gently and promised the sleeping figure that he would never desert her but would care for her forever. The memory of their few months of happiness was hard to forget.

Carman filled his life with work and managed to become a Director in the Telephone Company. His only fear was that his little girl Carmina would inherit his wife's madness. He watched her carefully for any sign.

"Daddy, why do you look at me so hard all the time?" Carmina complained.

"It's only because Daddy loves you so much my little one, only because I love you so much," he would answer.

Carmina was not at all disturbed by her mother's strange irrational behavior, but would hold her hand and walk her around the house or take her out to the garden where they would sit. Anna would sometimes talk to the child kindly, asking about her welfare and constantly begging the little girl to forgive her. Carmina would always say, "For what Mama, because you are sick, I know that you love me, and I love you Mama no matter how silly you are sometimes."

At this Anna would always laugh and say, "I am silly sometimes aren't I?"

"Yes you are Mama, but Daddy says that's allowed."

"Does he now" said Anna, "it's allowed. That's good to know." She would sit humming holding her little girl's hand wondering where the hell she was.

Carman would often take Anna for a drive in the car, which she particularly seemed to enjoy. Sometimes Carmina would join them and sometimes even his mother would come along. They would ride up to

Kensico Dam and Carman would be sure to hit all the bumps in the road if Carmina was along, just to hear her shouts of joy. It takes very little to keep a man content, as long as he doesn't ask for much and Carman didn't. As long a Carmina laughed, and his poor demented wife hummed happily on their sojourns on a Sunday afternoon, he was content. Life seemed to go on smoothly without interruption. Carman grew withdrawn from friends and family and concentrated on keeping Anna and Carmina content. He had almost forgotten how wonderful physical love was and refused to ever think in those terms in fear that he would be unfaithful to Anna. He could not forget his promise to her. Even though the woman to whom he made those promises was never going to be seen again, he was in constant fear of betraying her.

Sometimes even the best of intentions are abandoned. After leaving his employ to get married, Madelyn had returned. Although truthfully, Carman had never loved Madelyn, he certainly loved making love to her. Catching glimpses of her as she went about her duties was very disquieting. He tried to avoid seeing her but found himself restless and uneasy just knowing she was in the house.

He could not remember the last time he made love and knew that this was undeniably his problem. One evening as he sat in his living room reading the paper and smoking a cigar, visions of Madelyn completely invaded his peace.

"I need a woman," he thought "but where do you get one?" It had been a long time since he had ventured out into the seamy side of life. He didn't have a clue where to find one. Without hesitation he called Marty. Although he rarely saw his old friends he always stayed in touch with Marty. Awkwardly he tried to ask his friend if he knew where he could pay for a woman. When his friend finally realized what Carman was looking for he almost choked from laughter and had to hang up the phone. It wasn't long before he stood outside of Carman's door and knocked. When Carman came to the door he hugged his friend and the two of them shared their laughter. Together they tried to figure out how to get Carman "fixed up". Unfortunately, whenever either of them came up with a plan the other started howling. After a few drinks the friends settled down to talk of life and Carman, for the moment, forgot his need.

When Marty left, Carman felt embarrassed. I'm fine, he thought. I'm really Ok. I'm just a little tense that's all. Slowly he started up the stairs to his bedroom. It had been a long time since he shared a room with Anna. It was lonely sleeping alone. No matter, he thought, I'm almost twenty-eight. Soon I'll be middle aged. I should get some exercise. That sounds good. Talking silently to himself he never noticed the pretty woman smiling at him as he neared his room.

"Carman, what in the world are you thinking? You look so sad. Is there anything I can do for you," asked Madelyn?

"You startled me, I didn't see you there," he answered.

"Gee, Carman I'm sorry, you just look so mournful," she answered with a smile playing on her lips.

"How are you Madelyn, it's been a long time."

"Good Carman, I'm good. We're just having a few problems at home and I thought I might as well make some money instead of fighting all the time with my husband. I can stay out of his way and think things out and make a little money too. And that's about the whole story," she answered.

"Sound's sensible to me. If you need any help, let me know," he answered earnestly.

"To be honest Carman, I was wondering if you wouldn't mind if I...." She never finished her sentence but moved so close to Carman that her lips were almost touching his. She put her arms around his neck and pressed her body against him. Their lips met and Carman lost all will. He took her hand and led her to his room, undressing her on their way. With all his reserve he held back his need and undressed her gently, revealing her still lovely body. Without any hesitation she pulled him to her and gave herself willingly to him. Almost frantic at first, their lovemaking became more composed, almost rhythmic. They had forgotten how in tune they were with one another. It had been a long time for both of them.

In the days and nights that followed, Carman's guilt was replaced by a peace he had long forgotten. Madelyn and he never feigned love. They just satisfied one another's need. Eventually Madelyn left again and went home to her husband who she really loved. It was a shame, she thought, that the man she loved could never make love the way Carman did. She was a pragmatic woman and content with her lot in life.

Carman, on the other hand, was lost without her. He decided that he was after all, not quite old enough to give up sex entirely. In fact after Madelyn, he wondered if he would ever get sex again. Blessed with good looks and a charming personality, once he gave up his guilt, it was easy for him to find romance. Careful not to get emotionally involved, Carman never failed to inform his current inamorato of his wife and child. It was rare that a woman would make any demands of him. To his surprise, ordinarily, they did not want or expect anything more than a one-night stand

It wasn't long before Carman stopped his gallivanting. His roving days were short lived. Guilt reared its ugly head again and his conscience forced him to stop his roving and come home at night. Just about a week after he decided to be more prudent, Anna entered his bedroom and announced, "Welcome home, Carman" and left abruptly slamming the door. He could not believe that Anna had been aware of his indiscretions and sat with his mouth open gazing at the closed bedroom door.

Chapter Fifteen

Days and months ran one into the other. Except for visiting with his family at his mother's Sunday dinners, life was uneventful. Although not serene it was at least comfortable. The only thing that constantly played on his mind was his fear that Carmina would inherit her mother's sickness. Unknown to anyone he took Carmina to various children's doctors and was invariably told that symptoms usually appeared after eighteen years of age. Carman couldn't wait for that first fateful sign. A cure was unheard of and if Carmina was indeed cursed with her mother's illness, nothing could be done to stop it. He was told that not everyone manifests the same caliber of disturbance and that in some cases the sickness is never recognized or given a name because the manifestations are so slight. Except for an occasional lack of composure some patients actually lead relatively normal lives. Carman was constantly looking for Carmina to exhibit bizarre behavior, confused thought and chaotic speech. In his own mind these were the big three signs of schizophrenia.

The more Carman learned, the more he wanted to know. You could find him on any given Saturday afternoon in the library reading everything he could get his hands on about schizophrenia. He became somewhat of an expert, but to no avail Carmina was only ten years old and seemed to be a perfectly happy child who unfortunately had a very sick mother.

As she got older she became even more beautiful. She resembled neither Carman's family, nor Anna's. Carmina had the most beautiful blond curly hair and lovely dark green eyes. Both families were dark eyed and had either brown or black hair.

"Someone way back in the family must have come from the north of Italy perhaps even Switzerland," Mama would say whenever Carman brought up the subject of Carmina rare coloring.

"Mama please, who do you know in the family came from Switzerland", was Carman's familiar reply.

"Ah, I know a lot of people who came from Switzerland," Mama would say and than abruptly change the subject, for she did know someone who came from Switzerland who shared Carmina's unusual coloring. She was someone in fact who looked remarkably like her little Carmina when she was a girl. But Mama was not about to cast dispersions on her Carmina's heritage. She loved the little girl much too much. Anyway, Carmina was her granddaughter and that was that. Besides, only Mama had the long memory of her little friend with the beautiful blond hair and green eyes.

The economy in America was on the verge of bankruptcy. The stock market crashed and it seemed as though everyone in the neighborhood was looking for work. Carman had always taken care of his mother financially because his expenses at home were minimal. Anna's father made sure that his daughter and his grand daughter were financially independent. In advance of Wall Streets collapse, Anna's father had withdrawn all of his cash and converted all his holdings to gold. Carman, on the other hand, had no such holdings but managed to live from payday to payday with ease.

With all the time in the world on his hands he finally graduated from college. He was now working as an engineer and his salary kept him and his mother, and sometimes his sister and his friend Marty, off the bread lines. Fortunately, the Telephone Company didn't fold. Carman and his brother Steve were safe from the soup kitchens that were cropping up everywhere. Occasionally Carman was called on at work to again man the power lines and he would find himself hanging from a pole again. To his delight, he found contentment out in the field. Sometimes he even made repair calls. This was a new extraordinary experience for him. He had never been a repairman, but it seemed to agree with him. He found himself looking forward to being out of the office and would volunteer for any outside work. Times were hard for everyone in the neighborhood and sharing what you had with family, friends and neighbors was common. In was well known in the neighborhood that a free meal could always be had at the Duva's house.

Steve, Marty and Carman went to the closing of Guardo's Restaurant. No one in the neighborhood could afford a meal or even a meatball sandwich out so the old hangout was closing. The three friends sat at a back table and were joined by Guardo for a last farewell. All the animosity that had stood between Guardo and Carman had disappeared years before. Guardo secretly thanked God that he had not, after all, married Anna. Although not as beautiful as Anna, Guardo's wife could certainly make gorgeous children. Look at his Rosa, she was a beautiful child. Of course you could not deny those green eyes came from his mother, but the jet-black hair was his wife's. These thoughts were racing through Guardo's head as they tried to finish as much wine as possible. They laughed and drank and ate, not wanting the evening to end.

Carman looked up to see a vaguely familiar face smiling down at him. It was Guardo's mother Grace. He hadn't seen Guardo's mother in years.

"Eat and drink everyone for tomorrow my Guardo starts his new job in the Telephone Company," she exclaimed drinking a toast to her son. Everyone applauded, happy that there would be no bread lines for this family.

"Mama" asked Guardo, "what are you doing here at such an hour?"

"I came to see if you were alright Guardo, it's very late and your wife sent me to help you lock up. Come my son, it is time to go home."

Reluctantly, Carman, Steve and Marty left Guardo and his mother to close the restaurant for the last time.

As usual, Steve was sober and managed to get Marty and Carman home safely.

"I don't know how you do it Steve, you never get smashed," said Carman as he held his on to his brother for dear life.

"I can't explain it Carman, I drink like a fish and never get drunk," he replied.

"Steve, I may not be making too much sense but when was the last time you saw Guardo's mother?"

"Not since I was a little kid" replied Steve adding, "I remember her having the most beautiful blond hair just like our little Carmina. I never forgot it. I remember having a crush on her too."

"Get out of here. You had a crush on Guardo's mother, give me a break," said Carman.

"Hey remember I'm older than you are. I wasn't that young when she and Mama were friends. I didn't even know she was married until she brought Guardo over to play with you. It was then that I realized how much older she was. She certainly was a beautiful girl."

"Well, I can't get it out of my head. I get the feeling that I know her well," Carman said as he laid his head on his brother's shoulder.

"Don't worry about it Carman, it will all work out tomorrow."

"Ok Steve, tomorrow," said Carman as Steve half carried his brother home.

Very early the next morning Carman woke up with a start and ran into Carmina's bedroom waking her.

"What is it Daddy you frightened me," cried the little girl rubbing her eyes.

"Nothing Carmina, nothing, Daddy just had a bad dream. Go back to sleep. It was only a dream," Carman said as he stumbled out of his daughter's bedroom. It was only a bad dream. But in his heart he knew it wasn't a dream. But he couldn't think about it now. Not now, not ever if he could escape it, not ever

Inexplicably Anna turned on Carman. Gone was the peace that kept Carman at home and willing to give up any semblance of a normal life. Now at every encounter with Anna she would physically attack him and call him outlandish names. There was no definable reason for the outbursts. Carman tried reasoning with her, but he could not reach her. Her doctors were at a loss to explain why the sudden change. The only one who was able to calm her was Carmina, but how long could a little girl put up with the madness. Although Anna's doctors changed and substituted her medication, her symptoms worsened. The sight of Carman inflamed her so that he often arrived at work bruised and battered by the countless articles she would hurl at him if he came into her view. Finally it was decided that for all concerned, Anna should be put in a sanitarium to calm her and perhaps stop her violent episodes.

Carman realized after finding his little girl clinging to her mother and crying softly, how upset Carmina was at the thought of her mother leaving. Reluctantly he decided to move in with Mama for a little while hoping Anna would change. Believing she would in time rid herself of the animosity she felt toward him, he unwilling left promising Carmina he would see her every day.

"But Papa," cried Carmina when she saw her father leaving, "I don't want you to go away either."

"I don't want to leave you baby, but it's the only way. If you come with me your Mama will be inconsolable. It will only be for a short time. You'll see Mama will get better and I will come home."

Although Carmina was not convinced, she promised to give it a try and wait for Carman to come home to stay. Carman could not imagine a day without seeing Carmina she was his entire life. He didn't know how long he could live away from her. Hopefully, Anna would come around and he could go home in a few weeks.

After four years in the Cavalry and the seven years with Anna it was strange to find himself in his old room. He didn't remember the room being so large, but then he had always shared his room with someone else. If not with his brother Steve it would be some relative who needed a place to stay. Occasionally, a complete stranger shared the room with Carman and his brother. Those were the days when Papa wasn't working and Mama would fill up the house with boarders. There were times she would have a boarder sleeping in the kitchen.

Looking around the room Carman decided it wasn't bad at all. He could smell Mama's cooking and hear her singing softly and the feeling of being home was good. In fact this was probably the first time he felt completely at peace since he joined the Army. He lay back on the bed and nestled on the lightly starched pillows and smelled the scents of home. Not bad not bad at all, and with a deep sigh he fell into a dreamless sleep. He woke up to Mama's soft call, washed his face and headed in the direction of those delicious aromas coming from the kitchen.

Within a week, it was as if Carman had never left home. The only change was not having to answer to his parents for late hours or missed meals. Ordinarily he was too tired to go out after supper. It was his mother's cooking that kept him coming home every night. He actually gained a few pounds. He looked better than ever and except for missing Carmina he was relatively content. After a months absence from Anna he attempted to see her but her hostility was indisputable. Anna's doctors asked him to be patient that this condition could not go on forever. If the truth were known he wasn't in any hurry to get back to Anna. He was relieved of the burden of her schizophrenia and was at last, finding himself. Eventually he started to go out and play cards with his friends and occasionally had dinner with Marty or Steve.

His work became so diversified he hardly knew what to wear to work, so he took to leaving work cloths in his locker when called upon for outside pole climbing or his favorite, house calls for telephone repair. Before long without any thought he asked a female co-worker out to dinner. She was a nice girl in no hurry to form any permanent relationship. She was someone to share a meal and some harmless conversation. His intentions were completely innocent. On occasion he would ask some attractive woman he met, while repairing phone lines, out dancing. He had only one criteria, that the female companion not be Italian and definitely not be interested in him for any reason but pure unadulterated fun. He was convinced that Italian girls wanted only one thing and that was marriage. They seemed to him to be more serious minded than the occasional Irish girl he dated, who really enjoyed a good time with no strings attached. He refused to get involved with an Italian girl, for that to him meant trouble. They always insisted on you meeting their parents and picking them up at home. Right away there were strings attached. He never mentioned to any of his dates, that he had a wife and child. He felt it was unnecessary. After all he had no intention of getting involved with anyone. It was all for fun and games and life, was sweet again. His promise to see Carmina never wavered but he became reluctant to try and reach Anna. The freedom he now possessed would be difficult to surrender if and when Anna got better.

During this time Carmen was faced with the truth about his little girl.

One evening he came home late to find Mama sitting at the kitchen table looking at her treasured box of pictures of when she was a girl. Some of them were tintypes, where the picture was made on an iron plate. Amazingly these pictures were more lifelike and fade resistant than the new heavy paper ones. You couldn't tear one if you tried.

Mama had one of her tintypes in her hand gazing at it so intently that she didn't hear Carman come in. Seeing him she literally jumped out of her seat.

"Mama, what have you got there an old picture of a boy friend, let me see," he said laughingly as he playfully snatched the picture from her grasp.

"Please Carman give me the picture," she begged.

"Mama, please one little look" he said as he quickly glanced at the ancient picture. Taking a closer look he said, "come on Mama its not even a man, it's a picture of a little girl."

Carman lifted his eyes in disbelief and said, "Who is this girl Mama."

"Some girl I knew as a child, come on give it back to me and I can put it away" she said reaching for the picture.

"What girl Mama, what was her name".

"Hey Carman it was so long ago, I can't remember, you want a nice cup of coffee," she said trying to distract him?

"What was her name Mama," Carman insisted?

"Let me see," said Mama as she supposedly searched her memory, "I think her name was

Gracie yes Gracie Gasperino."

"And who did she marry Mama, who did Gracie marry," he asked although afraid to hear the answer?

"Well Carman that's a long story - Gracie was married very young and her poor husband died a few years later of consumption. After that she was so broken hearted she went home to live with her parents."

"Ok Mama, did she ever marry again?

"Well Carman after a lot of years she married again."

"And who did she marry the second time".

"Well Carman, I think it was," and here she whispered so softly that Carman had to bend his head to hear her words.

"I can't hear what your saying Mama, who?"

Reluctantly she said the words "Guardo's Papa."

"Holy Christ Mama."

"Please Carman do not curse Jesus."

"Oh Mama please, you've known all along haven't you," he whispered as the tintype shook visibly in his hand?

"No Carman, I don't even know now. What are you talking about? You mean you never heard of people looking like other people, who weren't from their own family? It happens all the time. You think your Mama looks like her Mama or her Papa? NO, I look like nobody, so what's the problem, you gonna make yourself crazy because of an old picture?"

"Mama, look at this picture, you would swear that my Carmina posed for it," he said putting the picture right in front of her eyes.

"There is a slight resemblance," she whispered pushing the picture away," but nothing extraordinary. What is the problem? Carmina slightly resembles Guardo's mother when she was a little girl. So I actually resemble Fortunato's mother, you think I really belong to the Fortunato's family?"

"Mama, you know the truth, you can't deny this picture. I only saw Guardo's mother for the first time since I was a little kid the night Guardo closed the restaurant. There was something so familiar about her I couldn't get her out of my mind."

"Of course there was something familiar about her, she was always here when you were little, and you just remembered her. She hardly goes out now because she takes care of her own mother. The only time I see her is when I visit her at home. I never saw any resemblance to my Carmina." said Mama urgently.

"Mama, I saw something, it's the eyes. When I saw her I saw Carmina's eyes."

"Oh Carman, the only thing you see is green eyes. They are just not that common in our family. Only my sister Bella had green eyes, as a matter of fact she's probably the reason Carmina has green eyes. "

"Come on Mama, Aunt Bella had hazel eyes."

"Hazel, green what's the difference it only goes to show you how different eyes are in one family. Now forget all this nonsense and go to bed, I don't want to hear any more. What you're saying is that my granddaughter is not my granddaughter? Are you crazy? That child is the image of me, with green eyes, now go to bed and leave me alone you're giving me a headache,"

Carman looked at his mother and saw the tears in her eyes.

"I'm sorry Mama, you go get some sleep, I'm just going to have a nice cup of coffee and then go to bed."

"No more crazy talk about my Carmina," she whispered.

"No more crazy talk about Carmina Mama." He kissed his mother and watched her walk haltingly out of the kitchen. He sat staring off into space as he drank the coffee that would help to keep him up the rest of the night as he thought about his tangled life and his little girl Carmina.

Since Anna's last release from the sanitarium there had been no new episodes of chaotic behavior. Inexplicably Anna turned on Carman. Gone was the peace that kept Carman at home and willing to give up any semblance of a normal life. Now at every encounter with Anna she would physically attack him and call him outlandish names. There was no definable reason for the outbursts. Carman tried reasoning with her but he could not reach her. Her doctors were at a loss to explain why the sudden change. The only one who was able to calm her was Carmina, but how long could a little girl put up with the madness. Although Anna's doctors changed and revised her medication several times, her symptoms worsened. The sight of Carman inflamed her so that he often arrived at work bruised and battered by the countless articles she would hurl at him if he came into her view. Finally it was decided that for all concerned, Anna should be put in a sanitarium to calm her and perhaps stop her violent episodes against her husband.

As the sun came up he finally fell into bed and slept for a few hours until the alarm clock woke him with start. He jumped out of bed hoping that last night was just a bad dream. But no, what he saw last night was real and today he had to hide all the evidence. He headed for the kitchen where Mama was making fresh coffee. The smell of the coffee turned his stomach.

"No coffee today Mama please," he said as he sat wearily at the kitchen table.

210

Mama placed a bowl of oatmeal in front of him. She had put cream and lots of sugar in it just the way he liked it and urged Carman to eat.

"Come on sweetheart, eat a little it will make you feel better."

Slowly Carman ate his oatmeal and some Italian toast with jelly. Gradually he did feel better as the food absorbed the acid of a gallon of black coffee.

"Carman," said Mama softly, "sometimes things happen that we can't change no matter how we try. Love happens too Carman, and no matter what we find out the love remains. You and I both love Carmina with all our hearts. That will never change, so we go on and forget the things we learn and only love." Carman looked at his mother and saw the tears running down her cheeks and realized he too had tears. He hugged his mother and said, "thank you Mama, all I want to remember is that you and I love our Carmina, and Mama. throw out that picture Ok?

"Ok, my Carman Ok," said Mama as she stuffed the picture at the bottom of her garbage.

"No man should loose too much," said Mama. You can loose a wife and get another, but a child, no. A lost wife is enough for my Carman," said Mama to no one in particular. As far as she was concerned there never had been any doubt in her mind that Carmina was her grand daughter. Picture, or no picture she knew her own and Carmina was hers.

1929

Carman sat watching the snow that was falling lightly now. Even the wind had calmed down. What a beautiful picture it made he thought. It looked as if it would be a beautiful day tomorrow after all. Well my love deserves at least that.

Now where was I in my meditation? If I can't sleep I might as well keep looking back on my life and maybe just maybe I could find some answers. I made so many mistakes in my life. Tomorrow will probably be my biggest folly.

Oh well, I've been in way over my head before and somehow I got through it. It was just my life I was responsible for then. Now everything has changed. If I could only find a way out I'd take it. Too many people are going to pay for my mistakes.

"Where the hell is the answer?"

I haven't been up all night since I realized that Carmina wasn't really mine. My life chanced swiftly after that, and here I am with my ass in a sling again.

I better get something to eat before all this coffee burns a hole in my stomach. I'm sure Mama left all kinds of goodies waiting for me in the kitchen. Sure enough when he walked into the kitchen, he couldn't help smile when he saw the food on the table. She had left all his favorites. He bit into a giant crumb bun but found it difficult to swallow. He wasn't hungry after all. He returned to the living room and continued his agony.

1926

It was difficult to get on with his life. His job was anything but boring and he actually enjoyed every facet of his work. He had time to go back to school at night and finally got his degree in engineering. There weren't any jobs on the market for engineers, but he felt good about himself with the degree. The co-eds at Pratt's Institute were more than willing to accommodate Carman in his endeavor, be it lovemaking or typing. His virile good looks got him whatever he wanted. He never realized what how much a part of his fate stemmed from his demeanor. He had a sweetness about him that had a disarming effect on people. The fact that it was genuine only made him more appealing.

At night when sleep would abandon him the longing for his wife and daughter immerged. He was surprised how much he missed Anna. Somewhere along the way he had fallen in love with this strange woman. His heart ached for his daughter. Little by little the visits to see her had dwindled down from almost every day to hardly at all. He stayed away because he felt as if her were an intruder in her life. Anna's parents spared no expense to give Carmina every advantage. Carman could sense a detachment from Carmina. He could detect relief in her voice if he called to say he would nct be over or one of their planned outings would have to be delayed. Without any planning, little by little he eventually lost all contact with his daughter. She became a memory of something precious lost, something else to be forgotten and put aside.

Eventually he left his mother's house and got himself a small apartment.

The all night card playing resumed and he was in a whirlwind of woman, booze and cards. Apparently he was content with his meaningless life. During this time Dominica left her husband. Carman's apartment seemed to be the perfect sanctuary and he welcomed his sister with open arms. Although living at Carman's apartment was very exciting for Dominica, Mama convinced her that ultimately she would get a reputation of being just like Carman, which could be deadly if you were a recently separated woman. Reluctantly she went home to live with Mama. Albeit not at all disturbed that his sister was taken home because of his lifestyle. He knew it would be short lived, and he agreed with Mama that Dominica's reputation was at stake. He would miss the late hour confessions to his little sister and her laughter echoing through the apartment at some of his ridiculous exploits. A good part of his diversion came from Dominica's shocked wonder at her brother's fantastic stories.

Steve came often to lecture him, but make little impact on what he was doing and where he was going. It seemed to all concerned, except Mama, who knew him best, that Carman was on the road to disaster. As a matter of fact all he did was play cards losing sometimes, winning sometimes, with hardly any change in his finances. Occasionally he would have one too many drinks and sing all the way up the stairs to his apartment. His standing in his little community was envied by most of the men and scolded by all the wives. Mama turned her nose up at all the woman. Her only fear was for the virtuous girls, but they hardly shared the same haunts of Carman.

Inevitably Carman curbed his card playing and drinking for they failed to fill the void in his life. With little else to do, he threw himself into his work. Overtime meant nothing to him. He became the guy you called when you needed someone to take your place. He was totally efficient in every facet of the Telephone Company. Had it not been for the depression, Carman would have risen to the top of his profession. As it was, he sashayed from executive to lineman daily. Wherever he was most needed, he worked. There wasn't a job that was too big or too small for him. The company loved him. It was because of the different hats he wore that changed his whole life. One prophetic day he was making seemingly harmless calls to patrons, questioning if in fact their telephones had been fixed properly. One after another boring call was made and the information jotted down for further consideration or crossed off his list.

He glanced at his list and noticed the name Katie O'Donnell. Carman had a special feeling for Irish girls and usually found them to be as sweet as honey. On the other hand he was very careful when speaking to Italian girls because they were trouble. The only thing on their minds was marriage and he already had an Italian wife.

As he dialed he was mentally hoping that Katie O'Donnell was young and unmarried.

"Is this the Katie O'Donnell residence? Carman asked the sweet voiced female who had answered the phone.

"Why, yes it is."

"This is the Telephone Company, we're checking to see if your telephone had been fixed to your specifications."

"Honestly, Mr. Telephone Company I wouldn't know," answered the sweet voice.

"But since I'm speaking to you, I can assume that it has."

"I guess you can Mister Telephone Repairman," she answered playfully.

Carman had talked to hundreds of woman on the telephone, but this one had the voice of an Angel.

"Goodbye, and thank you for calling," she said.

"Hold it", he replied, searching for a way to keep the young woman on the line.

"I'm sorry, but I have to get to work."

"At 2 o'clock in the afternoon," he replied.

"Some of us work strange hours, Mister Telephone, bye."

And the phone went dead.

Carman sat there looking at the telephone wondering why this girl's voice could have such an effect on him. Unwillingly he went on to the next call, but not before he copied Katie O'Donnell's telephone number in his little black book.

The following day Carman found himself looking for Katie O'Donnell's telephone number. Try as he might, he couldn't get the sound of her voice out of his mind. What a voice he repeated to himself, what a glorious voice, I've got to hear it once more. Maybe I'm really losing it; I could be mistaken nobody sounds so damn sweet. I can't just call. Or can I? Why the hell not? Why shouldn't I call, he raved to himself as he finally located her number and sat looking at it, afraid to dial. Carman you really are getting crazy, she could look like "Two Ton Tillie" for all you know. He had never considered making a date with her sight unseen, which just wasn't his way. All I need is to get seriously involved with someone. Christ I'm married. Lord, what do I do? I know, come on Carman you're a big boy, I call. What could happen? Right? Yeah right. But I'll never be free of Anna, and do I want to be? Jesus what am I thinking, the sound of a beautiful voice and I'm considering divorcing Anna? Carman my man, you've been alone too damn long, and you've been married forever.

Married at seventeen to Anna because of Carmina and now I'm thirty and alone, and my beautiful Carmina isn't really mine. I've spent less than a year with Anna and most of that time she's been nuts. Wow, I've been snagged and hung out to dry. No wonder the sound of a voice can take me over the top. Carman you've got to see whom this voice belongs to. Without hesitating he dialed Katie O'Donnell's number. He didn't recognize the voice that answered the phone and asked; almost relieved "is this Katie O'Donnell?"

"This is Katie, what can I do for you," she answered?

"I, I err, I'm calling about your service is it Ok.

"It sure is mister, didn't you call before."

"Ah, no, Carman stammered, still shocked at the sound of Katie O'Donnell's voice.

I'm really losing it he thought to himself; I even invent glorious voices.

"That's funny," Katie said,"my cousin said someone called from the Telephone Company checking on the repair.

"Oh" Carman said, nor knowing if he were glad or sad," I guess it wasn't a-a- noted in the register, sorry to bother you Madam.

"You can bother me anytime buster, feel free to call again," Katie answered laughingly. "By the way my cousin's name is Marie and you can probably run into her at the

Telephone Company, she works there as a night operator. That is, of course, if you're interested?

"I am, I am," Carman replied desperately trying to convey some kind of decorum, but stammering in spite of himself.

He finally managed to say, "Can you tell me at what office?"

"Fordham Road sweetie, and don't let on I sent you there, Marie would have my head. "Thanks."

"Fordham Road, I'll be damned," Carman said as he hung up the phone. He worked at the Tremont Office hardly a mile away.

Well now that I have the information, what do I do now? I must see this Marie. Maybe she's a dog. No, impossible, no one with a voice like that could be a dog. But how do I get a look at her? Stand outside of the Fordham Office and watch all the girls go by, hoping I can recognize her voice? This is crazy. Forget it Carman, go play cards tonight maybe you'll be lucky and pick up some dame for a few laughs. Yeah, that's what I'll do. I can't go looking for a voice.

But that's what he did. The card game was boring and he never noticed the young ladies who were there. He left early and to his surprise found he was leaning against the wall of the Fordham Telephone Company listening for a voice in a multitude of young woman leaving the building after their 3 to 11 shifts.

And there it was not a voice but a laugh that startled him so he almost knocked over a very pretty young lady. "Sorry miss," he said righting her on her feet as he searched frantically through the crowd sure he'd never find her. Then to his surprise a definite male voice called out "Marie over here."

There she was, skipping down the steps to this guy. Boy she was some looker, what a face, what a body. Well she was a little rounder than most of the girls he dated. But what a shape on her and that hair, she's a true red head. Wow, she's gorgeous and she's got a boy friend. Oh well Carman you almost met the girl of your dreams. He reached into his pocket, took out a cigar, lit it, and casually leaned against the wall of the Telephone Company watching Marie

"Something was happening with the guy she was talking to. Was he leaving, yeah he was. Nonchalantly, Carman sauntered within hearing distance as that beautiful voice called to her friend.

"It's Ok, I can go, and my brother will cover for me".

Linking arms with another really nice looking young lady, beautiful Marie walked off into the night, Carman watched Marie disappear into the darkness and something very strange happened to him, he suddenly felt unhappy. Boy Carman you really are a sorry case, you don't even know the girl and already you miss her. What the hell does that mean; he wondered as he puffed his cigar and walked off in the other direction.

Chapter Sixteen

As the days passed no matter what distraction he could think of, Carman was unable to stop thinking of Marie. His vision of her kept invading his consciousness. Fortunately he did not really know her and resolved to forget her as quickly as possible. Usually when confronted with adversity his best remedy was physical endeavor; to do something that would not hamper his mind but keep his body active and tired. Consequently he decided to redo Mama's house.

Mama was elated. The house had not been touched since Papa died.

Predictably, Carman got his brother involved and between the two of them they managed with very little capital to redo Mama's kitchen and added on a bathroom which, in itself, was the envy of the neighborhood. It took the brothers at least six full months to complete all the alterations. When they were finished Mama was so proud that she invited everyone she knew for a big party to celebrate her new home. Dominica was so impressed by her brothers' handy work that she threatened to move back in with her husband. Mama was certainly agreeable to that idea for she was lonely with Carman gone to his own place and now with all the extra room, someone should definitely move in.

In the end, Dominica's husband vetoed the idea. All he would need was Mama keeping tabs on him. His marriage was shaky enough. So Mama had a big refinished house and no one to share it with. With Carman living a Monk's life he decided to Mama's delight to move back home. There was absolutely no reason not to. He would have plenty of privacy if he were lucky enough to need it. It also gave Carman something else to think about, his Mama. She wasn't getting any younger and the toll on her since Papa died was dramatic. Within a week of the transformed Duva establishment Carman was back home as if he had never left. In reality it was a very good move for him, the loneliness he felt since the breakup of his home with Anna, slowly vanished. Just when Carman's life was on an even keel he accidentally ran into Marie.

It was a hot summer afternoon with the sun beating down relentlessly on Carman as he climbed pole after pole on Webster Avenue in the Bronx.

There was a break in the wiring for that area and no one had been able to pinpoint it. So again, Carman traded in his suit for some overalls and "took to the poles". Ordinarily the break in monotony was welcomed, but not on the hottest day of the year. There he was hanging from a pole on Webster Avenue when Marie came walking down the street. Luckily he didn't electrocute himself at the shock of seeing her but in his haste to climb down the pole to intercept Marie, he lost his footing just as she passed under the pole he was working on and he slid down literally knocking her off her feet.

Miraculously, neither one was hurt as they sat laughing at one another on the curb. Carman scrambled to get up and literally picked Marie off the ground. Confounded by her in his arms he just looked at her mesmerized by her understated beauty.

Laughingly she said, "You can put me down now, I'm perfectly fine".

"Are you sure, he managed to answer.

"Yes I'm sure."

Carefully he set her down and stood looking at her.

"Are you all right," she asked?

"No I'm not, he answered.

"Are you hurt," Marie asked wondering why she was so concerned about the man who fell off a pole on top of her.

"I don't really know, but I feel very strange," Carman answered completely baffled by his reaction to this girl.

"Come sit on the stoop a few minutes until you get your bearings. You took some slide down that pole. Is that the way you usually get down?

"No, he replied, I've never actually slid down an entire pole before; it's a first for me. I think I've got splinters on my entire body, or at least my clothes have, he answered as he looked at the array of wood splinters down the front of his work cloths. It's a good thing they make these cloths so thick, I'd have a heck of a time removing all of them.

"Are you feeling better? Aside from the slight bruise on your cheek you look ok", said Marie examining Carman carefully for any possible injury.

"No I'm really fine. I guess I'm just a little embarrassed falling down on you like that. I could have really hurt you, I'm awfully sorry."

"Oh I'm in one piece, nothing happened to me, not to worry, can you get up," she asked still concerned?

"Sure," he replied as he stood towering over her. He never realized how short she was. God she was cute, he couldn't seem to take his eyes off of her.

"Say, do you want to go for a cup of coffee or something," he said leading her down the street to a small coffee shop he noticed while working high on a pole?

"Well, I don't know. I don't even know your name. I mean is it all right to just knock someone down and then to take them for coffee? We really haven't been introduced you know and I certainly don't want

you to get the wrong impression of me. I don't have coffee with everyone I bump into." She rambled on and on unable to stop talking. She
was completely mesmerized by this complete stranger and didn't know
exactly what to do. And so she let him lead her into the little coffee
shop on the corner and sat down as he ordered coffee and donuts for
them. Finally her mouth just stopped talking and Carman said, "Are
you quite finished, I thought for a minute you were going to go into the
Gettysburg Address, do you always go on like that?"

"No, this is the first time," she said bursting out laughing delighting
Carman with the magical sound.

After exchanging names they sat talking for nearly two hours; not
even aware of the amount of coffee they had consumed. Conversation
came easily as they laughed and talked not even aware that Carman had
hold of Marie's hands and was rubbing them gently and unconsciously
as if he had know her all his life. Neither one knew how to end this
lovely afternoon. Carman had completely forgotten his pole climbing
and had left all of the Telephone Company's equipment lying in the
street, next to an open truck.

When reality struck, Carman threw some money on the table,
grabbed Marie's hand and whisked her back to his work area. He
breathed a sigh of relief when they arrived to find everything there
just as he left it. He sat Marie on the fender of the truck as he gathered all of his equipment into the back of the truck and locked the
doors securely. He lifted her down from the fender and said, "Ok Marie
where exactly do you live? I'm taking you home. I don't want anyone else
to fall on you ever again.

"Charles I live right here."

He was totally shocked at Marie calling him Charles. Actually he
had told her his name was Charlie. It was the way she said Charles that
thrilled him.

"Áre you ok?"

"Sure, I'm fine."

"We were sitting on my stoop before."

"Oh," he answered, realizing that she didn't live in the same house as her cousin Katie O'Donnell.

"Marie, would you like to have dinner with me sometime soon?

"That would be lovely Carman," she answered.

"How about tomorrow."

"Tomorrow's good."

"I'll meet you right here at seven. If that's ok," he replied.

"I'll meet you at the coffee shop at seven, ok?"

"Ok, I'll see you tomorrow"

He turned to his truck, got in and blew her a kiss from the window.

Carman flew to his office and quickly changed his cloths, called his brother Steve's office and learned that he had already left. He literally ran to the parking lot and headed for Steve's house and was there in a flash.

Walking right in, which was not his custom he headed to the back porch where he knew his brother would be sitting having, his one drink, as he contemplated the days events. Steve was shocked to see Carman standing in front of him.

"Where the hell did you come from was just thinking of you" exclaimed Steve.

"Steve I just had to see you, you've got to help me something wonderful happened to me today. Without further ado Carman launched into his encounter with Marie, adding his decision never to make contact with her after locating her at the Telephone Company.

"Wait Carman, slow down, tell me again about you first hearing her voice, amazed at his brother's story.

Carman took a deep breath and started at the beginning, leaving nothing out, aware of the look of astonishment on Steve's face. He ended with,

"I know this sounds bizarre, but I think I'm in love."

"Bizarre, nothing, you're just nuts, laughed Steve.

"Steve listen to me, I'm serious as all hell, God help me I'm in love Steve, you're got to help me, he added as he hung his head and covered his face with his hands, and sat warily in a chair next to his brother.

Realizing just how serious Carman was Steve got up and gently patted his back.

"Take it easy pal, we'll fix this. You can't be in love with Marie you're already married to Anna."

"Christ I know Steve, I know," he replied hardly audible.

"Ok Carman relax, you want a drink," asked Steve?

"Yeah, a drink would be fine, I really need one, I'm scared shit," he replied completely spent as he watched his brother disappear into the house.

He couldn't believe how upset he was, and how ridiculous he must sound.

My God, he thought she's just another girl in the long line of girls I've dated since Anna went into the sanitarium. I'm overreacting, I'm losing my mind, and I'm working too hard. Fall in love, how absurd how asinine, I'm not even sure of her last name and she's just a kid. I shouldn't be dating her anyway. I must really be crazy to come running here.

Carman sighed as he watched the sun setting behind the beautiful trees in Steve's garden. What an exquisite view, there were traces of a mountain range in his view that he wasn't even aware of. The magnificent colors of the flowers in the garden were beautiful. There were begonias, roses, impatience, flowering over the entire backyard. He never remembered seeing such vibrant colors. No wonder his brother came here directly from work in the evening. It was a brilliant spectacle of hues, tones and tints. The effect of his environment calmed him so that he was transfixed by the serenity.

By the time Steve returned with his drink, Carman was softly humming to himself.

"Boy, you certainly can switch temperament, can't you," his brother asked astonished at

Carman's transformation and surprised at the relief he felt."

Handing Carman his drink the two brothers sat and watched the sky darken content to be in each other's company.

Eventually Carman started to tell his brother about Marie, but without the exigency he had felt when he first arrived. Steve sat quietly and listened, alarmed what he heard in his brothers' voice.

By the time Carman returned home he had convinced himself that Marie was not a threat to him. After all wasn't she Irish, and wasn't it his experience that Irish girls would date Italians but would never consider getting serious with them. In the past he had learned that Italians were not welcome suitors in Irish homes. The reverse of that was also true. Whenever he went out with an Irish girl no matter how he seemed to care for them they never intended anything more than a casual acquaintance and lots of fun. This particular arrangement worked very well in the past. Why would it be different now? With a name like O'Donnell he had nothing to fear.

Dauntlessly the next evening he entered the little coffee shop on the corner of Marie's block and there she sat as innocent as the morning breeze. The last rays of the summer sun shone on her beautiful hair surrounding her beautiful face. Carman stood watching her until she called softly, "Charles over here I'm here." He stumbled awkwardly forward, righting himself in time to miss upsetting her table.

"Oh, Charles you are so funny," she laughed covering her mouth, her eyes shining.

He couldn't help but smile at her.

"Come with me I have a wonder full restaurant picked out for us this evening.

He decided not to bring Marie to any of his old haunts. The fact that he used his work name Charles Duval instead of Carman Duva was not unusual, after all Marie worked at the Telephone Company too - why confuse her with his two names. For the time being Charles would do him fine, he hardly felt like a Carman anymore anyway. The only time he ever spoke Italian was to his mother who refused to speak anything else.

Hand in hand Marie and Carman walked into Dominic's Restaurant, a short distance from Marie's house. It was just off Third Avenue and 180th Street in the Bronx.

Marie was delighted with Charles' choice, she had never been to this restaurant, but had heard from his brothers that the food was excellent, although a bit pricey. Thinking of her brothers, she could not wait to tell them were she had gone to dinner. She only hoped that her brother Gerry was covering for her, as promised. Not that she went out often, but Papa was a very strict Italian who did not believe a girl should go out without a member of her family with her. He was so old fashioned and so hard to please that it was a wonder that Marie adored him. Of all his children, Marie was Papa's favorite, but then again, she was his only daughter and aside from his old-world practices Papa did spoil her a little.

While they sat looking at the menu, the waiter asked if she cared to order a drink.

"A small glass of wine would be lovely," she replied.

Carman was surprised. Not one of the Irish girls he dated ever ordered red wine. It was usually some strange new cocktail he had never heard of. Maybe she wasn't Irish after all. No, he thought, she's got red hair and green eyes and skin as white as milk. No I never saw an Italian with that complexion. Dear God if she's Italian I'm a dead man.

After they had ordered, Carman casually said,

"Do you realize I don't know your last name?"

"For heavens sake, I can't believe I never told you. Why it's Pinto."

"Pinto," Carman said raising his voice, "Pinto, I thought you were Irish"

"Charles please everyone is looking at us, don't you like Italians."

"Of course I like Italians, I'm Italian, I just thought - well you really look Irish" he whispered, embarrassed by his outburst.

"Well Charles to be perfectly frank my mother is Irish and I do favor her side of the family. Is this a problem,"she asked a little dismayed by his reaction?

"Of course not I don't know what I was thinking. I just thought you didn't look Italian, that's all, there's no problem," he answered relieved that at least she wasn't all Italian, he was only half a dead man.

"Charles how could your name be Duval, I thought that was a French name, you did say you were Italian right."

"I'm definitely Italian Marie, have no fear, there was probably a mix up at Immigration when my father came from Italy."

"I know," Marie added," I don't think Pinto is our original name either. The only name I'm sure of is my mother's maiden name, O'Donnell. Even though the Irish spoke with a brogue when they came here it still was English, except of course the ones who only spoke Gaelic.

"So does your mother speak with a brogue?" Carman asked.

"No, not at all, my mother's people have been in America a long time, but they still consider themselves Irish. My father, on the other hand, came to America as a little boy and still speaks very broken English. Yet he considers himself an American."

"I can understand that," replied Carman," my father, God rest his soul, spoke English very well and considered himself American while my little Italian mother is just that "Italian".

"Oh Charles, I'm sorry to hear that your father has passed away. Tell me about him" Marie asked.

Carman answered Marie with stories about his father that he thought he had forgotten. He told her all about everyone in his family but neglected to tell her anything about Anna or Carmina. The evening seemed to fly by with each of them talking freely to one another completely at ease as if they had known one another for years instead of hours. Walking Marie home from the restaurant they made plans for the weekend. Arriving at her house Marie spontaneously gave Carman a hug and a kiss on his cheek and quickly ran up the stairs disappearing behind the door of her house. He stood for a minute looking at the closed door and finally walked to the corner to get a bus home. The feel of her sweet kiss on his cheek warmed him all the way home.

1929

He could still remember the look on Mama's face when I told her about Marie. The word livid always comes to mind. That little Italian lady literally spun around the kitchen, using words in Italian that he had never heard before and was reluctant to ask what they meant. Remembering, he could still conjure up that wonderful sensation he felt that night as he walked into his mother's kitchen. He felt so marvelous being in love that he never thought how shocked his revelation would be.

It was unusual for Mama to rant and rave. She invariably took any news he had to offer calmly with no reaction what so ever. Eventually she calmed down.

Perhaps it was the sheer honesty that his mother heard in his voice, whatever it was, her reaction had subsided and she calmly poured him coffee and continued to listen in wonder, to her son.

Oh yes, I remember now Dominica was there too.

1927

Hearing the commotion, Dominica appeared in the doorway.
"Hey Dominica, what are you doing here so late, every thing alright.
"Ah, Carman, nothing has been right since I married that maniac."
"Maniac, last week he was your Prince, what's changed."
"Nothing, it's too complicated to go into, so what's with Mama, I never heard her scream before and those Italian words. They must be too wild for even me to get the meaning."

"Who knows, I just told Mama I'm in love," answered Carman laughing.

"Oh Carman," Dominica whispered, "how wonderful. Do I know her? Can I meet her? It's about time you had some happiness; you make me so glad."

Dominica stood there with tears in her eyes, seeing her bother happy for the first time in years. "I'm so happy," was all she said.

"How can you be happy," shouted Mama." Do you not realize what this means? Torment horror, hiding and denial. You can only love one woman Carman and that one is your poor sick wife. What will happen to my Carmina, if you continue with this madness?"

"What madness Mama," he answered? "I hardly know the girl. I just know I love her. What can come of it, absolutely nothing? I am chained to Anna for the rest of her life, and there is nothing I can do about it. Do you think I could give up my Carmina? Even though, I never see her anymore she is still in my heart. No Mama, only a miracle could change my life. I just never thought I could love again. I'm sorry Mama," he continued, "I didn't want to upset you, I thought, I don't know what I thought, I just wanted to tell you. Nothing will come of it. I will end it before it starts.

"Oh Carman cried Dominica, I can't stand it. Why shouldn't you be in love? It's not a sin to love. It's why we're here. Life is so short and hard, it's only love that can make this journey worthwhile."

"Stop Dominica," exclaimed Mama. "What do you know of love? All I hear from you is Victor does this Victor does that. Here you are at midnight, when you should be home with your husband. Tell me my daughter what do you know of love?"

"Oh Mama, you're right. I shouldn't be here. I should be with Victor. You must forgive me Mama. I can't stop being your little girl and I want you to fix everything for me. Tonight Mama, maybe you have. What do I know of love? Not too much Mama, I've never had the experience. Victor on the other hand, really loves me. So, I should give his love a chance. Goodnight Mama," she said as she bent to kiss her mother.

"And you Carman, if you love this girl, reach for the stars." Brushing her brother's cheek with a kiss Dominica left.

"Carman, that girl is driving your Mama crazy. I can't have two of my children filling my head with dread. Go to bed, maybe tomorrow the love will go away."

Slowly Mama left the room leaving Carman with his thoughts of Marie.

No matter which way he looked at his situation, there was no avenue he could take that would not bring heartache to someone. Maybe Mama is right, he thought as he closed the kitchen light, maybe tomorrow I won't be in love.

Chapter Seventeen

For Carman tomorrow never came. After two weeks of agony, he succumbed and called Marie. Marie had also spent her days in agony, wondering why Carman had not called her. She was ecstatic when he did.

Without any fanfare, slowly and with little help from anything or anyone Carman and Marie fell deeply in love. The kind of love poet's write about and singers sing about and lovers revel in. Anyone seeing them walking together down a street could tell immediately that they were in love. There was little doubt how much they meant to one another. For Carman, there was no turning back. He didn't have the strength. The previous torment and uncertainty of his relationship with Marie were gone because of the love he felt for her. He knew he was treading on thin ice and disregarded the obvious consequences. Wearing blinders to hide the truth of his actions, he ventured on to the height of indiscretion.

Marie, gentle, beautiful and innocent rode the wave of love unaware of Carman's deception. Only her Papa was suspicious of Carman. Right from the beginning he felt that this man called Charles was much too old for his little Marie. There was a certain sophistication he sensed in Carman that was too worldly. He could see in Carman's face that life had not been kind to him. There was too much sadness in his eyes. Papa was aware that Charles had served in the Calvary in World War I, but taking that into consideration there was still too much sadness in his eyes. In Papa's estimation Charles was too old and had seen and felt too much to be an eligible suitor for his daughter.

Papa, in his wisdom, halted this run away romance before his girl could get seriously involved. Marie's Mother felt all the misgivings Papa had but realized that the affair was beyond recovery. Look what had happened to her and Papa. Both families almost disowned them for marrying outside of their nationality. Mama and Papa would laugh till today at what they had given up for their love. They spent many hours agonizing about Marie and Charles. Marie's Mother could still remember the burning desire that welled in her heart for Papa, and that nothing in this world could stop them from loving one another. Papa refused to equate the two relationships. What he and Mama had was real love, not this infatuation that his daughter believed was love.

Finally the decision was made and Marie was forbidden to see Charles. Being an obedient daughter she tried bravely to comply with her parents' wishes. Although they did not see each other they did talk several times a day by telephone. Reluctantly, Carman regained his senses and sided with Marie's parents, completely confusing her.

"Charles, I understand your unwillingness to interfere in my family's decision to separate us, but do you have to be so obliging," Marie cried. "I can't understand you."

"Oh my darling, if only I could explain. They're right," Carman answered sadly.

"Of course they're not right; don't be ridiculous, we love each other right," she replied?

"Sad but true my love, but sometimes love is not enough."

"What do you mean, not enough. Love is always enough."

"Oh my little angel, if you only knew".

"Charles, you must tell me what you're talking about. You're always alluding to something but you never tell me. Please, I must know why are you siding with my parents? Can it be that you truly don't love me, is that it? I must know now or I can't go on. You're breaking my heart."

"Marie, please know this," answered Carman, "in the entire world you are the one I love and until the end of my life that will never change but your parents are right. I'm too old for you and I have seen and done too many things to continue with this relationship. It must end. You've got to find someone else, and believe me you will. Meeting me has been unfair to you. You are too young and beautiful to waste your life on me. It is much better this way. I must never see you again my darling, please try to understand. There are things I can never tell you that will turn you against me. Let it end now before it's too late. Just know that I will love you forever."

Carman hung up the phone in despair. Marie sat with the receiver in her lap unable to understand what had just happened.

MARIE

When Marie fell in love with Charles, it was really for the very first time. When it ended she was overwhelmed and completely devastated. She couldn't believe that loving someone could hurt so badly.

Remembering her past experiences she recalled how sad she was when the boy next door found a girlfriend. It had never occurred to her during the years they played cowboys and Indians, or hide and seek, or for the times they shared an ice pop, or a candy bar, that he would choose someone else just when she realized how much he meant to her. She never forgot him. His name was Benny. Then there was the boy around the corner. His name was Herbie. He actually asked her to meet him in the Metro Movie Theatre. They would sit together in the children's section and he would buy her an Almond Joy candy bar. He also gently held her hand, and she was thrilled to her toes. But that romance was short lived when she witnessed his mother drag poor Herbie up to their apartment when she saw them talking in front of his building. He looked so small and frightened that she was embarrassed for him. He started to meet another girl at the movies, one that hadn't witnessed his humiliation. Then there was the boy on Washington Avenue. He was so handsome that girls would drool when they saw him. But he had a thing for Marie. He also had six toes on one foot, which he would show her upon request for free. He charged all the other kids on the block two pennies a look. Then at thirteen she met Johnny Carbone at the carnival on 187th street. He had the most beautiful black curly hair and he actually paid to take her to the Paradise Theatre. He also brought along a friend. That didn't bother Marie since she was unaware of the protocol of dating anyway. The list ran on and on getting closer to love all the time. Now there was Charles and all of the boys that she had seriously considered as her one true love disappeared without a trace. Who could possibly compare with her Charles? So sweet, so tender that the first time he kissed her she thought the world stood still.

Fortunately her parents had raised her with a good sense of morality. The twelve years of catholic schools with angelic nuns also helped her get through this difficult period. Without it she would have been lost. It was just so hard for Marie to stop imagining Charles making love to her. To avoid these images, she ate. Marie gained ten pounds, which on her little frame was not too attractive. The result of taking solace in food forced her to go on a vigorous diet, which kept her mind off sex. Fairly slim again, and much stronger from the experience, she vowed never to let food become a substitute. She was just in love for the very first time and she'd have to contend with it. Marie couldn't understand how she could live without Charles. She chastised herself for not sleeping with him and longed for what she had missed. At night she fantasized how it would be if she met him again, accidentally of course. She took comfort from these make believe scenario's adding and deleting events, almost believing they had happened. Tears would well up in her eyes whenever she thought of him.

Marie could not believe that her life was going on as usual. She ate, slept, and went to bed hiding her misery. His leaving her also embarrassed her. Her mother and father knew of her agony, but said nothing. They were relieved that the affair was over.

Her brother Gerry started to bring friends home to meet Marie until she begged him to stop. After awhile it seemed to everyone that she had recovered. It was all a façade. Try as she might, she couldn't forget him and spent most of her time hoping to run into him. He seemed to disappear off the face of the earth. No one knew where he was. He had taken a leave of absence from the Telephone Company and virtually vanished. Marie's pride forbade her from searching him out. Finally she was convinced he just didn't care about her anymore. Amazingly her life seemed to go on.

1928

A year went by before Carman was able to think of Marie without pain. He knew he owed her an explanation but he also was keenly aware that seeing her would be too dangerous and he would be back to square one. The fear of seeing her or hearing her voice kept him far away from New York. He managed to get a transfer to Boston and rarely came home except on holidays. It was during this period that he learned that his in-laws were planning to adopt his Carmina legally. He literally stormed their doors and reclaimed his little girl. Surprisingly, Carmina was delighted with her father's actions. Although she truly loved her Grandparents, she adored her Father. Together they made a home in the Italian section of Boston and they were content. Carmina went to a Catholic School and with special arrangement with the Sisters, stayed with them until her father picked her up after work. Carman could never have made such an arrangement on his own without the help of his friend Father Paul who seemed to have friends in all parishes. It didn't matter how long he stayed away from Marie he still loved her.

He reasoned that he would probably love her forever. But that was ok. He had Carmina to take care of and it was time they both visited Anna.

When Carman and Carmina arrived in New York is was like coming home. Carmina begged her father to let her visit her Grandparents. Although he was reluctant he finally agreed to let her stay with them and dropped her off to the waiting arms of his in-laws. When he saw how Carmina reacted to seeing her grandparents again he knew he had made the best decision. He was invited in and was treated like a returning hero. It was difficult for him to feel comfortable after all the anguish he had been through trying to get his daughter back. Watching them he felt like an intruder as they compared notes with one another on what had gone on in each other's absence. He was aware that Carmina and his in-laws corresponded regularly but he never realized how much his daughter missed them. He sat there listening to them and knew in his heart that his little girl belonged with them. The three of them looked like an ideal family, and as much as he knew he would miss his little girl, taking her away from them was not fair to her. He decided then and there that he would have to make new arrangements and return home for good so that Carmina could see and be with her grandparents as much as possible. He made his excuses and left with a promise to return the next day for a real family dinner. He kissed Carmina and left to the sound of her delightful laughter, something he had not heard for a very long time.

It wasn't as difficult as he envisioned getting a transfer back to New York and Mama was delighted to have him home with or without Carmina. Aside from the fear of running into Marie he was content. He had made an arrangement with the Similetti's that Carmina could stay with them as long as they promised in writing that they would never again try to adopt her away from him. They were so grateful to have Carmina under their roof that they would have signed any agreement. Carman was asked to visit at any time whatsoever. He began having dinner with his in-laws at least three times a week in order to make sure that he was part of Carmina life. The child was ecstatic with the arrangement and flourished.

Carman tried visiting Anna as much as possible but she was unaware of his presence most of the time. Occasionally she would recognize him and proceed to have a normal conversation with him. At these times she was eager to hear about her daughter but was reluctant to see her. Carman understood her hesitation it was hard for him to see Anna even when she was lucid. Her dazzling hair was replaced by one long pure white braid. Albeit the beauty of her face was still constant her eyes were vacant. He held back tears watching her earnestly trying to act rational. He always promised her to come back the following week, but was reluctant to return. He would force himself after a month had gone by to go back to the sanitarium. The dear Nuns who took car of her were quick to absolve him for his failing. He was inspired by their kindness.

Carman's life went on with little distraction except for work. Just when he thought that life had passed him by, Marie walked back in.

Their meeting was certainly not planned. Indisputable it was Carman's greatest fear. If you believe in fate then their reuniting was inevitable. Carman was just coming out of the side entrance of the Telephone Company when he literally bumped into her almost knocking her over. He caught her in his arms and looking into her beautiful eyes he just couldn't let her go. As if on cue they hugged and kissed one another as if nothing had happened in the interim. Finally, he took her by the hand to a little restaurant around the corner where they sat for hours recounting their love for one another.

He was lost in his love for her. Listening to Marie recount her family's joy at their separation brought Carman back to his senses. Without question he knew he was playing with fire, but he convinced himself that it was harmless.

They decided to meet secretly for the time being and to act toward one another as just good friends. They knew they were lying to one another but it seemed doable at the time. And so it all began again and it wasn't long before Carman took Marie to his bed. He never meant to hurt her he just loved her beyond reason. Their lovemaking was without exception the most ardent sensuous example of ecstasy he had ever experienced. For Marie it was her ticket to heaven.

Without any warning, she stopped seeing him and refused to take his calls. He was beside himself with anguish. What had he done? He had finally decided to divorce Anna and marry Marie. He knew he would never get an annulment from the church but he was certain Marie would understand and agree to marry him outside of the church. But he never got the opportunity. He did, in fact search out an attorney and ask him what he had to do. According to his solicitor it would be an easy process. But his beautiful Marie refused to see him or answer his letters. She quit the Telephone Company and had simply vanished from the earth. He haunted her house waiting to catch sight of her but to his amazement the family had moved and not one person in the neighborhood knew where they had gone. For two solid months he hounded anyone who could possibly know where Marie had gone. And then to his surprise he walked into his doctor's office where he had gone hoping for something to rid himself of the constant headaches he had since her disappearance, and there she sat quietly reading a magazine.

"My God Marie, what the hell is going on?" was all he said.

She looked up at him in complete shock and tried to run past him out the door. He grabbed her and literally threw her on the couch holding on to her for dear life. Immediately she started to sob uncontrollably. The sound of her crying brought their doctor to the waiting room.

"Come into my office you two and let's see what the problem is."

They both stood and followed the doctor into his office without any hesitation. Fortunately the nurse had left early and they were the only people in the waiting room. Dr. Callucci sat Marie down next to his desk as Carman watched as he asked her, "Is he the one?"

She nodded yes and continued to sob quietly.

"Carman do you have any idea of what this is all about. You seem to be unaware of what has been going on with Marie."

"Hey Doctor Callucci, I've been looking for her everywhere. Her family moved, she quit her job and no one knows where she has been."

"Ah, I see," he said and gazed at Marie affectionately. "It seems that I have been doctor to Marie for years, and although Carman is one of my new patients I feel I owe you both allegiances. Marie would you care to tell Carman what your condition is or would you rather I tell him?

"Please Dr. Callucci, please can you tell him."

"Alright child I will. You better take a seat Carman."

Carman sat down eagerly not caring what the problem was as long as he could be with Marie. The fear of her having an incurable disease ran through his mind but he refused to take that scenario seriously. Doctor Callucci looked around his office as if he could get some assistance from the walls and ceiling. Finally trying not to look as either of his patients he said in a whisper, "it seems our little Marie is going to be a mother."

Carman sat with his mouth open, unable to speak. Marie kept her eyes down and the doctor looked from one to the other waiting for some acknowledgement that they had understood him. At last Carman got up and knelt down in front of Marie taking her hand in his saying, "why couldn't you tell me?"

"Oh Carman, I felt so ashamed."

"Why, it's a wonderful thing, and you certainly didn't get pregnant all by yourself, right. I am the father aren't I?" he added hopefully.

"Oh my God Carman of course you are."

"Well then, I guess you two have lots of plans to make so why don't you get out of here and make them," said Dr. Callucci as he ushered them both out of his office. As they were closing the door he called out to Marie, "I'll see you the same time next week."

1929

I can't deny she certainly was a little chunky, but those eyes, that smile, that face. She was lovely, and I couldn't get her out of my mind. She believes everything I say. She calls me Charles, not Charlie, not Chaz, not Chuck like everyone else at work, but just Charles. When she murmurs my name in my ear as I kiss her I melt. God help me I love Marie. I think her family has swallowed my new identity. I never meant to deceive anyone. I just decided to use my Telephone Company identity to make life simpler. Explaining my real name and why I had to hide my heritage was humiliating. I never intended to fool anyone or go against my birthright. I just needed a good job and they don't hire Italians at the Telephone Company. Marie used her mother's maiden name to get a job as telephone operator. Why I didn't acknowledge my own deceit when I first met her I'll never understand. It never occurred to me that I would fall in love after all this time. It was when I finally decided to end my relationship with Marie that the reality of my affection for her emerged. Seeing her again was my downfall.

I'm sure she became pregnant at the end of last summer when we decided to go swimming at Star beach, an unusually small and secluded beach that ran along the shoreline past Orchard Beach. It seemed like a great idea at the time. I had to break off with this innocent girl before my desire corrupted her. My intentions were honorable, but my emotions won over. In trying to say goodbye to her I lost myself in her gaze. Words and feelings I never knew I possessed engulfed her. On a deserted little beach, in a far corner of the Bronx she gave up her virginity to me. I remember after it was over, we lay exhausted covered with one another, unable to let go. I had never experienced such emotion before. Sexual desire wasn't even a part of our coupling. A bond of love enveloped us beyond physical awareness. If it hadn't stormed we'd have stayed there for days or at least until someone discovered us. Huddled together and laughing hilariously the inevitability of our actions never entered my mind. The reality of my situation never occurred to me.

The fact that I have a wife in a mental institution and a little girl that I had to fight to get custody was conveniently forgotten. I decided then that I would make Marie my wife and absolutely nothing was going to stop me.

Ah, the best laid plans etc., etc. It would have been so easy if I had known Marie was going to have a baby. Now there was no time to divorce Anna.

1929

They walked out of the doctors' office hand in hand. Carman couldn't believe that it happened again. What an idiot I am he thought. How many times can I keep making the same mistake? It's too bad I never think. I've always considered myself to be an intelligent moral man, but in reality I take advantage of young ladies and occasionally I get them pregnant. My God, what do I do now? Look at this sweet girl holding on to my hand for dear life. I question that if she actually knew me, would she indeed touch me? Is love really that blind?

"Carman you look so sad. I know you don't want this baby."

He looked at her and as usual he lied saying, "how can you say that. Of course I want the baby."

"Are you sure?"

"Yes," he answered, "I'm sure.

"And you'll marry me?"

"Of course Marie, I love you."

"Thank God," she sighed. "Now you must speak to my father, ok?"

"Ok."

"Now?"

"Why not," he answered.

"But first you have to let me talk to him for just a minute. He is beside himself with worry.

"Sure Marie, but I don't even know where you live now. Was it really necessary to move, to get away from me?"

"Oh Charles I was terrified you wouldn't want me and the baby, and I felt ashamed that I had disappointed my parents. I thought my mother would die when I told her. My poor father wept. It was terrible. I never thought in my wildest dreams that I could make love to someone I wasn't married to. How could I let myself go like that?"

"Oh my little sweetheart, you just love me and I love you. It's that simple."

"But moving away, that must have been hard on your whole family."

"Oh Charles, they were moving anyway and I was grateful for the chance to get away from you."

"Do you think I would let you face this alone? Certainly it's my fault, not yours. You're just a sweet young girl who got mixed up with a scoundrel like me. I never want to hear you take the blame for this baby. It was my fault and I can't deny it. The truth is I love you madly and whatever the consequences I'm going to marry you and give this baby my name. Come on sweetheart let's talk to your father. Which way do we go?

"We just passed my house," she said as she turned him around and entered her parents' new apartment building.

When they got to her door she asked him to wait while she went in to speak to her father first. He nodded his head and she quietly opened the door. He took out a cigar lit it and found a windowsill to sit on while he anticipated the dreaded meeting with Marie's father. He couldn't imagine what to expect. The reality of the situation was just starting to permeate his gray matter leaving him with a feeling of dread. He smoked his cigar and waited. He was mystified by what would happen with his meeting with Mr. Pinto. He had almost finished his cigar when Marie finally opened the door. It was obvious she had been crying her cheeks were red and wet with tears. He took out his handkerchief and wiped them away.

He was outraged at himself for being the cause of all her humiliation.

"Don't cry anymore baby, I'll take care of everything," he said not knowing exactly how he was going to accomplish that.

Her father stood in the middle of the living room waiting for him. Her mother was sitting on the couch quietly drying her eyes with her handkerchief. Her father looked much taller than his meager five foot two. He head was cocked as if he was ready for a fight and there was fire in his eyes. His wife started to speak but he stopped her saying, "Not one word Mayme, not one."

He looked at Carman straight in the eyes and asked, "You're going to do the right thing?"

"Yes sir," answered Carman, not knowing what the right thing could possibly be.

"In church" he asked.

Carman nodded his head yes thinking oh sure why not, I always get married in church.

"As soon as possible?" he added

Carman nodded again not able to speak the words. In his head he kept thinking how can I do this without anyone finding out? My God, I'll go right to hell. I'll need my baptismal papers. But they have my real name on them. My army papers have my new name. I'll bring them too. He just kept nodding his head not knowing what Marie's father was actually saying. When we tell the priest that Marie is pregnant, I'm sure he'll bend the rules. What happens to Carmina now? What will happen if and when Anna gets out of the sanitarium? God if my father was alive I'd be a dead man now. How am I going to support everybody? Jesus can't do this. Then he looked over at Marie standing there in complete terror. He knew that whatever he did he'd have to protect Marie.

All these thoughts were running through his mind as Marie's father went on and on. Finally he stopped talking and just stood there looking at him. He knew he should say something and blurted out,"whatever I have to do to make things right, I'll do."

Evidently it was the right thing to say because he started to talk to Marie saying, "Marie, is good thing he no want to wait, he want to marry you right away. That is good thing. My sister Anna will make the dress. We have small party right here." Looking at Carman he said, "You can have your Mama come that's all, nobody else. I no want anybody here except my sons, my wife and your Mama. That's all. I want everything very quiet. No one must find out that my little Marie is." He couldn't finish the sentence because at that point, the stern never bending Papa was crying too. Everyone waited as Papa took out his handkerchief and blew his nose loudly trying to get control of himself. He finally was able to continue saying "nobody in this family ever got in trouble before. This is first and last time, we meet at St. Martins at seven o'clock, ok?"

"Ok," replied Carman.

Dear God if I get away with this, I can get away with anything, he thought. I should run not walk to the nearest train station and never come back. But he turned and saw his Marie bravely trying to smile with tears welling in her eyes. He put his arms around her and murmured how much he loved her and to please forgive him.

Mr. Pinto was hardly moved by the scene and told him to let his daughter go saying, that he had done enough harm already. Except for their appointment with the priest at St. Martin's, Carman was forbidden to see Marie alone until their wedding day. Unceremoniously he was shown the door. He stood dumb founded outside the apartment building wondering which way to turn. Aimlessly he walked down the street and finally came to a bar, walked in and ordered a double scotch. After several drinks, he walked home. Not knowing what he should do first. He was hoping to talk to Mama but she wasn't home. Just as well she would have stopped him from going to the church. He went through his army papers searching for his discharge papers with the name change. Luckily he found them and to his surprise he also found his baptismal papers. He looked at his watch and realized he had little time to get to St. Martin's to meet Marie and her father at the time specified. It seems Mr. Pinto was quite sure of Carman's willingness to marry his daughter and had called the rectory for an appointment when Marie had gone into her apartment to tell her father that Carman was with her.

As a matter of fact little Mr. Pinto was ready to take Carman on if he didn't agree. Old man Pinto was small in stature but as strong as a bull and as fierce as a tiger.

When Carman approached the church there was Mr. Pinto pacing back and forth, fearful that he wouldn't show up. The relief in Marie's eyes, when she saw her Charles, was indisputable

Fortunately, the priest at St. Martin's was very indulgent after hearing that Marie was going to have a baby. He dispensed with the reading of the bans at all masses. He barely glanced at Carman's army discharge papers and announced that the wedding could take place on the next Sunday. The priest was only concerned with Carman's baptismal papers. Since the war, frequently the name on a young man's discharge papers didn't quite match the name he was given at birth. Americanizing one's name was a common practice for some Italians. The priest being Italian himself knew how difficult it was for Italians to secure employment no matter how qualified they were and so he was content to marry Marie to a Charles and not to a Carman. He never once mentioned the disparity of names on both documents.

When they left the rectory a complete change came over Marie as she questioned her father about of all things, her wedding dress.

"Oh Papa do you think Aunt Anna can make me a dress in less than a week."

"Of course, she could outfit the entire family in a week. We go now and see her., and you Charles, you be here Sunday at two o'clock with a best man and your Mama, that's all."

Thinking quickly not knowing where he could find a friend who didn't know he was already married, asked Marie casually, "is your cousin Katie going to be your maid of honor?"

"Yes she is Charles, is that all right?

"Of course, I was just thinking, why not have her boyfriend stand up for me. He seems like a swell guy."

"Oh Charles that would be lovely. Katie will be so pleased; she and Fred are planning a June wedding."

"Could you arrange it for me Marie?"

"Of course Charles, I'll see them tonight."

With that Papa Pinto grabbed Marie and walked briskly home.

Carman watched as they turned the corner and again he found the nearest bar.

He walked to the back of the bar and found a deserted booth. He sat down and held his head in his hands.

"Come on Buddy, nothing can be that bad," said the bartender as he stood watching the young man who looked as if he just lost his best friend.

"That's what you think. Could you bring me a bottle of rye and a glass please?"

"Sure Pal, no trouble," he answered and headed back to the bar. He had owned this bar for many years and had found that the best thing you can do to help a poor chap like the one in the back booth, was bring him a bottle and let him drink himself to a good drunk.

By the next day he would feel so physically bad that his problems would fade with the onslaught of a hangover.

Miraculously he woke up in his own bed, and was sick as a dog. It took him several hours just to shower dress and try to hold down a cup of coffee. He didn't remember how the hell he got home but was grateful he had. He sat at the kitchen table and tried to make some plans. All he knew for sure was that he was getting married again on Sunday.

1929

I had only a few days to get as much as I could set up for my Carmina. I went to my in-law's house and had a long talk with the Similletti's. They couldn't have been happier with my suggestion that they should adopt my Carmina but that I was always to remain her father. They could make all arrangements for her school and take care of her finances but it was understood that I had to be informed of any important decisions that had to be made. They assured me that their lawyer would incorporate anything I wanted. They were thrilled at the news that I would be leaving the country for an extended time and was unable to take Carmina with me. It's amazing how they believed the lies I was telling them. They wanted Carmina and were willing to do anything I said to have her. When I asked them to also take care of Anna, they were of course completely willing to take on that responsibility too. They swallowed my story hook line and sinker. I told them I would be out of the country and unreachable for almost a year. In that space of time it would naturally be completely feasible that all decisions about Carmina would be theirs. Of course when I returned from my new job in about a year, important decisions about Carmina would again be mine. They agreed to everything. I told them that my new job with the Telephone Company was very sensitive and that in case of any real emergency they were to contact my brother Steve. In view of the depression, they seemed to understand my willingness to leave the country on assignment to a foreign land and not be able to tell them exactly where I would be. I explained that because of all the cut backs at the Telephone Company I was willing to take this out of country job, insinuating that it had something to do with the defense of the country. Once I got started lying I couldn't seem to stop. I went on and on and they, God knows why, believed me.

The hardest most painful lie was to my sweet little girl. At first she was very sad, but as I got into my ridiculous story she too believed that I was somehow saving the Telephone Company and Uncle Sam.

Twice in my life I have been completely disgusted with my behavior. The two times that I have made two sweet young ladies pregnant and telling my little girl the reason I could not see her for at least a year was a new important government job for the Telephone Company, was by far the lowest possible level I had come to. And she believed me. How could they all believe me?

My most difficult task lay ahead. How to tell Mama? Predictably, I didn't have long to wait. I was sitting in my room wondering how I could tell her without hurting her too much when she suddenly appeared at my door.

"So you gonna tell me what's been happening?"

"Come in Mama, come in. I was just thinking of you. Come sit down, do you want a cup of coffee?

"No sweetheart I don't need coffee. I need to know what is going on. You haven't stopped at the house. Steve hasn't seen you and even Dominica is worried. So you ready to tell me what's wrong. You look like you haven't slept in a week. Are you sick, tell Mama. Remember I am old woman and I've buried a son and a husband. So whatever is wrong is no problem for Mama."

"God, Ma I hope you can forgive me for what I am about to tell you?"

And so with all the courage I could muster I began my tale. Watching her face as I told her the whole story from the moment I met Marie until this afternoon when we made arrangements to marry was very painful. At times she smiled and I thought, maybe is wasn't so bad after all. When I got to the part about going to church to make the arrangements all the color in her face drained and I was afraid she was going to pass out. She just held her hand to her mouth nodding. When I finished I couldn't look at her face. I was too ashamed. I just hung my head unable to make any excuses for myself because there weren't any. Just when I thought I had finally broken my mother's heart, I felt her hand on my shoulder as she patted me gently and said, "We take care of this Carman. No worry, Mama is on your side. I stand by you when you marry this Marie.

We no tell anybody except Dominica and Steve. Maybe we get away with this. Can you go to jail for marrying two women? Ah, who's gonna find out. I think you have to move far away. So no one see you with Marie. Maybe you could go back to Boston. Who's gonna find you there. Then you must divorce poor Anna. Its one thing to sin against the church they don't put you in jail. But I think it's against the law and you can go to jail if they find you. I don't think that God will be too angry with you. You deserve a little happiness. As long as my Carmina is taken care of and I can see her whenever I want, there is no problem. You know Carman; maybe you give your Mama a nice Grandson huh?"

I stood up and hugged her and thanked God for the gift he made me by giving me Mama. "You sure are something Mama, one in a million."

"That's me; I think it would be a good idea if you come and stay with Mama when you get everything organized here."

"I think so too Mama. As soon as I can I'll be over your house."

She kissed me and left. I knew I had hurt her greatly when I looked out the window and saw her walking down the street wiping away her tears.

The next couple of days flew by quickly. I still had to work and try and make arrangements to go back to Boston. My boss thought I was surely losing my mind but I convinced him that I really missed Boston and since I did a good job there why not make it permanent. He said he'd see what he could do. In the meantime I couldn't bring Marie to my apartment. In an hour word would be out all over the Bronx and the police would be at my door. Franticly I jumped in my car and took off for Yonkers. I remembered an army buddy of mine saying what a great place Yonkers was. It supposedly was quiet and country like. So why not Yonkers, it would only be for a short time until I could get my Boston job back and it was far enough from the Bronx that we wouldn't be bumping into people who knew me and Anna.

Driving along the seemingly peaceful roads in Yonkers I was surprised to see a for rent sign on a pretty little house not far from the train station. Without hesitation I knocked on the door and to my surprise was able to rent the house for thirty dollars a month. That's what I was paying for my little apartment in the Bronx. All of a sudden my spirits seemed to lift thinking of how pleased Marie would be when she saw the little house. I had plenty of furniture that would do until we could buy whatever Marie wanted. It was too good to be true. Maybe things would work out after all. I drove back to the Bronx, hired a mover and had him take everything I owned except my clothes to Yonkers.

There must be something wrong with me I thought. I felt awesome knowing that the girl I love would be with me from now on. I started to look forward to my wedding. When I finally got to Mama's I was feeling pretty good. I would finally live in a house full of joy. I even bought a brand new suit and everything that goes with it. In spite of everything I knew that I could never live without Marie and if this was the only way to have her, so be it. Not since I came back from the army had I felt so marvelous?

Mama was busy at the stove cooking something excellent. It was late and tomorrow was the big day. I sat in my old room waiting to be called for dinner and suddenly I had little appetite. Mama called and I answered that I just wasn't hungry. I just sat there in the dark and smoked a cigar and all my memories flooded back to me.

I watched the sun come up and knew that I was going to go through with the charade. I dressed in my new suit and waited for Mama to get dressed. She knocked on my door and there she stood in all her finery with that little black piece of fur around her neck. We could never figure out just what kind of animal it came from but Mama never went anywhere important without it. We stepped into the glaring sun as it shone on the snow.

Gratefully my brother had shoveled the snow away from my car so that Mama and I could get to the church on time.

I parked the car and entered the church with Mama on my arm. I led her to a seat kissed her gently looked up and saw my beloved.

Looking at her I knew I had made the right decision. She literally glowed in the beautiful white dress she wore. She carried the flowers I had sent her. In my pocket was my Mama's wedding ring. All I needed now was a little luck.

The End

www.ingramcontent.com/pod-product-compliance
Lightning Source LLC
Chambersburg PA
CBHW070837280626
47161CB00015B/1016